I0699683

SINNERS AND SAINTS

Secrets and Promises

Book 3

Anna Wilcoxson

FROM THE TINY ACORN ...
GROWS THE MIGHTY OAK

To my grandfather,

Spirito Urbani, who started the journey.

The truth of love emerges most clearly
when the beloved person stumbles,
when his or her weaknesses or sins
come into the open. One who truly
loves does not withdraw his love
but loves all the more, loves in
full consciousness of the other's
shortcomings and faults and
without in the least approving them.

—Pope John Paul II

Preface

"Champagne, young lady?"

I looked up at the woman holding a tray of half-filled flutes. "Please," I said, trying not to sound irritated. "And for future reference, my name is Anna."

"The flight attendant blushed as if realizing her mistake. "Oh, yes, of course," she said, giving me a smile reserved for difficult passengers before moving on.

Young lady. My ass. Glancing at her carefully dyed roots, I figured the flight attendant couldn't be more than a decade younger than me. Just because I would be celebrating the big 6-0 in a few months didn't mean I had to be reminded of it constantly.

"Can I have orange juice instead?" a familiar voice asked. I turned to look at the passengers in the seat behind me. *Figures.* Terry, my younger sister, was always choosing the healthier alternative. Tino, two years older than me, accepted the glass of Champagne without complaint. Both siblings had asked if they could join me on my trip to Italy this time. No doubt to pass judgment on my latest crazy endeavor.

This was Tino's second trip to my grandfather's hometown. He had accompanied me to Scheggino four months ago to not only check out the apartment I had discovered but also get away from the drama of a difficult divorce. I knew he blamed himself for the break-up; he had been too busy or too reluctant to see the signs. The ordeal became a symbol of his emotional failings, and it had made him doubt his ability to find happiness with another. When he had suggested coming to Italy, I guessed he saw it as an escape, a chance to gain perspective. Travel has a way of broadening your horizons and teaching you things about yourself you didn't know before. Like learning the difference between a momentary whim and what is best for you in the long run.

My sister, Terry, had expressed another reason for joining us. With her kids grown and her husband nearing retirement, she had begun teaching music classes at Saint Vincent's Academy in the Italian community where we grew up. The stories she had heard about our colorful Italian relatives had piqued her interest. Maybe knowing about them would strengthen her relationships with her own family. I hoped that included me.

I settled back into my seat, took a sip of the bubbly liquid, and let my mind wander.

Being the middle child had its advantages. Early on, noticing a much-appreciated talent for entertaining myself, my parents often left me to my own devices. I spent my afternoons staging productions in the family's garage using neighborhood kids—demonstrating a vivid, if not always gifted, imagination. Since then, my siblings had gotten used to my creative ventures. When I told them I had made an offer on a run-down apartment in Italy, they barely raised an eyebrow.

Buying the sliver of stone in the little Umbrian village of Scheggino had not been a calculated decision—a head-over-heels moment would be a more accurate description. Typical Anna Wilson behavior: *leap before you look*. Five years ago, when Mom and I had vacationed in Italy, we were anxious to visit the town where my grandfather was born. Pulling up to the piazza in our rent-a-car and gazing at the historic castle and the ribbon of water running alongside it, I had felt an instant connection. Then, when two villagers told us a story about my grandfather's secret life more than a century ago, I was hooked. Before he left for America, in 1907, my grandfather Spirito had committed a murder and fathered two children with a woman who was not my grandmother. Agatha Altarocca, the woman left behind, had gone on to become a design icon known all over Europe, her two illegitimate sons comfortably ensconced in the hierarchy of the Urbino truffle dynasty.

And the surprises didn't end there.

After discovering the apartment and putting down a deposit, I returned with my brother to take title. Only then did I realized I was the proud owner of a smelly hovel lacking some basic amenities, namely a kitchen and a working toilet.

The good-looking owner of the Villa Urbino volunteered to put us up while Tino and I contemplated our next move. Agostino was kind and hospitable, and, more importantly, he knew a handyman who worked cheap. To a woman who had just bought property in a foreign country, that was like talking dirty. Maybe it was the growing attraction to my host or the inkling that my life was about to change—whatever it was, I felt my emotions kicking into high gear. My hot flashes vanished, and feelings I thought had died with menopause were clamoring for my attention.

Tino and I soon discovered our ninety-four-year-old Uncle SJ, Agatha's youngest son, and the last remaining link to my grandfather's other life, lived next door. It was time to meet the skeleton in my family closet. Much to our surprise, he welcomed us with open arms. SJ had been the chef for the Urbino Truffle Foundation before he retired. It had been a productive life but a lonely one. Seventy years ago, the love of his life had run away determined to leave the past behind. The mystery of what happened to Agostino's Aunt Giulia still haunted him.

"Let's go find her!" I said to SJ after he recounted the story. "What have you got to lose?"

"Nothing, except a sack full of regrets if I don't try," SJ answered.

Tino, SJ, Agostino and I took off for Turin following Giulia's trail, but we were too late. What we found instead was a daughter. Giulia and SJ's daughter, Mari.

There was one more surprise.

Mari had kept all the correspondence between her mother and her family back home in Scheggino. It revealed a heart-rending story and the discovery that Agostino was adopted, the identity of his real parents unknown. Quite a revelation for the nephew who had always thought he was related to the CEO of the world's largest truffle exporter.

"I want to find my real family," Agostino told us.

Mari handed over the letters with a cautionary warning. *Be careful when you start digging up the past. You may find a lot of dirt under your fingernails.*

~

I swallowed the last of the Champagne as I heard the plane's engines start up. A moment later we were racing down the runway leaving civilization behind. After we leveled off, I thought of Agostino, and a warm glow came over me. On my last day before returning to San Diego, tender words had been spoken and plans for the future made. Since then, I'd had time to think about our cultural differences and the logistics of a long-distance relationship, Would I finally find what I was looking for, or would this be one more in a long line of romantic delusions?

One thing was for sure. another exciting adventure lay just below the clouds—an adventure I hoped Agostino and I would share together.

By tomorrow night, barring any unforeseen disaster, I would be in his arms.

PART I

Chapter 1

A Little More Time

Scheggino, Italy, 2016

A RAY of sun, like a gilded finger, crept across the tangled sheets and lingered on the slumbering form of Agostino Urbino. The gray hair and weathered features—and the fact that he was not alone—testified to a life well lived. But it was the robust sound coming from his half-open mouth that suggested one of his priorities included a good night's sleep.

As the morning progressed, the gilded fingers reached into the corners of the room, illuminating a crumpled red silk dress and a pair of four-inch heels. A blonde woman stared back at me from the large Rococo mirror positioned at eye level to the bed, one long leg against her companion's thigh, and one hand spread across his chest.

It took me a second to recognize her. For a woman entering her golden years I didn't look half bad . . . even if the credit for the satisfied expression on my face belonged to the man lying next to me. I took it all in and blushed, if only for the sun's benefit, when I thought of last night.

Agostino and I had left my apartment in the middle of my homecoming party and walked to his villa with only one thing on our minds. On my last visit, there had been two failed attempts: one on a roof top deck where we were interrupted by an employee happy hour, and the other by an ill-timed farewell party improvised by well-intentioned friends. With only four months of phone sex to sustain us, we were both ready for some serious hip action.

We never even made it to the bed. The minute we crossed the threshold of his bachelor pad, I had him against the wall and was unbuttoning his jeans, my tongue inching past his abs . . .

"*Famme male,*" he shouted.

I did a quick translation in my head. *Do me bad.* I could manage that.

I stood up and leapt into his arms, my legs wrapping around him—or at least that was the intention. Either I misjudged where his hips were, or my spring wasn't what it used to be. As my legs came down, the force of my body pushed him off balance, and we both tumbled to the ground. I heard the thud of a skull hitting tile.

"Ow," Agostino cried out.

I put my hand on the back of his head. It felt wet.

"Holy crap, you're bleeding," I said.

Agostino looked at my hand and closed his eyes. "I'm going to die."

I felt the cut again. "A mild concussion at worst. You are not going to die—at least not tonight."

Agostino sat up and glared at me. "This is not exactly the way I dreamed things would go." He looked down. "Now it looks like we will have to start over."

"Not a problem," I said, helping him up and leading him to the bed. "But first, I need a first-aid kit . . . and scissors."

"Top drawer of the dresser." A pause. "Why do you need scissors?"

"I will have to trim the hair to clean the wound. Luckily the cut is right in the middle of your bald spot."

"Bald spot?" Agostino's voice rose a notch.

"Relax," I said, pushing him down on the bed. "Once I put the bandage on, you won't even notice it."

I made Agostino lie on his stomach while I patched up his head. This was not what I had planned either. Tonight was supposed to be the big event. Three months of fantasizing and now this. I turned him over.

Agostino's gray eyes were twinkling.

"It looks like you've made a miraculous recovery," I said, climbing on top of him.

I had never had an Italian lover before and was completely unprepared for the exquisite sensation of having every part of my body enjoyed and accompanied by romantic Italian words whispered into my neck. It was like overdosing on chocolate mousse cake—in bed. In my experience, the only dialogue American men seemed to have during intercourse was with themselves. I could see it in their faces as they hovered over me. "If I do this, will I have to commit? Will she want marriage or joint bank accounts? What assets do I stand to lose if it doesn't work out?" All that before the pants were even off. Then came the self-evaluation of how they measured up: size, technique, stamina—even while they were doing it. Like their performance mattered more than the experience.

When an Italian man makes love to you, there is no score card, no questionnaire, and the subject matter never feels anything but cherished.

Agostino's hand and the morning sun brought me back to reality. If he observed that my breasts were a little less than perky or my belly was no longer concave, he never gave the slightest indication. I felt like a beautiful woman in her sexual prime.

"I hope you don't have anywhere to go this morning," he said.

"Nothing pressing." I started giggling. "Well, apart from that . . ."

Sometime later, I reluctantly disengaged myself and sat up.

"Today is the first day of the truffle festival," I reminded him. "And I have a houseful of guests back at my place who don't know where I am."

"Oh, they know." Agostino was planting soft kisses along my spine, his fingers moving southward.

"Did you forget you brought Flavia and Mari to my party? How do you think they got home?"

"I'm sure someone offered to drive them." Agostino's fingers paused, and he looked out the window at the impressive villa in the distance. "I see cars at Paradiso Vinto. Flavia has guests. She and Mari are probably cooking breakfast for them as we speak."

I followed his gaze. The floodlights framing the dome of the villa up the hill were still on from the night before, and I could see lights in the cottages out back. "I am glad SJ made sure his niece would inherit Agatha's villa after his death. He supported Flavia's dream of owning a *casa de vacanza*, and now it is a reality. I just wish he could have been here to see it."

"Maybe he's looking down on it now. Who knows," Agostino said softly.

My eyes lingered on the view beyond the window. Fields of farro whispered in the early morning breeze, and beyond them, the mountains of Monteluco rose like sentinels over the undulating valleys of the Umbrian countryside. "This is the second time Mari has paid Flavia a visit. I think she likes it here in Scheggino."

"Don't forget, it was her mother's hometown," Agostino reminded me.

"And she and Flavia are related," I added. "Wouldn't it be great if she moved here to help Flavia? A pastry chef and a *maestra della casa* under one roof. What a great collaboration!"

"I am in favor of it," Agostino said. "Scheggino could use a *pasticceria*." He started tracing his fingers along the length of my thigh. "And speaking of collaborations, what do you think of ours?"

"I know we have chemistry."

"Passion is the most important thing, *sì?*"

"There are other things to consider. Whether we share the same interests and goals . . ."

We both laughed. Under the present circumstances, my words sounded ridiculous. Agostino's fingers started traveling again.

I put my hand over his. "We both have responsibilities today . . . and . . . and . . . I'm sore."

"You are what???"

"Sore. Out of practice. I need to develop the proper muscles again."

Agostino grinned. "Practice session tonight. First two hours are on the house."

"Seriously, we aren't spring chickens anymore."

Agostino swung his legs off the bed and stood up. "Speak for yourself. This rooster could go all day." He puffed out his chest and pounded on it with both fists.

"Cock-a-doodle-do-me-later?" I offered, but Agostino had already disappeared into the bathroom.

As soon as I heard the shower running, I started searching for my clothes. I examined the seriously wrinkled dress and a pair of panties thrown into a corner. Last night, my mind on other things, I had not thought to bring a change of clothes. I opened an armoire, and a wave of perfume hit me. Not *my* perfume. There were a few fancy dresses and shoes that Agostino had obviously neglected to get rid of from the last person who had spent the night here.

After Agostino went downstairs to the kitchen to make coffee, I investigated his dresser drawers. Underwear. And not just men's underwear. Given the mounting evidence, I couldn't help wondering how many *other* women were intimately acquainted with Agostino's Bachelor Pad. There would have to be a serious discussion about *that*.

I indulged myself in a nice hot shower and padded down the stairs barefoot wearing Agostino's unbuttoned button down shirt.

"It looks better on you," he said, coming out of the kitchen carrying a steaming cappuccino and a plate of flaky *cornettos*. He gestured to the empty seat at the table and told me to sit.

"*Grazie*," I said, acknowledging the compliment. "That leads me to the next question. All I have is a cocktail dress and stilettos to walk home in. How I made it up the hill in those shoes . . . Today, my feet are so swollen, I can't even get my big toe in."

"Last night, you were not thinking about that part of your body," Agostino reminded me.

"Damn right," I answered. "How am I going to get home? I can't walk barefoot on these Roman roads."

"I will drive you."

"But we walked up here together. You left your car in the village."

"I have my farm truck here."

I remembered Agostino's battered pickup, used primarily to haul pigs to the slaughterhouse. I could just see the old ladies in the village glancing up from their customary benches in the piazza, watching his truck pull up. Even they, remembering their more nubile pasts, could guess the woman descending from the cab in a dress and heels at sunrise had spent the night somewhere besides her own bed. Not that they would be surprised. The American lady, who had bought an apartment in her ancestral village of Scheggino, was already the subject of much speculation. From the start, my efforts to learn about my kin had been met with cool indifference. Even if my grandfather was born here, I was still a stranger to them. And now I had just spent the night with a man whose relatives owned the biggest truffle operation in Italy. I could hear the tongues wagging already.

I polished off a *cornetto*. "I accept your offer."

"Which offer is that?" Agostino said, eyeing my legs.

"To be driven home in your slaughter truck. I just hope there are no dead carcasses still in the back."

"I will check," Agostino promised. He pushed another *cornetto* toward me.

I plucked the pastry off the plate and took a bite.

"Anna, before you left, I told you I was going to try to find my birth mother."

I jerked my head up. "You found her?"

Agostino shook his head.

"What about adoption records? Did you check the hospital in Spoleto?"

"*Sì*, I check the hospital records . . . even the cemetery. Nothing to show who gave birth to me. The name of my real mother is still a mystery."

"Have you told Beniamino about this?"

Agostino took a deep breath. "I did not tell him right away. *Nonna* Gabriella did not want me to."

"Agostino, doesn't he deserve to know? After all, he is your uncle."

"Technically, this is not true. I can no longer claim to be related to the Urbino truffle dynasty. Finding out after all these years that I do not belong with these people—that I am a stranger—is something I am still trying to work out. Gabriella is the only one within the family who knows."

"Why are you keeping it a secret?"

Agostino hesitated before answering. "Gabriella has always been afraid that if Beniamino's family found out, they would treat me differently. Not like one of their own."

"She has a point. Your whole association with them could change. Are you prepared for that?"

"They are bound to find out anyway. I had to convince her that holding back the truth about my birth was a mistake. If Beniamino heard it from someone else—not family—it would be worse."

"I agree. It would look like you were hiding it for other reasons. You are Gabriella's only heir... at least in their eyes. Coming clean about your parentage is the right thing to do." I looked at him with renewed respect. "It is obvious Gabriella is on your side. She loves you no matter who you are."

Agostino smiled. "I think she does too."

"So, what happened?"

"She invited Beniamino and me to her villa to discuss it."

"Oh, boy. I wish I'd been there. How did he take it?"

Agostino stood up and walked to the French doors and looked out. "Not well."

"Buon giorno, Beniamino." Gabriella extended a ring-encrusted hand to the man striding across the room toward her. "It is good of you to come. I know how busy being the CEO of the Foundation can be."

The stocky, well-dressed man took the hand of the ninety-nine-year-old woman in the wheelchair and kissed it. "For you, Zia, I will always make time." His keen brown eyes traveled to the man standing nearby. He nodded.

"Agostino, always a pleasure."

"We have some news—about Agostino here—that I think you should hear." Gabriella gestured to the sofa. "Why don't you both sit down."

Both men settled into seats at opposite ends of the couch.

"What news?" Beniamino asked.

Gabriella addressed Agostino. "Perhaps you should be the one to tell him. Start with the trip to Turin you took with your new relatives."

Beniamino raised an eyebrow.

Agostino opened his mouth to speak but when Gabriella kept talking, he shut it.

"You remember that American woman, Anna Wilson, who has been sniffing around trying to find information about her family?"

Beniamino nodded. "I remember her. She came here some years back with her mother. Quite a duo they were . . . two peas in a pod as the Americans say. I let something slip about their relative, Spirito Urbino. I mentioned he fathered a child . . ."

Gabriella cut in. "Someone in the village told them about Spirito's secret life and the woman who gave birth to that child."

"Yes, we all knew Santo was Spirito's and Agatha Altarocca's child." Beniamino's eyes had turned wary. "What else are you talking about?"

"Agostino tells me Spirito fathered another child with her. SJ Urbino. Your father's chef at the Headquarters," Gabriella replied.

Beniamino's eyes slid over to Agostino. "How did you find out?"

"SJ told me himself," Agostino said. "How did *you* find out?"

Beniamino shifted uncomfortably. "Papa always knew. One day he just told me. I was sixteen. After forty years, it wasn't such a big deal. After all, our family shared some blame in Agatha's predicament. Is this what you wanted to tell me?"

Gabriella spoke up. "Agostino, get to it."

"It was Anna's idea that we take the trip to Turin with SJ. He wanted to find out what had happened to the love of his life. You remember, the girl who ran away seventy years ago to escape her family's misdeeds." His eyes slid back to his uncle.

"You are talking about Giulia."

"I am. When we got to Turin, we learned Giulia was dead, but her daughter, Mari, was still alive. SJ's daughter. You see, SJ and Giulia had been . . . well . . . intimate the night before she left."

Ben gave him a *do I really need to hear this?* look.

Gabriella sighed. "Agostino, the letters . . ."

Agostino nodded quickly. "I was getting to that. Mari gave us letters Giulia had written her mother during her absence. The letters told us something we never knew about our family."

Beniamino looked at his watch. "All this is ancient history. I'm sorry but I really don't have the time . . ."

"I suggest you make the time." Gabriella's eyes narrowed as she looked at her nephew. "Because what we are about to tell you will knock your *calzones* off."

I took a sip of my cappuccino and looked at Agostino. "So, you told him."

"I told him." Agostino sat back and crossed his arms. "We'll see how they treat me now. The truth is, I don't care. My side of the family were farmers, not truffle hunters. We were never part of their money-making schemes to take over the industry. After my father died, I remodeled this home and turned it into the hotel you see today. I do not belong in Beniamino's world, and now I know why."

It sounded cold. I knew he didn't mean it. I could only guess what it must feel like to learn that your real family are people you don't even know. "You are your own person, Agostino. You are free to have the life you want now."

He looked at me head on. "I know one thing. I want you in it," he said.

I made him wait a good minute. "What about the clothes upstairs?"

"What clothes?" Agostino looked uneasy.

"Unless you have some tendencies I don't know about, you need to clean out your closet . . . and your drawers," I added.

Agostino smiled weakly. "I will tell her to come and get everything tomorrow."

"I have a better idea. Donate it."

He reached out and grabbed both my hands. "Enough about this. My bachelor days are over. Now, we talk about *us*. We must make plans."

"Plans?" I repeated. "I am here for a month, and my brother and sister are only staying a week."

"I am talking about the rest of our lives."

I withdrew my hands. "Agostino, we just made love for the first time. Don't you think it's a little early to be talking about a forever future together? Let's see where this goes."

The look on his face made me wish I could take back those words. He looked disappointed, like I had failed him. The truth was, I had been through this once or twice before. Relationships that started with an intense physical attraction and then fizzled out when my lover's dirty clothes, his unmade bed, and the unwashed dishes in the sink were no longer a charming indication of someone who had better things to do. Or when the opposite happened— when I cared more deeply than he did. I had learned to be wary of that first blush of love. I knew my assessment of mutual compatibility was all too often influenced by what happened between the sheets.

"I don't understand," Agostino said, his eyes anxious. "We are good together, yes?"

Good together was obviously a reference to sex. Even *I* knew the answer to that question required finesse. "For an emotional person, like myself," I began cautiously, "I will admit to having once or twice mistaken sexual passion for something more."

Agostino looked hurt. "Is that what you think is happening here? *Lussuria invece d'amore?*"

I translated the Italian in my head. *Lust masquerading as love.*

I took the kid gloves off and pointed a finger at him. "Don't tell me you don't know what I'm talking about. The women's clothes hanging in your armoire . . . was that love? And what happened? You are alone."

"A man has many needs . . . companionship for one . . ."

"And sex for another," I countered.

Agostino searched my face. "I don't deny my past, but what I feel for you is different." He drew in a shaky breath. "I do not mind to say that it scares me . . . a little . . . but I know that I have a responsibility to take seriously this feeling that you are a gift to my heart."

Wow. *Gift to my heart.* That was a first. Were all Italian men this romantic . . . and emotionally fragile? I suddenly realized how my fickle nature could hurt this man. I needed to be very sure of the sincerity of my feelings. I put the kid gloves back on. "Just give me a little more time to get there, okay?"

Chapter 2

Cheap Rates

WITH A quick glance in the rear of Agostino's truck—it was empty—I slipped into the passenger seat, and we headed down the road into town.

By 9 a.m., the gray mist in the hollows of the valley had thinned, revealing patches of blue and the promise of a spectacular spring day in Umbria. When we reached the outskirts of the village, I saw a parade of booths lining the road. Craftsmen and artisans were already setting out displays of their handmade products while butchers strung up sausage links alongside slabs of porchetta on the back walls of their shacks. Rows of freshly baked focaccia, still warm inside brown paper bags, tempted the few hungry customers passing by.

The owners were calling out greetings: *"Fresca* this morning! *Compri adesso.* Buy now!" A few booths down, fancy bottles of essential oils and lotions culled from the nearby fields and forests of the Valnerina were lined up, waiting to be sampled. The artisans paused from their labors and waved as Agostino passed, his truck a familiar sight to those working in the fields in the early morning hours.

Since I had bought the apartment only four months ago, I had not been to the annual festival that drew hundreds of people from all over Umbria to the little town of Scheggino. The Urbino Truffle Foundation sponsored the event, providing entertainment and the ten kilos of truffles needed to make the giant omelet. The grassy banks of the Nera River that ran through town had been chosen as the location for the twenty-foot waffle iron. In full view of the crowds, a vat containing a combination of egg and truffle would be poured into the iron round and after twenty minutes, a group of the strongest young men of the town rotated it by hand to cook both sides. When the eggs were set, the iron was pried open and pieces of the omelet cut up and served to the crowds. It was a tradition that had been going on for almost a century and showed no signs of stopping—even amid modern concerns about sanitation and salmonella. In close to a hundred years, no one had died or sued the Urbinos for food poisoning. Later, when evening settled over the town, there would be musical performances on the stage erected near the fountain commemorating Pietro Urbino, the patriarch of the Urbino Truffle Foundation. The music and the festivities would last well into the night and start right back up the next day.

Agostino pulled up in front of the *alimentari,* the Italian equivalent of the mom-and-pop shop back home. It was the convenient alternative for those who didn't want to drive the six kilometers to the big box store in Spoleto.

With a careful look at the benches in the piazza—*no signoras*—I gave him a quick peck on the mouth and hopped out. "I can walk from here," I said.

Agostino stuck his head out of the truck. "When will I see you again?"

"You have guests staying at your villa tonight, right?"

Agostino nodded his head. "*Sì,* all the rooms are reserved. On festival night, we always have a big dinner. I started this tradition when we first open the villa as a hotel thirty years ago. It is one of the biggest nights of the season for us."

"Do you need help?" I asked, secretly hoping my services in the kitchen would not be required. I had no intention of ruining a time-honored family tradition.

Agostino gave me an amused look. "I have all the help I need *but* thank you for asking." It was safe to conclude he had no illusions about my culinary skills.

I hesitated a moment. "What are you making for dinner?"

"Regional Umbrian dishes," Agostino said, vaguely, as if withholding a treasured secret. "Come, and bring Tino and Terry."

My curiosity was piqued. I gave him a mock bow. "We will be honored."

"*E dopo?*" Agostino had a gleam in his eye. "Maybe we go up to my room for dessert?"

I put a finger to my lips. "Only after the guests have retired. I have a reputation to maintain."

"Enjoy your reputation while it lasts, *cara.*" He laughed. "After one week, all of Scheggino will have their windows open to listen to your screams."

"Speak for yourself," I shot back. "I wasn't the only one screaming."

I stepped out of the cab, stilettos in hand, watching the truck make a precarious U-turn. As Agostino passed, he twirled his tongue at me before clattering off the way he had come.

"*Buon giorno,* Anna."

I turned around to see Sabina Garibaldi keying into the *alimentari.* She was staring at my outfit with a big smile on her face.

"Great," I muttered. The owner of the market lived three doors down from me at the top of the castle and was the biggest gossip in town. *Now everyone will know where I spent last night.*

"I saw GianPietro's truck up by your house this morning," she informed me. "You have a *backup?*"

Backup. The Italians had adopted the word from us at some point, probably because American overconsumption caused most of the plumbing problems in little village hotels. I had learned the meaning of the word last summer when I discovered an overactive sewer was one of the features in my newly purchased apartment. Agostino had introduced me to GianPietro, a talented, if eccentric, plumber who had not only coaxed my pipes into submission but also replaced a kitchen that the previous owners had thought necessary to take with them. In one afternoon cleaning out the bathroom, GP and I had become kindred spirits. In my view, one can never have too many close friends who know how to unclog a drain in a property you own halfway around the world. As I headed up the winding cobblestone labyrinth inside the castle walls, I prepared myself for the worst.

Built in the 1200s, the towering medieval fortress, complete with its own private church, was once the property of a certain Cardinal Graziani. Through the years, the rooms had been reconfigured and sold off as private residences—kind of like a condo complex from a thousand years ago with an infrastructure just as ancient. No wonder I had plumbing problems.

Fortunately, the charm of the castle outweighed its shortcomings. Negotiating the labyrinth of stairs, I saw pots of neatly tended geraniums on the porches of stone cottages and clotheslines strung across the passageway, displaying freshly laundered undergarments. I ducked my head to avoid a pair of polka-dot granny pants. All around me, melodic Italian voices called out greetings to one another from tiny windows flung open to the bright blue sky.

Reaching the third level, I saw GianPietro's Ape; the tiny truck's vintage hubcaps glittering in the sun. A short distance away, a petite woman with a carrot-colored pixie haircut was sweeping the leaves off her doorstep. Her deep-set brown eyes lit up when she saw me.

"Anna!" She took in my wrinkled dress and bare feet and the heeled shoes dangling in my hand. She didn't say another word, but her eyebrows spoke volumes.

Leonia and her father had been the first friends Mom and I had made on our trip five years ago. Enzo had known Spirito as a boy, and it was from him we learned why my grandfather had left the village for America at the turn of the century.

"It was a lovely party last night," Leonia said, finding her voice. "Even if the guest of honor left early."

I smiled awkwardly, my bare feet feeling the rough stones and the wind whipping around my thin dress. "I . . . uh . . . we . . ." I stammered.

Leonia gave me a quick hug. "No need to explain. I'm sure there was a *very* good reason." Her bright eyes looked at me hopefully.

I'm sure she would like nothing better than to get a full report, but now was not the time.

As if guessing my thoughts, she said, "GP has been at your house all morning. Maybe you'd better get up there."

I took my cue gratefully. "See you at the festa later?" I asked her.

She nodded her head, and I started up the ramp to my apartment.

Reaching the top, I listened for a moment outside the open wooden doors leading to the courtyard I shared with three other apartment owners. A highly imaginative Italian expletive came from the other side of my front door.

"*Leccaculo!*"

I heard it again, this time louder, followed by a burst of laughter.

I pushed open the door, winked at my sister, and addressed the figure hunched over my sink. "GP, you are poisoning the image of plumbers all over the world. Don't think my sister doesn't know what that word means."

GP didn't even turn around. Legs spread to get a better stance, he had both hands wrapped around a wire contraption and appeared to be snaking out the kitchen drain. The jeans he was wearing were so dirt encrusted they could have stood up by themselves, and the odor of sewer pipes mixed with bubble gum hovered in the air around him. Every few minutes, he would lift his gnome-like head and blow a big round bubble and watch it pop.

Terry was sitting on a kitchen chair nearby, her eyes on GP's slowly emerging butt crack. "I know what *culo* means," she said and averted her gaze, fastening her large brown eyes on me. "I can only guess about the rest of it."

I turned to my sister. She was dressed in running clothes, her small spare frame bursting with energy. Chestnut colored hair grazed the chin line of her heart-shaped face. She was a dead ringer for our great grandmother, Teresa, right down to the tiny mole above her pert mouth.

Far from being grossed out, Terry seemed to be enjoying the spectacle of an Italian plumber hard at work. A thought occurred to me. Maybe if she found GP's performance entertaining, I didn't need to cart her around to all the usual tourist traps I assumed she wanted to see. Maybe a little small-town drama would suffice.

GP's head came up. "Your brother put garbage down here"—he pointed to the sink—"I not surprised. Wherever the Wilsons go, plumbing problem follow."

"Tino thought you had a garbage disposal," Terry explained. "He found out you didn't have one a little too late."

GP turned to me. "What is this 'garbage disposal?'"

I thought for a minute. No one in the United States had ever asked me that question. "It is an appliance that fits into the drain. Americans use it to grind up their leftover food."

GP made a face. *"Strana."*

"What do *you* do with food scraps?" I asked him.

GP held up a finger. "First, Italians eat almost everything they cook. Except maybe for bones, there is nothing left over. What we don't eat, we feed to the animals or put in ground to make soil better."

"Compost?" Terry offered.

"Sì. Nothing go to waste."

I pondered this bit of information. "You know, Americans could learn a thing or two from you people about recycling. The amount of food we throw away could feed a small country . . . *and* their pets."

"Our pets eat specially prepared food that comes in big sacks and looks like breakfast cereal," Terry added.

GP shook his head. *"Stranissima!* You have appliance that grind up food to go down drain and buy food for dog separate. Why you not skip a step and serve leftovers to dog? Then you no have to pay plumber to fix this . . . *thing."* He scrunched up his nose and pointed to the sink.

I shrugged my shoulders. "It's the way we do things, GP. We like to make life as complicated as possible. They pay plumbers well in America, by the way."

GP's eyes lit up. "How well?"

"Over $100 an hour," Terry said.

GP's *serpente* clattered to the floor. *"E vero? Cento dollari per ora?* Maybe I take my family to America."

"Plenty of work," I assured him, "But *here,* the Americans pay Italian wages. *Hai capito?"*

GP's face fell. *"Sì, ho capito."* He picked up the snake and went back to work.

My eyes wandered to the bare table and bags of trash near the front door. It looked pretty tidy, considering there had been a room full of revelers eating and drinking when Agostino and I had ditched the party last night. "Thanks for cleaning up, sis. Where's Tino?"

"He went down to the *alimentari* to buy some supplies."

"That's odd, I didn't see him on my way up. He must have used a different set of stairs. In this castle, there are five different ways to get to the same spot." I glanced at the empty shelves. "Sorry about the lack of supplies. I meant to stock up but . . ."

Terry's eyes swept over my cocktail attire. "You had other things on your mind. So, how did it go?"

There was no use evading Terry's scrutiny. Siblings can't be fooled. Before I could answer, I heard footsteps just outside the open front door. I put my finger to my lips. "Tell you later."

"The prodigal daughter returns," Tino said walking into the apartment and setting down the bags of groceries. "Don't bother to thank me. I took Mari and Flavia home. Agostino brought them here, remember?"

I looked contrite. "Thank you. Were they upset?"

"Not really. We all knew you were both chomping at the bit."

"That obvious, huh?"

Tino ran a hand through his full head of gray hair and grinned. With his blue eyes and square jaw, he bore a striking resemblance to the framed portrait of Spirito in the family home in San Diego. "By the way, your hosting skills need honing if you want to entertain guests from across the pond," he said, extracting a bottle of Scotch from one of the bags. "Staples," he commented when he saw my face.

GP looked up and pointed a finger at Tino. "Keep him away from sink . . . and toilet, if you know what is good for you. Your brother is trouble."

Tino laughed. "Good thing you gave me your phone number, right GP?"

GP's eyes narrowed. "I am not . . . how you say . . . 'on call' all day. My hours are 8 a.m. to 8 p.m. After that, I charge American rates."

I turned toward the stairs. "Sounds reasonable, GP. Now, if you will excuse me, I am going to change clothes. I looked at the stilettos in my hand. "It's going to be a jeans and sneakers day."

I walked up the flight of stone stairs where the three bedrooms and full bath were located. Terry had set herself up in the smaller room, the one I intended to use as an office. It had a futon and two nightstands from the early 1900s that a neighbor had donated in my absence. They were as ugly as sin but refusing her gift would have been bad form. Tino's room had a low ceiling and was shaped like a tube, but it was large. I had outfitted it with a bed, a dresser, and an armoire from the 1960s. The midcentury craze had not yet infiltrated Scheggino, and furniture from that era could be had for the price of hauling it out of people's storage. I had already accumulated a few pieces. Both bedrooms had a view of the village piazza *if* you looked beyond the crane positioned in the middle of the first level of the castle. Installed when a major remodeling project began a few years ago, the crane captured the lovely ambiance of scaffolding and steel from all of my west-facing windows. Whenever I poked my head out and looked up, there was always a large piece of stone suspended directly overhead.

The last room was the master. Sixteen-foot ceilings with the original crossed wood beams and a French door that looked out on the garden of Cardinal Graziano's villa. The view was worth the price of the entire apartment.

I sat on the edge of the bed and sighed with satisfaction. Apart from owning property in my ancestral village, another dream had come true. A home full of family.

Chapter 3

Buried History

THE TRUFFLE festival was in full swing by the time Tino, Terry, and I walked down to the center of town. We had made a quick detour to the second tier of the castle to visit my great uncle Georgio and cousin Renata. Their two-story house was on a large piece of land with a courtyard and a slew of out buildings secured by an iron gate. In the early 1900s, the property had belonged to my grandfather, Spirito, and as legend would have it, a murder had taken place there. Spirito had hoisted a rifle into one of the holes that shared an outside wall with the castle and shot the man who raped his first love, Agatha Altarocca. Today, the spot is fondly remembered by the town as the site of "Spirito's Revenge."

Terry was fascinated by this morsel of Scheggino lore and didn't seem the least bit disturbed by the fact that her grandfather had killed a man in cold blood. She wanted to hear all the details, demanding to be led to the site, and even putting her finger in the hole where the shot was fired.

"The man he killed, the one who raped Agatha, was an Urbino. A relative of the wealthy family that owns the Truffle Foundation, right?" Terry asked Renata.

Our cousin, an attractive middle-aged woman who could have passed for Sophia Loren's sister, dropped her voice to a whisper. "It is true, what you say, but on the day of the festival we should not talk of "Spirito's Revenge." This day belongs to the family that pay for all this." Renata gestured to the crowd at the base of the castle. "Come. Papa is already down there. Let us go see if they start making the omelet."

After we negotiated the stairs going down, we strolled along the narrow walkway that ran alongside the river. There were crowds of people swarming the booths and taking in the tentative April sunshine. Midway across the bridge, we stopped and leaned over the railing. I could see the town's dignitaries gathered on the opposite bank next to the giant waffle iron. A temporary wooden platform and microphones had been set up where Beniamino Urbino and his wife, Donatella, were seated. They turned and waved to the people on the bridge behind them, and the crowd responded with a roar. Suddenly, there was a movement in the mass of humanity lining the path to the river, and a very attractive woman in her late twenties emerged and walked toward the stage. She wore a hot-pink linen suit, a yellow striped silk blouse, and stilettos the color of cotton candy. Her legs, tanned and shapely, could have stopped traffic on the Autostrada A1.

Terry whispered in my ear, "That is Pamela, the mayor of Scheggino, right?"

I nodded. "When Tino first came here with me, he dubbed her "The Sex Goddess." That was before he got wise to the fact that Italy has evolved. Today's Italian women no longer tolerate titles like that. Now, he just calls her 'Goddess.'" I glanced at Tino, whose love-sick expression said everything. I waved my hand in front of his face a couple of times. He didn't even blink.

I turned back to Terry and Renata. "Tino doesn't have a chance. Pamela is married to Beniamino's son, Giovanni." I pointed to a man with a ruddy complexion, jet black hair, and a well-cut suit, who was sitting between his father and Donatella. "He will take over running the Urbino Truffle Foundation someday."

"How is your Agostino related to these people?" Terry asked.

My eyes widened. "Whoa there. *My* Agostino? Let's not get hasty here . . . we are in the early stages."

Terry snorted. "Uh huh. That *well-fucked* look is all over you, so don't tell me nothing happened last night."

I sighed. Soon the whole village would be linking our names together like we were already married. I wasn't sure I was ready for *that*. "Let's get back to your question about Agostino's relationship to Beniamino Urbino's side of the family," I said. "Everyone in town has always believed that Agostino's father was the great nephew of the founder of the Urbino Truffle Foundation."

"*'Has always believed,'*" Renata repeated. "Has this assumption changed?"

I debated momentarily whether I should keep Agostino's news a secret, but then I thought of Renata's connection to our family. I was sure she could be trusted because it could reflect badly on her if she spread malicious gossip about someone I was involved with. I looked at my companions intently. "This is classified information. Not for village consumption. Do you understand?"

Both ladies nodded their heads solemnly.

"A very important piece of information was discovered recently. Namely, Agostino found out he was adopted."

Renata's eyes widened. "I want all the details."

"Me too," Terry chimed in. "I think I have a right to know my future brother-in-law's true heritage."

I knew she was joking but my heart jumped into my throat anyway. "I feel the need for an espresso coming on . . . one heavily laced with grappa. Anyone coming with me?"

Terry and Renata nodded their heads vigorously. Tino kept his eyes on the candy-colored figure taking the stage. "I'll catch up with you later," he said.

I wagged my finger at him. "Stay away from the mayor. You are no match for Giovanni or his family. We don't want to find your headless corpse swimming with the fishes at the bottom of the Nera."

Terry, Renata and I strolled through the densely populated piazza and found an outside table at Avelino's Bar. The tiny hole in the wall flanking the SS45 highway had served morning coffee and evening cocktails to the residents of Scheggino for over a hundred years. New owners had come and gone, but the name had never changed. After giving the waiter our orders: three double espressos—one laced with grappa—my companions gave me their full attention.

"You remember when Tino and I came here three months ago to meet our long-lost uncle?"

Renata looked sad. "I heard about SJ's passing. *Condoglianze.*"

"*Grazie.* He lived a long productive life and at the end of it, fulfilled a dream. I am grateful that Tino and I had something to do with that."

"Your trip to Turin . . ." Terry began.

"Yes. Tino and I wanted to get better acquainted with this uncle we had never known. One night when we went to his villa for dinner, SJ told us a story of someone he had loved and lost seventy years ago. Giulia, the girl next door."

"Girl next door," Renata repeated. "You are talking about the family that owns the Villa Urbino?"

I nodded. "Giulia was Agostino's aunt."

Terry groaned.

"Long story short, I challenged our uncle to try and find her. I volunteered Tino and myself as chaperones and then coerced Agostino to join us."

"Did you find her?" Renata wanted to know.

"By the time we got to Turin, we were too late. Giulia had died two years before. Her daughter, however, was very much alive. It turns out, the union between Giulia and SJ had produced a daughter he knew nothing about."

Renata leaned forward, her eyes twinkling. "This sounds like a novel. Get this down on paper, and you could make a fortune."

I waved my hand dismissively. "The subject of skeletons in family closets has been well mined. Besides, if I start telling stories about Scheggino, I will lose all my friends and a *very* good Italian lover."

"I met Mari." Terry said. "She is the lady Agostino brought to your homecoming party. Remind me how this ties into Agostino's being adopted."

"Giulia had kept up a correspondence with her family back in Scheggino all the years they were separated. Mari kept all the letters. The true story of Agostino's birth was in those letters."

I took a sip of my espresso and smiled. "*Now* is where the story gets interesting."

Renata signaled the waiter and pointed to my cup. "I'll have what she's having."

"Make that two," Terry said.

"Agosto Urbino, the man everyone thought was Agostino's father, was the son of Gabriella Amedeo. She is the grandniece of the founder of the Foundation. Agosto was a hopeless romantic. He was fifty when he fell in love with a forty-year-old schoolteacher from a small town near Castelluccio. They married, and Cecilia became pregnant the next year. The pregnancy did not go well. Two weeks before her due date, she started hemorrhaging and was rushed to the hospital. After many hours, she gave birth to two baby boys. One came out dead and the other ended up in the ICU. Cecilia died a few hours later. Agosto took the news badly, threatening to kill himself right there in the lobby. That is where Dr. Sabatini entered the picture."

Renata stared at me. "Dr Alessandro Sabatini? He was the town's physician for many years."

"And an in-law of ours. My great aunt married him, don't forget," I told her.

Terry groaned again. "That's the trouble with small towns. Too many relatives. Just get on with the story."

"Dr. Sabatini happened to be at the hospital that night because a patient of his was giving birth—an unwed mother who wanted to give her baby up for adoption. He ordered Agosto to go home, where he was sedated and monitored, while everyone awaited the fate of Cecilia's second child. The baby died in the early hours of the following morning. Hearing the news, Dr. Sabatini made a quick decision. He apprised his patient of the circumstances and asked her if the Urbino family could adopt her baby. She agreed. Next, he arranged for the bodies of Cecilia and her babies to be brought to Gabriella's home, where she and Giulia's mother prepared them for burial. They sealed up the coffin with both babies inside. Dr. Sabatini then paid a visit to Agosto's villa to tell him that Cecilia's second baby was going to live. Five days later, Agosto came home from his wife's funeral to find the little baby they named Agostino waiting for him."

A silence fell over the group. Finally Renata spoke up. "The story is chilling but it shows how powerless humans are against the cruel hand of fate . . ."

"And how decisions made by others can determine the future of an innocent child," Terry added.

I nodded my head in agreement. "Not to mention that when that child grows up, like Agostino, he may someday want to learn who his biological parents were and why they gave him up. The answers may not be easy to accept."

"Did the father ever find out Agostino was not his?" Terry finally asked.

"No. Gabriella never told him or anyone the real story. When the letters were uncovered, Agostino and I went to the *comune* to corroborate the information. There were lines blocked out in the ledgers and enough tampering to make us suspicious. With the letters as proof, we went to his grandmother's villa where he confronted her. Faced with the evidence indicating the death of Cecilia's two children, Gabriella broke down and admitted everything."

"What about Agostino's biological mother? Is there a hospital record of the child she gave birth to?" Renata asked.

"No record of his birth or the name of his mother. It doesn't make sense unless she was from another region. It would have to be somewhere nearby because she gave birth at the hospital in Spoleto. It is the only medical facility in this part of Umbria."

Terry's lips were set in a thin line as if she was thinking through the story from a practical standpoint. She had always been the analytical one in the family—a strong and steady counterpart to her older sister's impulsive nature. She was the one who had steered my mother's real estate "hobby" into a viable business, creating a comfortable living for herself and her siblings. Anything she said about this story would not only make sense but also be devoid of any sentimental partiality.

"Let me get this straight," she began. "Except for some letters from an

Urbino relative and records from a *comune* whose facts may or may not be accurate, you have no concrete proof this story is real. There are no witnesses still alive except Gabriella. The memory of a 100-year-old lady under pressure is suspect at best. Dr. Sabatini is dead, and the birth mother has chosen to remain anonymous. Why doesn't Agostino just let it all go? Why does he want to dig it up again?"

Renata's eyes suddenly lit up. "Speaking of digging, I know one thing Agostino could do to get to the truth. Exhume the bodies."

"What???" Terry and I cried out.

"Open Cecilia's coffin and see if there are two skeletons in there with her."

"That is insane," I shot back. "Agostino would never consent to it."

"Don't be too sure," Renata countered. "Italians dig up their relatives all the time. It is no big deal."

"Yeah, I have heard about your bone box system," I said.

Terry sat up. "Bone Box? What is that?"

I looked at Renata. "Do you want to explain?"

Renata smiled. "I am happy to. You see, cemeteries in small towns tend to be small and community land scarce. Sometimes there is room for only one burial plot per family. There is no way the bodies of generations of family members could all fit, so we consolidate the old bones into one container to make room."

Terry looked horror-stricken. "But that is positively barbaric! Why don't you cremate?"

"Catholics frown on cremation," I told her. "It comes from an ancient belief that the corpse has to remain intact so the soul has time to leave the body and go to heaven."

"That's not exactly correct," Renata cut in. "The nix on cremation has to do with bodily resurrection, not soul ascension."

"Now that you mention it, I remember that from Catechism class. I always wondered, what happens to the people who go to hell?" Terry asked.

"If you ask me, *they* are the ones who should be cremated," I cracked. "Their souls are going to burn anyway."

Renata eyed me sternly. "Only God gets to decide who goes where. Maybe we should leave the cremation decision up to Him."

Chapter 4

Can of Worms

I LOOKED down at my empty cup and then at my two companions. "I don't know about both of you, but my head is spinning, and I'm seeing eight eyes staring at me instead of four. I'm taking a walk."

Terry rose and grabbed the arm of her chair to steady herself. "Let's see if the omelet is ready. Truffles and eggs sound pretty good right now."

After I paid for the espressos, we crossed the piazza and headed toward the crowd of people lining the bridge. Suddenly, a huge roar came from the banks of the river.

"They've just turned the waffle iron over," Renata yelled, grabbing my arm and leading me down the embankment. "You can't miss the next part. It is the most truffle you will ever see in your lifetime!"

By the time we elbowed our way through the crowd, the waffle iron had been cracked open, the yellow and black mound sizzling under the hot sun. Two burly men with long meat cleavers were cutting the omelet up into squares and shoveling them onto aluminum pans to be taken to nearby tables. An assortment of stray cats and dogs were busy licking the bits of half-congealed egg that clung to the sides of the waffle iron. No one shooed them away. I spied Tino at a table piled high with paper plates, plastic spoons, and napkins. Pamela was next to him, doling out plates of food to those already lined up.

"Tino looks positively Schegginese," Terry remarked, watching our brother interact with the crowd. "Mom would have been proud."

"Yes, she would have." I laughed. "And first in line to sample the omelet."

"I suspect Tino's motivation for helping out revolves around a certain dignitary. An excuse to brush shoulders with the mayor, perhaps?" Terry added.

At that moment, we watched Pamela reach across the table in front of him to retrieve more plates. We both looked at each other and laughed.

"Let's go give him a hard time," I said, grabbing Terry's hand and heading for the end of the line. Coming Renata?"

My cousin just stood there shaking her head. "Are you kidding? Did you see all those animals around the waffle iron? I always skip this part of the festivities."

I glanced over at the dogs flicking their tongues up into the still hot grill and then at the people sitting nearby spooning mouthfuls of food into their mouths.

"Are you feeling brave, today?" I asked my sister.

Terry considered my question briefly. "What's the worst that can happen? Salmonella only lasts a week, right?"

"Right," I said. We got in line.

After piling our plates full of food and giving Tino a few veiled remarks as to why he was suddenly a paragon of charity events, Terry and I made our way to the river's edge. We sat down on the grass and dug in.

Groups of families had joined us, clusters of parents and their children filling up the space in front of the kayak shed. The multi-colored boats tied together made a comforting scraping sound as they jostled for space along the muddy banks. Men in orange vests were walking back and forth to the shed, setting up rafting gear and getting the kayaks ready. After eating, many families would climb aboard and paddle their way down the not-too-dangerous rapids toward the nearby village of Ceselli.

I looked across the water to the opposite side of town. The pale pink walls of the castle stood out sharply against the mountainside. Along the edge of the Nera River, the sycamore trees were beginning to sprout, their new leaves reaching out over the water to meet the branches on the other side. To the south, plots of well-tended vegetable gardens stretched in an unbroken line of green.

A sigh of pleasure escaped Terry's lips as she popped the last bite of omelet into her mouth. She turned away from the mesmerizing flow of the river and looked at me. "Our grandfather's village is delightful . . . and I'm not just talking about the truffles. I am glad I decided to come."

I knew what she meant. This trip was an important step for the two of us. Being so close in age—ten months apart—had always been a challenge. We both wanted to be the favored one in our mother's eyes. Her opinion meant everything, spurring us on to compete for her affections through accomplishment. It became a competition of who could climb higher on the ladder to success. Our mother's standards were high, and her methods of pushing us to succeed were not always conducive to maintaining sibling harmony. Now, with our careers behind us, priorities had changed. Our current definition of success was measured in terms of personal growth. Practicing tolerance and forgiveness had become the goals to shoot for. I knew Terry had come not only to learn about her past but also to find common ground for the future.

"I'm glad you're here too," I said.

Terry glanced over at Tino piling used plates into a garbage bag. "Tino seems happy. Why can't you find him a nice Italian girl who will cook and clean for him?"

I snorted. "Not like his first wife, you mean. Jinelle treated him like her own personal houseboy."

"Yeah, she was a piece of work, wasn't she? She never had a clue how selfish she was."

"Too busy checking her makeup in the mirror to notice her character flaws," I said. "Not that we are prejudiced or anything."

"We are just looking out for our brother's welfare," Terry said.

"Right," I said, watching Pamela and Tino sharing a laugh. "A job that requires constant attention."

"Wasn't there a girl he met a while back when he took Mom and Dad to Scheggino?" Terry asked me.

"Our cousin Brunetta. Dr. Sabatini's granddaughter."

"She was a cousin?" Terry made a face.

"Step-cousin," I answered quickly. "Dr. Sabatini had a wife before he married our great aunt Teresina. Brunetta's mother, Pepina, was the daughter from his first marriage."

Terry put up her hand. "Enough! Another one of those too-complicated family relationships. So what happened?"

"Brunetta and Tino apparently hit it off, but Tino couldn't move fast enough, and she ended up marrying someone else."

Terry laughed. "Typical Tino. A lifelong commitment phobe, and when he does take the plunge, he marries a real ball buster."

I thought for a moment. "Do you want to meet Brunetta? She and her husband live in Bergamo but they still own Dr Sabatini's *palazzo* in Spoleto. They come here a couple of times a year. They might even be here now for the festival. I can call them."

"Sure. I would love to see if there are any embers still burning between Tino and his old flame." Terry said.

"Let's just hope Brunetta's husband is not the jealous type," I shot back.

Terry and I settled back on the grass, listening to the sounds of the celebration in the piazza. Across the river, from somewhere inside the castle, rose the plaintive notes of a saxophone.

Terry's ears perked up. "Do you hear that? That music is live, and from the sound of it, the artist is no amateur."

A man's voice interrupted her. "The artist you are referring to is Sergei, our resident celebrity. He played for some of the best bands in Italy when he was young. He will be in our lineup for tomorrow night's performances."

I turned around and looked up. A distinguished older gentleman in an expensive gray striped suit stood behind us. He had the look of a man who was used to being treated with respect.

I scrambled to my feet and held out my hand. *"Saluti, Signore Urbino. Come stai?"*

The man returned my handshake and then glanced at my sister. It was obvious he wanted an introduction. *"Scusa,"* I stammered. *"Questo è la mia sorella, Teresa."*

The man turned to Terry and smiled. *"Beniamino Urbino. Piacere."*

Without missing a beat, Terry stood up and embraced him with a kiss on each cheek, Italian style. Instead of being offended, Beniamino seemed pleased.

"Call me Ben," he said in English. "I see Anna has brought yet another relative to our part of the world."

"I arrived yesterday, but already your little town has made quite an impression on me," Terry said.

I winced at the word "little." The CEO of the Urbino Truffle Foundation probably was hoping for a more lavish endorsement.

He turned back to me. "I understand you have bought an apartment inside the castle. Does that mean you intend to live here?"

"Only part time," I responded. "I brought Terry along so she could meet our relatives, Georgio and Renata."

Ben's brow furrowed. "I see you have done some homework on your ancestors. I will warn you, family ties run deep here, and some of them come with a history all their own."

"I am learning that I have to be careful who I decide to pick a fight with," I cracked. "I may be insulting a relative."

Ben laughed uneasily. "There has definitely been some inbreeding in Scheggino in the last hundred years. On the other hand, sometimes we discover that a person we always thought of as kin is not even related to us."

I perked up. "Are you talking about your nephew, Agostino, by any chance?"

Ben looked quickly around to make sure no one had heard. His response was clipped. "You should know. *Tu hai aperto il barattolo dei vermi.*"

I did a quick translation in my head: *You opened the can of worms.*

Beniamino was right, of course. I had started the ball rolling with that trip to Turin. Little did I realize we would find the secret of Agostino's past through Giulia and her mother's correspondence. I had hoped the discovery that Agostino had been adopted would be taken in stride by the rest of the Urbino clan—that they would still regard him as a cherished family member. Looking into the cold eyes of Beniamino Urbino, I wasn't so sure.

There was an uncomfortable silence before Terry came to my rescue. "My sister is notorious for stirring things up. Don't take it personal. She really can't help herself."

"It would seem so," Beniamino answered. With a slight nod to my sister, he walked back to the stage area.

"*Great.* I just made an enemy of the most powerful man in town," I said. "Why didn't I keep my mouth shut about Agostino?"

"Technically, he brought it up," my sister reminded me. "Your response was what he objected to. Like I said, you just can't help yourself. I have no doubt, before long, all of Scheggino will be avoiding you like the plague. All except Agostino, of course. He will have his hands full cleaning up the mess you make."

Chapter 5

Siren Song

THE SOUND of the sax grew louder now, cutting through the stillness of the afternoon like the wail of an impassioned lover.

"Sergei must be practicing for tomorrow night's performance," Terry said. "Do you want to take a closer look?"

"Sure, it's about time I met the resident celebrity."

We gathered up our trash and started walking up the embankment toward the piazza. I caught sight of Tino and a few of the local boys hauling bags of garbage to the recycling bins.

"We are going to listen to the rehearsal," I called out to him, pointing across the river where the music was playing. "Do you want to come?"

Tino shook his head. "I've got to help Pamela with the clean-up."

I raised an eyebrow. "Oh, so it's *Pamela*, now, is it?"

Terry rolled her eyes. "What men will do for love."

We crossed the bridge and headed south where a row of craft booths lined the narrow walkway that led to the west end of town. A crowd of mostly older women had gathered in front of a half-open iron door at the base of the castle. Looking up to the third level, I could just make out the kitchen window of my apartment.

Renata called out to us. *"Vieni dentro.* Come in. Sergei is finishing up his session. One more song."

I walked into the crowded room where a group of women had drawn up chairs, obviously intent on getting a preview of tomorrow night's performance. I saw an older man who looked to be in his late sixties seated at a pianoforte, picking out the notes of a song. His head was bent over the keyboard, bushy white eyebrows framing eyes the color of a cool winter morning.

"Cazzo!" I heard him swear as he ran his hand through a mane of shoulder-length white hair. There were two other men grouped around the pianoforte, one on drums and the other fingering a bass viola. On the opposite wall were a kitchen countertop, a sink, and a rather expensive-looking cooktop. It seemed a bit unorthodox, I thought, having a rehearsal in the kitchen, but maybe the acoustics were good. Renata pulled out two barstools from underneath the counter, and Terry and I sat down.

The drummer, a middle-aged rock-and-roll type with hair grazing his shoulders and a five-o'clock shadow darkening the lower half of his face, shouted above the din. *"Dove sta la pianista?"*

"Valentina ancora non è arrivata," Sergei answered, his voice sounding resigned. He was fingering the keyboard uncertainly. "I would play it, But I don't remember the notes."

"His pianist is late," Renata whispered to Terry and me. "He has one more song to rehearse... his signature piece, 'Caruso.' He needs a piano accompaniment."

"Lucio Dalla's song? I know it!" Terry blurted out. "It's part of our band's repertoire."

"You have a band?" Renata asked.

"In San Diego. We do weddings ... and funerals. Mostly church stuff."

"Since when does an American church band do Italian love songs?" Renata persisted.

"There are a lot of Italians in my neighborhood," Terry explained. "But we are nothing even close to this level."

Suddenly Renata was dragging Terry toward the glowering figure seated at the pianoforte. "Sergei," she cried out, "my cousin knows the song!"

"Oh no," Terry protested. "I couldn't possibly ..."

Sergei turned, his gray eyes trained on my sister. "You know how to play?" He pointed to a portable keyboard set up in a corner. "On stage we use this."

"Electric piano? Yes, but . . ."

His eyebrows relaxed, and one side of his mouth turned upward. "Excellent. Come." He rose and escorted Terry to the instrument and gestured for her to sit. "You will be my accompanist for this rehearsal." He reached over and flipped the pages of sheet music until he found what he was looking for. "My arrangement," he said proudly. "You read music?"

Terry swallowed hard, a cold sweat breaking out on her forehead. "I read music, but this is the first time I have seen this. Don't expect it to be perfect."

Sergei patted her shoulder like she was a precocious student. "One thing you will learn very quick when you work with me. I never settle for less than perfect." He picked up his sax and nodded to the two musicians. "Now, we begin."

Sergei's version of the song started with a piano solo, followed by the introduction of drums, then vocals, sung by the bass player. At first, I could see Terry was nervous, her notes self-conscious and hesitant, but as soon as the other instruments kicked in and the sound of Sergei's saxophone filled the room, Terry was holding her own.

Almost immediately, the sensual sound of the sax and the man playing it pulled me in. His notes spoke to me, intimately, as if he and I were the only ones in the room. It was like he was making love to me with his instrument. My breath quickened, and I felt the pounding of my heart. Glancing around the room, I noticed all the other women were having the same reaction. Most of them were past fifty, their faces plastered with foundation to hide the lines, salon-colored hair carefully sprayed to cover the bald spots, but it was their eyes—alive and shining—that told me a different story. A story I could relate to. Inside we were all young, and the music made us forget that we weren't. The man with the sax also knew. He was aware of his power and used it confidently: the legs set apart, the tight jeans hanging low on slim hips, even the flexing of the muscles in his arms as his fingers flew over the buttons. Never mind that he was at least ten years older than me, this man was reeking of sex. For a split second, I pictured myself splayed out on his kitchen counter, begging for it. I felt my face grow hot, and beads of sweat gathered between my shoulder blades and trickled down my back. My dress felt sticky and my thighs moist.

As the wail of the sax reached its climax, Sergei abruptly pulled it away from his mouth and wiped the spittle with the back of his hand. An audible groan ran through the crowd, and the ladies moved toward the musicians, applauding wildly. With all the attention on Sergei, it was the perfect moment for me to escape. I pushed through the crowd and out the door, onto the cobbled walkway. *What had just happened*? Was I aroused or was this another hot flash? I felt like some oversexed geriatric living out all my sexual fantasies before menopause kicked in. I thought of Agostino, and a wave of guilt washed over me. This was exactly the kind of behavior I hoped I had outgrown.

As I turned to go inside, I heard a female voice at my elbow. "Your backside is all wet. Let me give you my sweater." I felt gentle hands placing a cardigan over my shoulders. I turned around to see a woman about my age, slim and elegant in a long tunic pantsuit. She patted my arm. "Happens to me every time I hear him play, too. I always come prepared."

I fingered the knitted cloth, grateful beyond belief. "But I don't know you. How do I give this back?"

"You will be at the concert tomorrow night, yes? You can give it back to me then. Come prepared with a change of underwear . . . you will need it." The woman flashed me a conspiratorial smile and walked away.

Sergei and Terry were conversing with the other musicians when I went back inside. As I walked toward them, Sergei put a hand on Terry's shoulder and whispered something into her ear.

"Hey sis, I am so proud of you," I said, joining them.

Sergei turned to look at me, his eyes lighting up. "I saw you in the audience." *Of course, his deep throated voice was even sexier than his sax.* "You are Terry's sister, no? You play an instrument too?"

Terry spoke up quickly. "Anna is a dancer."

A bushy eyebrow went up. *"Se vede.* I see that. *Ballet Classica?"*

I nodded and gave him a mischievous smile. "Tutus and pointe shoes all the way, but I can still shimmy with the best of them, given half a chance."

He studied me with renewed interest. "So, you like the way Sergei play?"

It would have been so easy to bat my eyes and contribute to his already oversized ego, but I resisted. "I thought my sister did a great job," I said shortly.

"*Sì, fantastico!*" Sergei's hand slid from Terry's shoulder to her elbow. "Maybe if my pianist not show up tomorrow, you will play for me?"

Terry's eyes widened. "How many songs would I have to learn?"

"Five or six. We work all night, here, in my house."

The clicking of high heels across the kitchen floor made everyone turn. An auburn-haired beauty, about thirty-five, showing an ample amount of cleavage and a fine set of legs, strode toward us. Even from three feet away, I could smell the gin.

"*Scusa, mi dispiace che sono in ritardo.*" She gave Sergei a special look as he stood there watching her. You could have cut the sexual tension with a knife. There was no doubt in my mind she had changed her underwear a few times too.

"I am sorry also you are late, Valentina," Sergei replied in English, obviously for our benefit. "Maybe you spend too much time at the bar?"

Valentina bristled. "Well, I am here now. Let's rehearse."

"But we are finished. This beautiful lady filled in for you." Sergei winked at Terry.

Valentina's eyes narrowed to slits. "*Va bene.* I guess you will not need my services tomorrow night." She turned to Terry. "*Buona fortuna.* He is not easy to work with, you will see." With that parting remark, she turned on her heel and walked away.

"How soon can you rehearse?" Sergei said to Terry loud enough for Valentina to hear.

Terry blanched. "I am honored to be asked, but there is no way I can accept. I'm just not good enough to do what you ask. I would demean your performance."

"Don't worry, *cara*," Sergei whispered as Valentina pushed her way through the crowd to the front door. "Valentina will be there tomorrow night. She behave like this many times before but she always show up. The audience is like a drug for her."

Terry looked relieved.

"You are still welcome to rehearse with us later tonight. I cook dinner, and we do a run-through of all the songs at midnight."

"Thanks," Terry said. "I'm not used to night club hours . . . and I'd have a lot of explaining to do to my husband back in San Diego. I call him every night at 9 p.m."

Sergei looked disappointed. "Perhaps your sister would like to join us?" He gave me a sexy smile. "I make a *pasta amatriciana* that will bring you to your knees."

I was sure he wanted me on my knees, but it probably wasn't to eat pasta. I pictured the kitchen counter fantasy I'd had earlier with a room full of horny musicians watching. Not even I was brave enough for that.

"Another time, perhaps, but we will be front and center watching you on stage tomorrow night. You can count on it."

Chapter 6

Trouble in Paradise

"PRETTY HUNKY for an old guy, isn't he?" Terry whispered to me as we pushed through the crowd of blue haired groupies and stepped outside.

"Sergei? I hardly noticed." I pulled my borrowed sweater closer around my shoulders.

Terry laughed out loud. "Like hell you didn't. I saw you squirming along with the rest of them in there."

"And you were completely unaffected, I suppose?"

"Not completely. Why do you think I declined his invitation?"

I studied her. "I thought you had to check in with Mark at 9 p.m. or he would have the *carabinieri* out looking for you."

"That was just an excuse. I have been tempted before. One minute you are playing music together and the next . . . well . . ."

I thought about my kitchen-counter fantasy. "Yeah, I get it," I replied.

It was late afternoon by the time we reached the old piazza. The festival was showing no signs of slowing down, and I knew the people of Scheggino would be partying into the wee hours of the morning. I caught sight of Sabina Garibaldi busy replenishing her display of Urbino Truffle products outside the *alimentari*.

"Agostino was in here earlier looking for you," she called out to me. "He says he needs you to help serve tonight at the villa. He has a full house." Her eyes were twinkling.

"Me?" My brow furrowed, and Terry cracked up. My talents as a waitress were well documented in the Wilson family archives. One summer, right out

40

of high school, I had talked my way into a job serving the 7-a.m. shift at a huge hotel chain on the beach. The second morning on the job, I dumped hot coffee into the lap of the hotel's CEO during an important staff meeting, He was irritated, no doubt, to think anyone of my limited abilities could have been hired in the first place. I was given my waltzing papers the next day.

"There must be some mistake," I muttered to Terry, quickly dialing Agostino's cellphone. After six rings, I heard a harried, *"Pronto?"*

"Agostino, are you expecting me to help tonight?"

I heard laughter on the other end. "Who told you that?"

"Sabina. She said you were looking for me. Listen, I thought I made it clear about my skills in the kitchen."

More laughter. "She's pulling your arm. Emilio from *Ristorante Il Ponte* is here."

"It's *leg*, Agostino. 'Pulling your *leg*' is the expression. If you are going to speak American slang, at least try to get it right."

"And if you and I are going to have a life together," Agostino snapped, "you must learn your way around my kitchen."

Great, I thought. Barely forty-eight hours into my arrival, and we were already arguing. Just hearing the words "life together" and "my kitchen" sent a cold chill up my spine. Agostino had his sights on the altar while mine were still focused on the sax player's instrument.

"Are Tino and Terry coming for dinner?" Agostino's voice was calmer, now. "I reserve a table for three. *Va bene?*"

"Va bene, caro," I said softly and hung up. My lack of expertise in the field where Agostino made his living was a problem. If I was serious about him, and making passionate love together should be an indication of that, I needed to make an effort to fit into his life. I just hoped he would be equally open to fitting into mine.

•⁓⁓•

Tino, Terry, and I passed through the open gates of the Villa Urbino just after nine. I felt a twinge of guilt when I saw every space in the parking lot was filled.

Agostino had a packed house, and I hadn't lifted a finger to help.

Perched on a cliff overlooking the valley and the town of Scheggino, the Villa Urbino had been built, originally, as the home of Agostino's ancestors. After his father's death, the seventeen-year-old Agostino, now sole owner of the estate, decided to try his hand at renting out rooms and catering events. He soon found that hosting lavish wedding receptions, a rite of passage for every well-to-do Italian family, was more lucrative than farming. Except for the herb and vegetable gardens and the half a dozen pigs he still kept for the occasional mega feast, the fifty-three-year-old bachelor had hung up his hoe and become a hotelier.

In 1980, flush with the cash from his growing business, Agostino had set about remodeling the original villa to better suit his needs. In the main house, walls separating the living quarters were torn down to create a large dining area and dance floor. Small windows became French doors opening onto an outside patio with a pool and cabana. The servant's quarters lining the cliff were reconfigured into guest rooms. The new rooms all had views, private baths, and windows designed to catch the romantic sunsets that splashed above the mountaintops.

As we approached the French doors leading to the dining room, I saw that most of the tables were occupied. The atmosphere was festive—white linens, silver cutlery, the room echoing with laughter and conversation. Emilio was on the opposite side of the room uncorking a bottle of wine for an impatient group of well-dressed people. He looked up and pointed to a table for three near the kitchen. We made our way over to it and sat down.

"I was hoping Mari might be joining us." Tino sounded disappointed.

"You said you dropped her and Flavia off at Paradiso Vinto last night," I said. "I'm guessing she's there helping out with the guests."

A few minutes later, Emilio joined us. He handed out a couple of menus. *"Ciao, benvenuti. Scusa,* I cannot stay and chat. I am the only waiter this evening." His eyes nervously scanned the entrance as another group of people entered the dining room.

I shooed him away. *"Vai, vai.* Just tell Agostino we are here."

"Certo, but he very busy," he called over his shoulder.

Tino had put his glasses on and was studying the elegantly printed paper. At the top it read: *"Festa di Tartufi 2016.* Villa Urbino."

"Agostino is offering a set menu this evening," Tino said out loud. "Antipasto will be *bruschetti misti di Scheggino."* He glanced at Terry.

"The word '*bruschetti*' I recognize, and '*misti*' means 'mixed,' right?"

"Good girl," he responded. "Next, for the *primo piatto,* we have *interiora di maiale."* He put down the menu, his gaze focused on something in the distance. "I remember that dish. Pig entrails. SJ served it the first night I had dinner at his house."

I chuckled. "I can't tell you how much I enjoyed watching you choke it down." I turned to Terry. "Tino knew he would have insulted our uncle if he didn't at least try it."

"I wish I could have known him," Terry said wistfully.

"You two would have hit it off," I assured her. "He liked spunk."

"And pigs feet," Tino said, glancing back down at the menu. "That is the *secondo piatto* on this menu in case you were wondering."

Terry made a face, and we all laughed, but for Tino and I, there was a sadness in the sound. A sadness that only comes when the memory is painful. The void a loved one leaves behind is not easily filled.

I put my hand over Terry's. "Before he died, SJ taught me a valuable lesson. One that took him seventy years to learn."

"What was it?" Terry asked me.

"Not to wait too long to tell someone you love them."

Terry's eyes filled, and she squeezed my hand. "Why is it my emotions are totally out of control here . . .?"

"Your Italian side is coming out," Tino suggested. "It happened to me the first time I came to Scheggino."

"Me too," I said.

A clatter and a loud *"Cazzo!"* echoed from the kitchen.

Terry nudged me. "Why don't you go help Agostino? After all, you will need to learn *some time.*"

I shot her a *what does that mean?* look. "Not my forte. I could do more damage than good."

"Go on," she coaxed. "He will be grateful."

The kitchen was a disaster. All six burners on the Biagio stove were flaming; pots bubbled with ragu and something pink and squishy covered the top of a big oval pan. I grimaced. *Pig entrails*, no doubt. Below the stove, the oven door gaped open, a fiery heat blasting the tiny space. A very sweaty Agostino was pulling out pieces of meat in an enameled pan. I inhaled. *Zampe di maiale.*

"Clear!" he yelled, brushing past me to the butcher block table, both hands enmeshed in heavy duty potholders. As he laid the pan down, the sizzling meat and the drips of sweat running down Agostino's face made me feel even hotter. I backed away and started for the dining room.

"Where are you going?" he called after me. "Throw on an apron and start serving!"

Agostino started portioning the meat onto plates and spooning sauce with a big steel ladle. "These three dishes go to the Castagnola table," he said without looking up.

"The Castagnolas? Uh . . . which table is that?"

"The one with three kids banging their forks on their water glasses."

I grabbed one steaming plate and placed the other one into my arm, then I picked up the third.

Agostino looked at me. "You got this, right?"

"No problem. I used to wait tables at a breakfast joint in college," I said, with more confidence than I felt.

The plate that was balanced on my arm slipped as I started for the table with the clanging forks. Six sets of impatient eyes were looking at me, mouths practically drooling. I picked up my pace, my hands slick with sweat. Midway across the room, I knew I wasn't going to make it. The middle plate went first, careening off before sliding under two white tablecloths and just missing my black silk skirt. Plate number two slipped off my right hand and crashed to the floor, hot brown liquid splattering all over someone's stockings and high-heeled shoes. With the remaining plate in my hand, I walked over to the hungriest looking Castagnola boy and placed the *zampe di maiale* in front of him.

"*Buon appetito*," I said.

He dug in without even looking at the mess on the floor.

It had gotten quiet—all eyes focused on me. I was horrified. I caught a glimpse of the woman I had dowsed wiping pig grease off her leg. I stuttered an apology. She waved her napkin at me and said, "*Ero un cameriere anche io. Non preoccuparti.*" I translated quickly: *I was a waitress once too. Don't worry about it.*

I flashed her a grateful look. "Emilio," I called out, "clean-up near table two."

A minute later, Emilio rushed out of the kitchen with a mop and pail. Right behind him was Agostino.

"I thought you said you waited tables in college," he yelled, hands on hips and eyes blazing.

Everyone sat back like they were watching a movie. You could have heard a spoon drop.

I calmly undid my apron and handed it to him. "I did. I just never said I was good at it."

Agostino turned me around and started retying the apron. "You are not getting off that easily. I need another pair of hands and you are it. For the rest of the evening, however, you will be carrying only *two* plates at a time."

In the next hour and a half, I managed to tip over only two glasses of wine and serve one table their entrees twice. No one complained. Even Agostino seemed pleased, giving me a tap on the rump when I brought the last of the dirty dishes into the kitchen. When the crush subsided, I stumbled back to my guests, slipping off my heels under the table as soon as I sat down.

"Well," Terry said, "it was worth waiting thirty minutes for the main course just to watch you make a complete ass out of yourself."

I shot her a withering look. "You could have helped too, you know."

Terry shook her head. "No way. *I* am under no pressure to make a good impression for my future husband."

Before I could answer, Agostino slipped into the empty chair next to me. Tino quickly poured him a glass of wine. "Excellent job. The meal was fabulous," he said. "Even if the help could use a little more training."

Everyone laughed except me.

Agostino smiled and grabbed my hand. "Not to worry. Once we are married, I will teach you everything about the business. No more dropping plates."

Terry's eyebrows went up, and I felt like running for the door.

Agostino downed his wine and looked at me. "Speaking of marriage, I am reading the book our former Pope, Giovanni Paolo, wrote when he was a young priest. It is called *Love and Responsibility.*" His expression changed as if he was considering something important. "You are Catholic, no?"

"*Recovering* Catholic," I muttered.

Agostino cocked his head. "Recovering? What does that mean?"

How could I explain that I could still feel the sting of my knuckles being rapped by a rosy-cheeked Irish nun when I had expressed doubts about the existence of Heaven? Or that I hated the Bible's assertion that, even if a person lived an honorable life, if they didn't accept God they were damned to hell? Another point of contention was my suspicion that the concept of a heavenly reward had originated not from God, but from man to avoid the finality of death and to keep society from behaving badly. The Catholic doctrine, as I perceived it, did nothing to shed light on these doubts.

Staring at Agostino's puzzled face, it occurred to me this might be an important conversation to have with him in the very near future. I wondered if he would be open to hearing it.

Terry spoke up. "Agostino, are Italian couples reading this book?"

"Per sicuro. It has become a popular book for today's *fidanzati."*

"A sort of couple's manual for a successful marriage?" Tino asked.

"Sì. They read it to prepare them for what lies ahead . . . the ups *and* the downs."

"I wish I had read that manual before I got married," Tino said.

"The chapter I am reading now," Agostino continued, "talks about the mindset couples must maintain to avoid temptation. Staying true to one person. It seems an important thing for me to think about . . ." He looked at me. "Especially now."

"What kind of temptation?" Terry asked. "As if I don't know. Italian men are notorious for cheating on their wives."

"You think the women don't do it too?" Agostino shot back.

I was thinking about the concert rehearsal earlier and all those squirming females. A cheating woman seemed entirely within the realm of possibility.

"Basta. No arguing tonight." Agostino reached for the carafe of wine and refilled everyone's glasses. "Tell me about your day. Did you enjoy the festival?"

"Amazing. Helping out made it feel very personal," Tino said.

I rolled my eyes. "I'm sure it did . . . the mega-wealthy Urbinos slinging eggs and truffles for the masses. Kind of like our American politicians showing up at soup kitchens around election time."

Tino smiled. "Say what you want about the Urbinos, but Pamela is different. Did you know she grew up on a pig farm? Now look at her, running the town."

"It pays to marry well," Agostino said dryly.

"Guess what happened to Terry today?" I was anxious to get the subject off matrimony. "She stepped in for Sergei's no-show pianist at his rehearsal. You should have seen her! You never would have known she wasn't part of his band." I looked at Agostino. "He must have been something in his day. How old is Sergei?"

"Seventy-one. He gave a concert in the piazza last year to celebrate his seventieth birthday."

"Mmm, I would have thought younger. Is he married? Children?"

Agostino glanced at me. "Not that I know of. Why do you ask?"

"Just wondering. All the ladies in town seem to have their eyes on him."

"Talk about temptation!" Terry's eyes were twinkling. "If I wasn't married . . . that guy is a hottie."

"Sex on a stick," I said, without thinking. The minute the words were out of my mouth, I regretted them.

The table fell silent. Agostino put down his glass.

"Sex on a stick," he repeated, his eyes narrowing. "What does this mean?"

"It's just an expression," Terry said quickly.

"Meaning?"

"Uh, maybe lickable . . . like a popsicle?" Tino suggested.

I winced.

"It means slimy, Agostino," Terry said. "You know, lecherous."

Agostino wasn't buying it for a minute. He turned to look at the two of us. "So, you think Sergei is sexy?"

I looked at Terry for support.

"For an old geezer, I guess he's not half bad," she said.

I caught her eye. *Brilliant, sis.*

Agostino sat back and regarded me coolly.

It was Tino who finally cracked the icy veneer that had spread across the table during our conversation. "Jet lag is kicking in, and it is way past my bedtime. If you give me the car keys, I can take Terry back to the apartment."

The implication that I might not be going back with them wasn't lost on anyone. I glanced at Agostino. He had his arms crossed in front of him, and his lower lip was protruding. He didn't even look at me.

My feet felt for my shoes under the table. "I think we are all feeling it."

As if on cue, everyone began stacking plates and glasses and loading them into the dirty dish cart that had materialized with Emilio. Agostino just sat there, brooding.

I put my hand on his shoulder. "I could come back later . . . to help clean up?" The tone of my voice suggested a wealth of possibilities.

Agostino looked up, his brows knitted together like an oversized scarf. "That won't be necessary. Like you American women like to say ... 'Not tonight, dear. I have a headache.'"

Chapter 7

Dirty Dancing

"ARE YOU wearing *that* tonight?" Terry was eyeing the red silk dress I had just zipped myself into.

"Orders from Agostino."

"So, he broke the ice and called you this morning?" Terry asked, pulling on boots. I noticed she was wearing a much more conservative sweater set and slacks.

"He said to meet him at Sergei's concert tonight and I'd better look sharp . . . something about being a decoration on his arm." I dragged out the heels I wore yesterday. My feet hurt just looking at them.

Terry frowned. "Decoration? What are you, a trophy?"

"Maybe he's just proud of me."

"And maybe he wants a certain someone to know you're taken." Terry grabbed her coat. "And since when did you start following orders from jealous boyfriends?"

"Since I spent a very intimate night promising to love, honor, and cherish every part of his body," I answered.

"That was your first mistake. Jumping in the sack with him on your first night back. By the way, from what I have seen so far, Agostino is taking this relationship far more seriously than you are."

I sighed. "How come I always get it wrong when it comes to men? I was so hot for him when we were on SJ's adventure to Turin, but now, I have cold feet."

"Maybe it's all that talk of marriage," Terry suggested. "You don't know each other well enough for that. It would scare me too. And this long-distance thing . . . have you considered how it's all going to work?"

"Of course not. All I was thinking about was . . . well . . . you know."

Terry shook her head. "You are following typical Anna Wilson behavior. Somehow, I had hoped you, at fifty-nine, had outgrown that."

"Well, you would be wrong." I slipped into my red wool coat and cinched up the waist. "Let's try to enjoy ourselves tonight. Did you bring an extra pair of panties just in case?"

Terry held up two fingers. "And a pack of panty liners. No sense in leaving anything to chance."

Black-clothed stagehands were adjusting multicolored lights on the outdoor stage when Terry and I crossed the bridge to the piazza. The sky had turned dark. I searched the crowd of well-dressed women, but I didn't see Agostino.

"My two American *dolcezze*" a voice behind me said. I turned around and stared into a pair of gray eyes underneath two bushy white eyebrows.

Sergei laughed at the shocked looks on our faces. He was appropriately dressed in tight jeans and a leather jacket; three gold chains nestled into exposed chest hairs. He had "American Rock Star" written all over him. "I am happy to see you both here. Come, I take you backstage. You see everything up close."

"I can't," I began. "I'm meeting someone."

Terry shot me a *don't you leave me alone with him* look.

I searched the crowd again. "I'm going to keep an eye out. If I see Agostino, you are on your own."

Sergei escorted us to a space toward the rear of the elevated platform. Sound technicians were hauling equipment up the small flight of stairs leading to the stage, wires trailing like snakes behind them. I caught sight of Valentina primping in front of a makeshift mirror.

"I guess you're off the hook," I whispered to Terry.

Sergei had disappeared into the area reserved for the musicians. A moment later, I heard his band warming up. Terry and I found a pair of oversized amps to perch on feeling like two over age groupies. Through the gap in the curtains, I could see a sea of lined, heavily made-up faces looking at the stage. A sense of suppressed excitement, like at the rehearsal the day before, was in the air. Every one of those ladies was waiting to be reminded of a time when love hurt so good.

Is Agostino out there looking for me? I wondered.

I turned to my sister. "I've got to find Agostino and at least tell him where we are. I promise I'll be right back."

Just as I got up to leave, an important-looking man sporting headphones and a T-shirt that read, "Bruce Springsteen, The Glory Days Concert," motioned for Terry and me to follow him.

"Sergei needs you on stage," he said.

Terry and I looked at each other. I spoke up. *"Scusa, perche?"*

"Search me," the stagehand said. He looked very proud of himself for having mastered American slang.

The three of us climbed the short stairway to the stage as the music began. I could hear a drum solo, the strum of an electric guitar, and then a burst of applause.

"I know this song"—I grabbed Terry's arm excitedly—"'Hungry Eyes'! Eric Carmen's big hit in the '80s. A panty-wetter if there ever was one."

Terry rolled her eyes. *"So* cheesy."

"Hey . . . *Dirty Dancing* is one of my favorite movies, I'll have you know," I shot back.

The man with the headphones was talking to someone as he led us to the edge of the stage. "I got 'em here." He listened to the voice on the other end and looked at me. "Take off your coat."

I was about to say I had no intention of freezing my ass off when Sergei strolled on stage and picked up his sax. The applause increased as he raised the instrument to his lips. When he played the first notes, like a lover's heart ripping open, I could picture every woman's nipples within a 2-kilometer radius snapping to attention. Mine were no exception.

Maybe it was the slow, languid saunter, the eyes holding mine as he walked toward me. Maybe it was the sound of the crowd in the background, egging me on, hungry for a show. My performing instincts kicked into gear, and the thrill of being on stage again, of unleashing my creative spirit and commanding an audience, took over. I knew I wanted this. I turned toward the audience and saw a look of horror on a face standing at the edge of the crowd. In that moment, I knew I was not going to go quietly into the kitchen of Villa Urbino tying my apron and rolling up my sleeves. If Agostino wanted a life with me, he had to accept that this need to perform—even if only once in a while—was something I would not give up.

Terry gave me a little push. "Show those Italian women how to do a proper American shimmy," she whispered.

With the image in my mind of Jennifer Grey and Patrick Swayze swiveling in each other's arms, I flung my hair back, sucked in my stomach, and strutted toward center stage.

Later that night, alone in my bed, I reflected on my performance and cringed. Had I really lain across the piano with my leg in the air? Was that me sashaying around Sergei while he leaned in, the brass thing between his legs perilously close to the edge of my dress? Had the crowd really screamed for an encore? The only thing I remembered with absolute clarity was that, when I looked out into the crowd a second time, Agostino was nowhere to be seen.

"He totally played you," Terry said, pouring liquid into two cups from my blackened Pedrini expresso machine. She had just come back from an early morning run as the picture of health. I, on the other hand, had circles the size of craters under my eyes, and my feet were soaking in a pan of Epsom salt.

"What do you mean?" I asked her.

"Musicians do it all the time. They take a likely victim, usually from the audience, and use them to get the crowd going. Didn't you ever see Bruce Springsteen's video of 'Dancing in the Dark'? That's why Sergei led us backstage to begin with."

"If I remember correctly, someone pushed me out there, whispering something about swiveling my American hips," I reminded her.

"Shimmying shoulders," Terry said. "You were not forced into that performance . . . just encouraged. Besides, so what? You enjoyed yourself, right?"

I colored and looked away. "Agostino didn't even stay for the end."

"Yeah, he left right after you started wiggling your tush up and down Sergei's backside."

I paled. "I did *that*?"

"You don't remember?"

"Sometimes when the creative energy is on you in a performance, you don't always remember every move. You just remember the feeling."

Terry raised an eyebrow. "And how was it?"

"It was a blast."

Terry laughed. "I could tell. You share that with Sergei, don't you?"

I looked up sharply. "I . . . I guess I do."

"I saw Agostino's face last night when you strutted onstage," Terry said quietly.

I sighed. "I saw it too."

"And yet, you still went out there . . ."

My eyes blazed. "It's part of who I am. Should I stop being myself just because he doesn't like it?"

"I think Agostino is worried. He can't share with you the joy of performing like Sergei did. That's why he's jealous." Terry sat down. "Look, last night's little performance showed Agostino who you truly are. Most of your life you danced on stages far bigger than Scheggino's. He needs to see all these different sides of you before he starts talking about marriage."

"And I need to see what kind of life we could have together before I go any further down the aisle," I added. "I wish I had kept my panties on that first night. It would have made things a lot easier going forward."

Terry gave me a sly glance. "And what about Sergei? Was that just acting on your part?"

"He's the kind of guy I thought I had outgrown. The one who doesn't need me. I've always been attracted to that."

"Sergei is not long-term material, I hope you know," Terry reminded me. "Or maybe that's the point. Maybe you are not really interested in what Agostino has to offer. Maybe all you want is a fling."

"I will tell you one thing—the fact that Agostino is assuming I want the same things he does without even asking me what *I* want is beginning to be a serious turn off."

Terry stood up and stretched her hamstrings. "Excuse me for being the one to bring this up, but if you start something up with the sax man, you will lose Agostino."

"After last night's performance, I probably already have."

That realization hit me hard. On the other hand, how could I be in a relationship with a man who didn't understand a very important part of me? And it went both ways. I needed to accept the way he was, not the way I wanted him to be. We weren't there yet. Maybe we never would be.

My cellphone rang. I grabbed it and looked hopefully at the name. My heart fell. "*Brunetta*," I mouthed to Terry.

Terry unlaced her running shoes and headed for the stairs. "Tell her we want to pay her a visit if she's in town."

Chapter 8

Dishing the Dirt

IT HAD taken a little persuading to get Tino to come along.

"We're going to Brunetta's after lunch. It will be a one-hour visit, tops. Pepina is inching past ninety, so her attention span will be short."

"Will Brunetta's husband be there?" Tino asked anxiously.

"I have no idea," I said.

Brunetta and Pepina's residence in Spoleto was behind a discount clothing store on a busy street. They owned a three-bedroom apartment in a non-descript building whose walls looked like they hadn't been cleaned in decades. The first time I visited, I asked her why Dr. Sabatini had chosen that particular location. Brunetta had said it was close to his office in the city and near the freeway where he could get to his patients in Scheggino. It was obvious her grandfather valued convenience—and his patients—over aesthetics.

I pulled into an empty parking place in front of a window displaying cheap dresses and a large red "*Sconti!*" sign. We all got out and started walking down a narrow passageway behind the store. I stopped in front of the five-story cement block. "Brunetta's *palazzo*," I announced.

Terry stared. "This is a *palazzo*? Somehow, I envisioned one of those fancy city houses built for old money in the *Seicento.*"

"In Italy, a *palazzo* is just a big building with a lot of apartments in it. It does not mean 'palace.'"

Terry looked disappointed.

I scanned the names on the intercom and found Pepina Marconi. I pressed the button and a godawful buzz emanated from the entrance to the building.

"Grab it quick," I told Terry. She pulled, but it didn't open.

"Try again," she told me.

I pushed the button, it buzzed, and Terry pulled. Nothing. Just then, we spied a woman from the other side exiting. When she opened the door, I called out a cheery *"ciao"* and we all rushed past her into the foyer. The dingy walls and gray cement floor had all the ambiance of a parking garage. I glanced at the peeling red paint and broken lights above the elevator door. "Let's take the stairs," I suggested.

"I remember this place now," Tino said as we climbed to the third level. *My* trip to find my roots with Mom and Dad. Nineteen ninety-five, I think it was."

I glanced at him. "That's where you met Brunetta for the first time . . . before she was married."

"Yeah," he said shortly.

We found 321 and rang the bell. A minute went by. I rang again. Another minute.

"Call her," Terry suggested.

I dialed Brunetta's cellphone. *"Pronto,"* a voice responded.

"Brunetta, we're here."

"But I did not hear the intercom . . ."

"We buzzed it twice and finally got in when someone was going out."

"Merda. That thing never work. *Aspetti."*

A few minutes later, the door swung open. I hadn't seen her for almost a year, and Tino hadn't seen her in twenty. Her look had changed. The conservative shoulder-length hair had been cut short and the ends were purple-tinged spikes stiff with hairspray. She was wearing a low-necked sheer blouse, tight jeans, and a pair of stilettos. Her eye makeup was black and thick.

Tino sucked in his breath.

Brunetta wrapped her arms around both Terry and me and kissed our cheeks. Then she stepped back and gave Tino her full attention. "You are not changed from the last time I see you."

Tino dipped his head to acknowledge the compliment. "But *you* have—for the better," he quickly added.

Her eyes lit up.

"Come inside," she said to all of us. "Pepina is expecting you."

Brunetta led us through a hallway where stacks of books and knick-knacks covered all the available surfaces. The clutter continued as we entered the main living area. There was a musty smell, and light from the sliding patio doors illuminated layers of dust. Beyond the glass, I spied a cement balcony and a view of the apartment building next door.

Brunetta shoved aside a pile of newspapers on the sofa and told us to sit. "I will see if Mama is ready," she said.

While we waited, I looked at the pictures on the walls. Most of them contained a gaunt, serious looking man with a closely shaved haircut and thick glasses. Dr. Sabatini, I guessed. On another wall, I saw photographs of the town of Scheggino from many years ago. I looked closer. In one, there were tables filled with soldiers at what looked like Avelino's Bar. Some of the men had swastikas on their sleeves.

"That was taken before the Americans came, when we were losing the war but no one wanted to admit it."

We all turned. Brunetta was standing in the doorway, her broken English replaced by a lightning-quick Italian. "Scheggino was one of the last holdouts of the fascist regime."

She walked toward the photo and pointed to a woman at one of the tables. "My grandfather's first wife. Pepina's mother. She worked at the *comune* during the last days of the war. Organizing events for the soldiers. In case you didn't know, my grandfather, Dr. Sabatini, was a fascist." She said the words matter-of-factly.

I had heard this before. It was part of our family lore. The man who admired Mussolini but would give the shirt off his back to help someone in need.

"We almost lost him one night to the *partigiani.* It was only because he was so loved by the town that he escaped being killed. A man came to our house and warned him. He got out in time." Brunetta's voice was cold and metallic sounding. I wondered how she and Pepina felt about her grandfather's politics and whether they had the same beliefs.

As if reading my thoughts, Brunetta continued. "Pepina did not agree with Hitler's reign of terror, and she knew her father never practiced that doctrine. He was a good man."

She did a quick shake of her head, indicating the subject was closed. "Come. Mama is ready to entertain you in her *suite.* The last words were uttered with a roll of the eyes.

We walked down another dark hallway. I passed a half-open door and caught sight of an unmade bed and piles of cast-off clothing thrown carelessly across a chair. "Vito did not come down with you?" I asked, catching up with her.

"He'll be down next week. He's in Lake Como doing some repairs for George and Amal. Children can be so hard on houses."

I heard a giant exhale from Tino.

At the end of the hallway, we stopped in front of a closed door. Brunetta rapped softly.

"Prego," a reedy voice called out.

Crossing the threshold was like stepping back to the 1920s. Silver Art Deco wallpaper lined the walls of a small sitting area adjacent to the bedroom. A metal and glass coffee table and several slipper chairs were grouped in the center of the room. Nearby, a tiny lady sat in a wheelchair; her hair was perfectly coiffed, and her made-up face looked out the window to a view of another apartment building.

Brunetta walked over to the wheelchair and whispered in the old woman's ear. "Mama, the relatives from America are here."

Pepina turned her head slowly and took us all in. The eyes underneath the creased lids were sharp like cut black glass. She gestured to the chairs, and we all sat down.

"These were my father's rooms," she said in Italian. "Alessandro never changed the décor, and I can't bear to, either. A bit outdated . . ."

I looked at the walls again, this time noticing a photo of a frail-looking woman with deep-set brown eyes and high cheek bones. Behind her was an iron gate with a plaque. I rose and walked over to take a closer look. *"Eremo delle Grazie"* was written in bronze letters on it.

I turned back to Pepina. "Who is the woman?"

Either Pepina didn't hear me, or she chose not to answer. She settled into her wheelchair and eyeballed Terry. "You are the one I haven't met yet. First time in Italy?"

"The first time in Umbria."

Pepina nodded. "It's about time." Her eyes moved over to Tino. "I remember that drive we took to see the cemetery in Scheggino. When you came with your parents. How long ago was that?"

"Twenty years ago, at least," Tino answered.

"Are you married yet?"

"Married and divorced, I'm afraid."

"Brunetta waited quite a while, and then Vito came along."

Tino turned red.

Pepina's eyes rested on me. "So, you bought a place here. Why Scheggino and not Spoleto? That damp little town, always shadowed by mountains—the smell of dirt and pig shit in the air—you could have bought something in this building . . ."

Cement as far as the eye can see? Not in a million years, I thought to myself.

"Scheggino is where my grandfather was born," I said instead.

"Ah, yes. Spirito's hometown. I seem to recall he couldn't wait to get the hell out of it. Lucky for you."

Brunetta gave us a long-suffering look. The caregiver's burden: to listen to a bitter old woman at the end of her life. The memory of my uncle patting my hand with a face full of joy at the end of his flashed through my mind. *I should be so lucky to die like that.*

Pepina suddenly reached out, her blue veined hand clutching mine. "Forgive an old lady. Sometimes I think I've outlived my ability to be kind." She shifted her legs under the blanket and cracked a smile. "It's been a while since I heard anything about Scheggino. *Dammi il sporco.*"

.   So she wanted me to dish the dirt. "I'd be happy to," I said, getting comfortable.

Pepina and Brunetta listened in uninterrupted silence as I described meeting the uncle I never knew and our adventures in Turin with Agostino. When I got to the part about Giulia's letters and an unwed mother's decision to hand over her baby to the Urbinos, Pepina began to get restless.

"Do you think the *comune*'s records were tampered with?" she asked.

Tino nodded. "The lines about the second baby living for only one day were blocked out . . . as if someone were trying to hide the fact that it died."

"Do you think Agostino's family did it?" Pepina asked.

"It would make sense," I cut in. "Without any record of a second death, the unwed mother's child could become the baby that lived."

Pepina's eyes narrowed. "Has Agostino found any information about his real mother?"

"So far, nothing. Spoleto's hospital records don't even show her having given birth to Agostino."

Pepina turned to her daughter, and a look passed between them.

It suddenly occurred to me that Pepina might already know about this. Dr. Sabatini could have told her. After all, he was there the night it all happened. I leaned forward. "Did your papa ever tell you this story?"

Pepina's eyes flicked to the photo of the woman by the gate before they came back to me. She gave a nervous laugh. *"Non l'ho mai sentito."*

On the way home to Scheggino, everyone in the car had an opinion.

"Pepina knew more than she was telling," Terry said.

"Then why did she say she had never heard it before?" I asked. "Do you think she was trying to hide something?"

Terry nodded. "She was lying. I was watching her body language. The minute you mentioned the unwed mother, she started to twitch."

"And Brunetta knows too . . . You saw that look they gave each other," I said. "We know the woman who gave up her baby is Agostino's real mother. If they knew her, why have they kept it a secret?"

Terry thought for a moment. "Maybe it has to do with the circumstances surrounding her death?"

Tino groaned. "You two are doing a lot of assuming from just some funny looks and twitching. Even if she does know something, Pepina may be withholding information for privacy reasons. The birth mother may have wanted to keep her identity a secret from Agostino and his family. Did either of you consider that?"

Tino had a point. If the mother wanted privacy, she had a right to it. "Should I tell Agostino about today?" I asked them.

Terry studied me. "If you do, he will want to see Pepina and talk to her. He will not let it go. Once you open the can of worms . . ."

Can of worms. Those were the same words Beniamino had used.

"Just remember," she added, "Tino and I will be leaving in three days, and if you open the lid, you will be dealing with the smell *on your own* long after we are gone."

Chapter 9

History Lessons

THE OLD Roman road that ran from the southern edge of Scheggino to the next village was five kilometers long. One side was a lush green hillside; the other dove straight into the banks of the Nera. Whenever it wasn't raining— or sometimes when it was—I allowed myself the luxury of experiencing it.

The next morning, when I started my run, the mountains were higher than the sun and I could hear, rather than see, the river running alongside me. As the sky lightened, it revealed itself: dark green and restless, rushing past the scraggly ferns that scraped the water like fingers. Halfway through, near the town of Ceselli, it bottomed out under a crumbling bridge. I paused to catch my breath, feeling the cool moist air against my face.

From the bridge, I looked across the water toward the village: little towers of stone jostled each other for a view of the surrounding countryside. The Valley of the Nera lay serene, a quiet hush of nature, as the sun burst over the eastern crown of Mount Sibillini. I breathed in a few mouthfuls of air and turned back.

Forty-five minutes later, Scheggino came into view. Seeing me, a rooster strutted toward the middle of the road and began to crow. A group of hens scurried toward him, their eyes wide with fright. _They are running to the rooster in hopes he will save them._ "Good luck, ladies," I called out. They looked behind at me and kept running.

Passing under the arch that marked the southern edge of town, I saw the glass and steel door of Sergei's house. I stopped and glanced inside.

A figure sat at one end of a cushioned banquette that ran the entire length of the wall. Past the banquette, a series of stone stairs without railings zigzagged up to another level. As I stood there, Sergei looked up from his book and gestured for me to enter. I raised the iron latch and pushed open the door.

"You are awake," I said, in Italian. "I thought all rock stars slept late."

He smiled. "They probably do. I'm jealous. Your Italian is improving faster than my English."

He lifted the empty cup in his hand. "Cappuccino?"

"*Per piacere.*"

As he headed for the kitchen, I eyeballed the house. The day of the rehearsal, I had been too distracted to notice. Cave-like stone walls rose to a height of more than twenty feet and rounded to a coved ceiling. To my left, a walk-in fireplace with a blackened wood mantel flickered with the light of a dying fire. In the center of the room stood a gigantic glass tabletop supported by a piece of iron angled to the floor. It looked suspended in midair.

"I've never seen a table like this," I said.

Sergei stood in the doorway to the kitchen with two steaming cups in his hand. "That's because there's only one. I designed it."

I walked around the table, noticing how one section of the glass slid back and forth, adjusting to the distance from the banquette.

"The adjustable glass makes it easier to eat without spilling food all over your lap," Sergei said, coming toward me. "My own invention. You see, I eat all my meals here . . . when I'm not outside."

"Absolutely amazing . . . everything . . ." My eye continued up the exposed staircase to a second level where an arched window had been cut into the wall above me. An elegant urn rested on the sill framed from behind by a yellow light. "I feel like I'm in a museum."

Sergei acknowledged the compliment with a slight nod. "*Grazie.* Please sit while I replenish the fire."

His hands sifted through the carefully stacked wood next to the fireplace. He placed two large logs into the fire and splashed them with liquid from a bottle lying nearby. As the fire roared up, he turned toward me, wiping the soot from his hands onto his sweatpants. The sex symbol entertaining a crowd of hungry-eyed women had disappeared. What I saw instead was man with multiple talents and a creative eye, a man who enjoyed his solitude as much as entertaining a crowd. A much more complex man than I had originally given him credit for.

I picked up the book he had been reading and thumbed through the pages. The title, "*Le Storie di Mi Papa,*" in big bold letters, stared back at me. "Stories My Father Told Me," I translated.

Sergei joined me on the banquette. "It is a book on Umbrian lore. Tales of people who populated this part of Italy many years ago."

"I know about the noble families and cardinals," I said. "And the farmers who worked their land but couldn't own it. They had to give back almost everything they grew. They were treated no better than slaves."

Sergei corrected me. "Landowners and farmers were not the only ones who lived here. There were others. Men from the east—from Syria—who came to escape persecution, hoping to find peace and solitude."

"Who were these men?"

"*Ereme.* Hermits, you call them in English. They lived in caves and cottages all over these mountains. Later, Saint Francis of Assisi founded a sanctuary at the top of Monteluco. He and his followers lived there for a few years in the late 1200s. It still exists—you can visit the cells. In fact, there is a wonderful trail that runs from Spoleto to the top of the mountain. As a young man, I hiked it on a regular basis. The monks carved it out originally. It is called La Via di San Francesco."

I looked at him admiringly. "I'm surprised—and pleased—to see you care about the history of your region. I am equally fascinated with the early inhabitants. In fact, I have walked the Via delle Mura Ciclopiche in Spoleto a few times on my way to the duomo. I have seen signs for the trail on that street," I said.

"And a short way from the sanctuary there is an old monastery. Michelangelo hid inside its walls to escape the Spanish troops infiltrating Rome.

Then, in the '30s and '40s, members of the church used it as a retreat.

"A monastery?" My eyes lit up. "Is it open to visitors?"

Sergei shook his head. "It is a private residence now. The hermits are long gone, but the monastery has some recent history that is interesting. A dentist from Rome bought it as a *casa de vacanze* in the early part of the twentieth century. Arrigo Lallo. It is rumored he had some very famous clients. Mussolini for one, the Italian Royal Family for another. The book says he invented the best-looking porcelain dentures in Italy."

I glanced at Sergei. "You're making that up."

"I swear, it says it right here."

I looked down at the page where his finger was. There was a black-and-white photo of an iron gate surrounded by woods. Next to it was a post with a sign that read, *"Eremo delle Grazie."*

"Was that the name of the monastery?" I asked, pointing to the sign.

Sergei nodded. "Originally it was called 'Eremo di Santa Maria delle Grazie.' Arrigo shortened it."

I gazed at the photo. *I've seen this before, but where?* Then I remembered. The picture of the woman by a gate at Pepina's house. The sign in the picture was the same as in the book.

I scanned the page quickly. "Does it say who lives there now?"

"The dentist's nephew inherited it in 1952. That's all the book says. He could still be alive . . ."

I stood up. "I'm going to find out. Can you tell me how to find the Via di San Francesco?"

Sergei closed the book and set it on the table. "I'll do better than that. Meet me here tomorrow at sunrise, and I will take you there."

I stared at him. "Are you talking about a hike?"

"Seven kilometers. All of it straight up."

I saw the twinkle in his eyes. Was he challenging me? It took me about three seconds to respond. "What time is sunrise?"

The corners of his mouth began twitching. "Six a.m."

When I closed the door behind me, Sergei was wiping down the table and gathering the empty cups. The sax man had shown me a different side of himself this morning. I had seen the sympathy in his eyes when he talked about the hermit caves, the monastery, and the men seeking solace in a life of prayer and solitude. Watching him move through his giant cave of a house, I wondered if, at times, he felt like one of them.

I turned away, feeling like an intruder, and began climbing the narrow steps to my apartment. My thoughts drifted to Agostino. I hadn't seen him since the day before yesterday—the night of my impromptu stage performance. Should I call and clear the air? After the intimacies we had shared—both physical and emotional—I owed him that much.

I whipped out my phone and dialed his number. At 8 a.m., I knew he would be having breakfast, feet up on the dining room table, reading *Il Messaggero*. I let it ring ten times before I hung up.

Climbing the last set of stairs, I lifted the latch on Cardinal Graziano's old wooden door. It was amazing how complicated things had gotten in little more than forty-eight hours.

Chapter 10

Sacred Ground

THE FOLLOWING morning I awoke to a sleeping household. When I had suggested the excursion to Monteluco the night before, Tino did not seem overly anxious to participate. Hiking up a mountain at sunrise was obviously not his idea of a preferred activity. As an alternative, he offered to drive Terry into nearby Spoleto for breakfast and a little sightseeing.

Originally an Etruscan stronghold, the town of Spoleto had been a favorite vacation place for numerous popes, including Alexander VI, during the early part of the fifteenth century. The Borgia Pope and his mistress produced a slew of kids there, and if legend can be construed as truth, the oldest, Cesare, not only killed his brother and had an incestuous relationship with his sister, Lucretia, but he also resigned as Cardinal because he was a heretic. Then there is the little matter of the beautiful Lucretia's favors being sold to the highest bidder for the Borgia family's personal gain. There is no proof any of these events actually happened, but that doesn't stop tongues from wagging even to the present day. What *is* a fact is that Lucretia Borgia ruled Spoleto as governor from 1499 to 1500. It would seem she got her revenge by proving she had a brain.

"Make sure you see the Borgia fortress, and then walk the hundred steps to the duomo on Via delle Mura Ciclopiche," I told both of them. "It is part of the Via di San Francesco pilgrimage that winds through town and ends up at the top of Monteluco."

Terry looked interested, but I suspected Tino had other plans. "We will meet you at the top for lunch. *By car,*" he informed me. "I take it the place is civilized enough to offer refreshment?"

"There is a snack bar where you can get a *porchetta* panini you won't soon forget," I promised.

By the time I walked down to Sergei's house at six, he was already in his Volkswagen, waiting. "Today, I will be giving you an opportunity few foreigners get: a guided tour of the route many Schegginese men—and women—took to get to the town of Spoleto. Before there was modern transportation, this road was the only way to get to the other side of the mountain."

"I know a little about that," I offered. "My grandfather and his brothers made the trek often when they were boys. It was legend in our household."

Sergei glanced at me. "I'm impressed. It's quite a hike. I'm dating myself here, but before I went to Terni to study music, I often made the climb. For enjoyment and exercise, of course, not because necessity demanded it. I used to compose songs in my head while I walked."

Sergei drove the Cabrio expertly through Scheggino's narrow streets and through the long tunnel toward Spoleto.

"So you were always drawn to music?"

"Always," he said. "My lucky break came when a local band in Terni needed a sax player at the last minute. I auditioned, and the next thing I knew we were headed to Greece for a twelve-month gig."

"How old were you?"

"Eighteen. I had no clue what the life of a traveling four-piece jazz band would be like, but I learned quick. Stay away from the groupies—especially the female ones—and focus on the music. No distractions."

"Apart from the groupies, was there anyone special in your life?" I asked.

Sergei paused. "There was one," he said quietly.

"What happened?"

"I lost touch with her. Not my choice." Sergei's voice had grown distant, and I sensed he was absorbed in his own thoughts. I sat back, marveling at the comfortable silence between us as the sky began to lighten. It was like I had known him forever.

We turned left at the Spoleto Sud sign off SS3 and parked by the Romanesque church of San Pietro. There were already four cars lined up along the side of the road.

"Hikers always know where the free parking is," he said.

Sergei had dressed appropriately in heavy-duty hiking boots, a thick jacket, and a wool cap and gloves. Having hiked the Alta Via 2 in the Dolomites the year before, I was equally prepared. At 6:30 a.m., the sun was still below the mountains to the east, and the road leading to the trailhead was just a dark strip of asphalt.

"The Rocca Albornoziana is up ahead." Sergei pointed to an impressive arched bridge spanning the valley. "Suicide bridge some call it. Eight hundred meters high and no barrier. Italians believe if you want to do it, no one should try and stop you."

I winced.

We passed a ruined cottage and found the beginning of the path. The metal trailhead sign read, "Monteluco, 5 kilometers."

"Three miles," I calculated. "Next to the Dolomites, this is nothing."

"Just remember, it's all straight up, and there are no snack bars along the way."

I felt insulted; his comment obviously hinted that I was some sort of weakling. Breezing past him, I shouldered my day pack and started climbing.

As the sun rose over the mountain, the light filtered through the leaves of the trees: shades of blackened green and pale gray contrasting with the emerald spears of the ever-present fern. The path, rocky at times, switchbacked steadily upward, making us forget how steep the climb was. Every so often, there was a break in the foliage, and I caught a glimpse of the shining city of Spoleto below us. Midway through the climb, we passed a tiny house with an arched doorway, a stone roof, and a bench where pilgrims could rest. A statue of a Madonna sat inside a niche surrounded by bunches of dead flowers.

We both paused to extract bottles of water from our packs.

"Tutto bene?" Sergei asked, his eyes on me as he lifted the bottle to his lips.

"Benissimo," I panted.

Sergei wiped his mouth and recapped the water bottle. "The monastery is not far from here. Who knows? Maybe the gates will be open, and we can have a look around."

I felt a surge of energy as I gave my pack another hitch and started moving. Another series of switchbacks later, we found it.

The iron gates were not only closed, but also, there was a chain around them and a *"Per Vende"* sign hanging off one of the rungs. I looked through the bars. Even though the plaque identifying the property was half-covered by an overgrown vine, I recognized it as the same one in the photo on Pepina's wall. I sighed. "It looks like Eremo delle Grazie has seen better days."

Sergei examined the overgrown shrubbery beyond the gate. "The professor must have given up trying to maintain the place. This happens so often now—the cost of maintaining these huge villas becomes impossible, and the only solution is to donate them to the city as a museum or sell them to a vacation rental group. They alter it and turn it into a hotel."

"And hermit cells become suites with attached baths," I said sadly. "I understand the financial predicament of the owners, but irreplaceable artifacts and a sense of history are lost when that happens."

"I guess it's better than seeing it dissolve into a ruin." Sergei looked ahead to the next switchback. "Let's keep moving. We still have a way to go before we reach the sacred wood and Saint Francis's sanctuary."

I took another sip from my water bottle. "At least we can be fairly certain *that* will never become a hotel."

Sergei laughed. "Not if the Franciscan monks have anything to say about it."

The sacred wood had been used as a place of prayer and inspiration by Saint Francis and his followers in the thirteenth century. Now it was a well-tended space with wooden benches and outcroppings surrounded by a crude adobe wall. Sergei had grown quiet as we walked the area. I sensed he was feeling the peace and serenity the monks had found there so long ago.

"You seem so different here . . ." I began.

"Different than the man making love to a crowd of women with his sax?" He gave a short laugh. "That is an act. It's what performers do . . . it has nothing to do with who I really am."

I smiled. "I'm glad you realized that shimmy up your backside wasn't the real me either."

Sergei chuckled. "Of course. A stage performance is but a glimpse the audience gets of the work of an artist. Hopefully, that particular evening, the glimpse was a favorable one. And as you know, part of the live performance experience is guessing what the crowd wants and giving it to them."

"Terry says you played me." I gave him a sly look.

Sergei held up a hand. "Guilty as charged. I confess I needed a little help that night. To get in the mood. Thank you for being my inspiration."

"You're welcome. You mentioned giving the crowd what it wants but a good performer gives of himself as well. Otherwise, it is not sincere. An audience can feel that."

Sergei looked at me. "You are right. That is why I rarely perform anymore. It is getting harder to give that way and I don't want to cheat them."

I was intrigued. "Are you talking about your audience or the world in general?"

"Both. For so many years, my contribution to others was my musical talent. I made people happy when I played. As I got older, when I saw that my music gave them back a piece of their lives—memories they had left behind— it still felt good. But lately, my heart is not in it anymore. I still want to give of myself . . ." Sergei's voice trailed off, and he looked toward the chapel at the far end of the sanctuary.

"In what way do you want to give?"

"That is what I am trying to find out," he answered quietly.

We exited the wood and made our way down to a large grassy meadow beyond the forest. Families were beginning to arrive for the day, bringing blankets and coolers filled with food to the picnic tables set up along the edge of the wide-open field. Kids were scrambling out of cars, already kicking soccer balls and chasing each other as the sun climbed higher in the sky. A white Cinquecento rolled up, and a head popped out the window on the driver's side.

"I'm starved," Tino called out. "Where's the snack bar?"

I pointed to a shack with yellow awnings and a patio cluttered with outdoor tables and chairs.

As soon as Terry's door opened, Sergei was there, offering her his hand and helping her out of the car.

Terry gave him an appreciative glance. "Next time I'm going with *you*. All I saw of Spoleto was the inside of a Fiat showroom in the industrial section. We never even made it to the duomo." Her eyes swept over the two of us. "How was the hike?"

"Magical," Sergei answered in English, flashing her a smile. "But it would have been much better with you."

The sax man act was back on. I wondered if what he said was true—that he was a different person when he was playing music. There seemed to be a public persona that he turned on and off—probably the result of his years dealing with admirers and fans. I could relate. In the past, during a performance or when I was signing autographs backstage, another side of me would emerge. It had come out the other night when Sergei and I performed together. Today, climbing the mountain, and enjoying the quiet beauty of the sacred wood, we had discarded the public image and shown different sides of ourselves. I felt honored that he could be that way with me.

The *porchetta* panini was as good as I remembered. Slabs of salt-encrusted pork, sliced thin and layered between hunks of shepherd's bread. The Wilsons ordered glasses of prosecco, and my hiking partner had a Schweppes.

Out of the corner of my eye, I watched Sergei. He seemed relaxed, his long legs splayed, and his eyes half closed as the morning sun beat down on him. He had taken off his jacket and sweater, and his white T-shirt was stretched taut against his pecks, the sleeves cutting across lean, muscled arms. He opened his eyes suddenly and looked at me. I looked away, embarrassed that he had caught me staring.

He scooted back in his chair and stood up. "I just remembered there is a little cemetery not far from here that many do not know about—families who have lived on the mountain. I have not been there in many years. Who is interested?"

Terry and I were up in a flash.

Tino remained seated and squinted up at Sergei. "How far is not far?"

Terry pulled him out of his chair. "That's what a glass of prosecco will do to you before noon. We are *all* going."

Tino looked at his watch. "I forgot to tell you. Flavia invited us for a farewell dinner tonight at Paradiso Vinto. Mari's leaving tomorrow for Turin."

"We have plenty of time. I promise, you will not be disappointed," Sergei assured him.

Tino sighed.

The four of us walked to the other side of the meadow. There were several large villas built in close proximity to each other facing the broad open space. They looked deserted but well maintained.

"Vacation houses for the wealthy families from Rome," Sergei informed us. "They come here to escape the heat in June and stay through summer."

Looking up at the clay tile roofs half-hidden by trees, I couldn't help thinking how much fun it would be to sneak onto the grounds and have a peek inside.

Sergei seemed to read my mind. "There are caretakers around even if you don't see anyone. Don't even *think* about trespassing."

He led us around the high stone walls and down a road toward the southern side of the mountain. As Terry matched Sergei's quick stride, I dropped back to keep pace with Tino.

"Did Mari say if Agostino would be there tonight?" I whispered.

Tino shrugged. "She didn't. I guess we'll find out when we get there."

Sergei stopped before a broken-down adobe wall and opened the gate to the tiny cemetery. As we stepped through the high grass, I noticed crumbling headstones with names that were no longer legible next to modern slabs of marble less than a year old.

"It looks like it is still being used," I said to Sergei. "There are graves here that go back to the 1800s." I walked along, reading the names of the families: "Baccaria"; "Parenzi"; "Proietti." I stopped in front of a block of stone set in one of the outcroppings. It looked like a crypt carved into the rock. There were names engraved onto its surface. "Arrigo Lallo," I read out loud. "That's the dentist—the one who owned the monastery."

Sergei joined me. "That is him. He die in 1952, the same year his son must have acquired the Eremo."

My eyes traveled to the two other names below. "Elena De Glielci Lallo, *Morto 1945*"; "Pio Lallo, *Morto 1995*."

"Arrigo's son was named Pio, wasn't he?" I asked Sergei.

"*Sì.* It looks like he die fifteen years ago. He outlive his wife by fifty years."

"She was young. I wonder what she died of . . ."

He stepped closer and read the words inscribed at the top of the crypt. "*Sotto l'ombra della montagna la mia anima riposa.*"

"Under the shadow of the mountain my soul is at rest," I translated. "It seems Arrigo and his family had a strong attachment to this place."

"There is another rock crypt over here," Terry observed, pointing a little farther down. "All with the last name De Glielci. That must be Elena's family."

"That's her!" Tino called out and pointed to a small grave a little apart from the others. "The girl in the photo at Pepina's house."

I hurried over to where he was standing. "So, you saw the picture . . ."

Terry followed me. "I saw it too, *and* I noticed Pepina kept glancing at it during our conversation."

I bent closer to examine the oval picture on the headstone. The black-

and-white image of a frail young woman with soulful eyes stared back at me. "Angelina Lallo. *Nato 1931. Morto 1963*," I read aloud.

"There is nothing else written, and she is not with the other members of the family," Terry said.

"Almost like she was an outcast . . ." I whispered.

Tino laughed. "Maybe they just ran out of room."

"Then, why is her grave the only one without a verse or a memory? She wasn't a child; she was thirty-three when she died." I looked at Sergei for an answer.

Even in the late afternoon sun, his face looked pale. "Sergei, are you okay?" I asked him."

He seemed ill at ease as he consulted his watch. "It is later than I thought. We must be getting back." He turned abruptly and walked toward the entrance to the cemetery.

"Wait," Terry said, turning to me. "I don't understand why Dr. Sabatini would have a picture of Angelina in his bedroom. Was she a close friend?"

"Or a patient?" I suggested.

Terry's eyes widened.

Tino held up a hand. "Enough. I think I see where this conversation is headed. Creepy old cemeteries have a way of contributing to already overactive imaginations. Time to go."

Closing the gate behind us, I turned for one last look at the solitary grave at the edge of the cemetery. "I know I could be opening a can of worms," I told the group, "but Agostino deserves to know about this."

We walked back to the car in silence. Sergei had grown quiet as if deep in thought. I caught up with him. "What happened back there in the cemetery? You suggested we see it, and then after a few minutes, you wanted to leave."

"Like I said, it had been many years . . . it was all so different."

"Different how?"

Sergei seemed to struggle for an answer. "There are a lot more graves now."

I was curious. "Did you recognize any of them? Is that what upset you?"

"Sergei!" Tino called out, cutting the conversation short. He had reached the car and was unlocking it with his remote. "You don't by any chance want a ride down . . . ?"

Sergei hurried on ahead and joined him. "Actually, I will take you up on that offer. Going down can sometimes be harder." He pointed to his shins.

Halfway down the mountain, Tino glanced at me in the rearview mirror. "Don't forget you are taking us to the airport tomorrow. We need to be there by 3 p.m."

Sergei looked surprised. "You are leaving? You just got here."

Tino laughed. "Seems that way, but it's been six days already. Time flies when you are uncovering family secrets."

I sat up straighter. "Wait...are you saying . . . ?"

"I'm saying Pepina is family, and she's got a secret. Anyone can see that. It remains to be seen whether it has anything to do with that woman in the cemetery and Agostino. That old lady is going to be a hard nut to crack."

I sighed. "I wish you both weren't leaving."

"I am going to Rome in the morning. I could drive you," Sergei volunteered.

"What time?" Tino asked him.

"Six."

Tino and Terry were silent.

"I'm going anyway," I called out. "I've already booked a room at the Hotel Metropolitan for tomorrow night. I haven't made my Caravaggio pilgrimage yet this trip. Going into the churches where his work is displayed is a ritual with me."

Sergei turned and looked at me. "Santa Maria del Popolo? Or San Luigi dei Francesi?"

"Neither. San Agostino. *La Madonna di Loreto,*" I answered.

I heard a low whistle from the front seat. "I guess you *do* know your Caravaggios."

Chapter 11

New Beginnings

THE DOME-topped villa stood at the end of a long winding road, the rows of cypress tress leading to it outlined sharply against a blood-red sky. As we drove through the gates, I admired, once again, the stunning architecture of the villa my grandfather's secret love had designed. Paradiso Vinto had been built in the 1940s by Agatha Altarocca, the creative force behind the Urbino Truffle Foundation. Later, SJ, her son and my uncle, had left his mark by planting the surrounding vineyards and adding guest cottages at the back. After SJ's death six months ago, Agatha's niece had transformed the five-bedroom Romanesque-inspired villa into a hotel.

The winding road ended in a parking space for guests to the right of the property. Terry got out of the Cinquecento and looked up at the impressive stone structure. "Wow. You told me about this place, but the reality exceeds all expectations. *Nonno* Spirito's mistress built this?"

I glanced at Tino before answering her. "We don't think of her quite like that. Agatha was Spirito's first love—the woman he would have married if the Urbino scion had not raped her and forced Spirito to take his revenge."

Tino intervened. "Well, Spirito wasn't exactly *forced* . . . Let's just say his actions were justified—at least in his eyes."

I waved my hand dismissively. "Whatever. The fact is, because of that incident, they both went on to live separate lives. But they never stopped loving each other. She had two children with him, don't forget."

Terry spoke up. "But he must have loved *Nonna* Marianna too. Their marriage lasted fifty years. I wonder if it is possible to have feelings for two people at the same time." She gave me a sideways glance.

I felt myself blushing. "I believe it is possible. It just makes things a little more complicated."

As we walked under a vine-covered trellis toward the villa, the remnants of a spectacular sunset washed the sky behind rose-tinged clouds. Reaching the entrance, I noticed a new addition: a rustic wooden sign hung from iron chains above the front door.

"Paradiso Vinto," Terry read aloud. "*Paradise Won*. I get it," she said simply.

I pressed down on the latch of the massive arched door, and it swung open.

Flavia had made a few alterations since inheriting her cousin's private residence, but the carefully curated ambiance created by the original owner remained intact. Beyond the black-and-white tiled foyer, the main floor opened to a huge space filled with a sprinkling of modern sofas and chairs. Glass and stone sideboards and wrought-iron floor lamps added seamlessly to the mix. On the opposite wall, an enormous accordion door revealed a panorama of the Valnerina in all its glory.

Tino pointed to the domed ceiling. "Central vaulted construction . . . like the Pantheon in Rome," he told Terry.

"It looks like it's been here that long," Terry answered.

I spoke up. "Agatha designed it to look that way. The villa was constructed using only ancient building materials and methods—like the castle in Scheggino. Not an inch of wallboard anywhere."

"*Sei arrivata!*" a cheerful voice called out from another part of the house. A few moments later, a tiny woman in her fifties walked toward us. Her graying hair was tightly pulled back in a bun, and she was wearing an apron with the words "*Maestra della Casa*" written on the front.

"*Scusa.*" She wiped her hands on the already greasy apron. "We are making *pizza al forno*."

"My favorite!" Tino said, enfolding her in a warm hug.

"There are no guests today, so I decide to try new toppings. You will be the . . . how you say . . . pigs?"

"*Guinea* pigs," Terry said.

Flavia favored us with a big gap-toothed smile. *"Grazie.* I learn English . . . slowly. Tonight, we will have pizza *con mozzarella* cheese, truffle, and mushroom. And Mari has made her special tiramisu for dessert. Come." She took Terry's hand and led her to the dual-sided walk-in fireplace.

Bisecting one end of the great room, the massive stone *camino* created a separate dining space perfect for making pizza or grilling meats directly in the fire. I looked through the open arched doorway to the kitchen and saw a woman bent over a farm table. As I walked toward her, she looked up from the pile of dough and grinned.

"Anna! *Scusa!*" Mari brushed a strand of hair from her flushed cheeks with the back of her flour-encrusted hands. She had her mother's Mona Lisa smile and my Uncle SJ's blue eyes.

Guilia, Mari's mother, had left Scheggino at eighteen, already pregnant with SJ's child. Unmarried and ashamed, she had begged her stepmother to help her find a safe place away from prying eyes. The *Duchessa* Sabauda, anxious to be rid of her husband's baggage, sent her to Turin, to work in the kitchens of the Italian Royal family. There, Giulia had learned her trade, brought up a child without a husband, and earned the trust of Her Royal Highness Princess Marie-Jose. When the Savoias were exiled in 1947, Giulia took her severance pay, and some savings, and opened a *pasticceria.* Mari had grown up working side by side with her mother, and when Guilia passed away, Mari assumed ownership of the shop. Later, when we arrived in Turin, she met the father she never knew existed.

I leaned against the broad soapstone counter watching her hands work the dough. "How does it feel to come back to the town where . . ."

Mari paused and looked up. "Where my mother grew up? It feels wonderful. She often talked about Scheggino when I was a child." She saw my puzzled face and rushed to explain. "Even though there were difficult memories for her, there were good ones too. When Mama was alive, I always hoped we would visit, but it never happened."

"You are here now," I said. "Somehow you found your way back. In some strange way, it seems prophetic."

Mari nodded. "It does. And knowing Flavia is the niece of my grandmother, Agatha Altarocca, makes it seem even more so. Scheggino is a very special place—a place where one could start a new life if one wanted to."

Seeing the look in her eyes, I couldn't help wondering which one of us she was talking about.

I heard a noise in the garden, and a minute later the pantry door opened.

Agostino stopped when he saw me. "I didn't know we were having guests." His voice sounded strained.

I felt an ache in the center of my chest when I looked at him. It seemed like three weeks rather than three days since I had held him in my arms. I noticed, with a growing sense of guilt, that his face was drawn and there were circles under his eyes. "I didn't know you were invited either . . ." I started to say.

Agostino gave a short laugh. "If you had known, maybe you would have thought twice about coming?" His voice had an edge to it I hadn't heard before. An edge tinged with bitterness.

Mari quickly stepped in, putting her arms around both of us. "Of course, you were *all* invited."

"Agostino, my man," Tino said, pouring him a glass of Montefalco red from the sideboard as the three of us walked into the dining room. "Terry and I are leaving tomorrow too. Anna is taking us to the airport, so it will be an early night tonight. I'm sorry to leave so soon, but I still want to have a job when I get home. Unfortunately, luxury car engines do not sell themselves."

Agostino addressed both Tino and Terry, his manner courteous but distant. "I am sorry to see you go. I hope you will return soon."

"First chance I get will be this summer," Terry answered. "Ever since I took that job teaching music at Saint Vincent's, I'm on a school schedule. I plan to stay longer next time." She smiled at him, and his face relaxed a little.

The conversation had a false ring to it—everyone walking on eggshells until Flavia gave each of us a job. Tino uncorked the wine, Terry sliced the fresh mushrooms, and I grated the truffle and the parmigiana cheese. She wisely assigned Mari the more difficult task of sliding the pizza pan into the fire and, under her supervision, taking it out at precisely the right moment. As I watched the two women work together, I saw a natural synchronization of movement between them. After only a week, Mari was fitting in like she had lived here all her life.

The pizza preparations proved to be a welcome distraction, and as the tension in the room eased, we all sat down to eat.

"*Scusa,* my American friends, but what I have to say next will be in Italian." Flavia reached out and patted Mari's hand. "We have some good news. Do you want to tell them?"

Mari shook her head shyly. "You go ahead."

Mari has decided to open a *pasticceria* right here in Scheggino."

A chorus of *auguris* rose, and glasses were raised.

"It will be located on the hotel grounds. Agatha's design workshop hasn't been used in decades, and it is the perfect size. Enough space for the ovens and racks and living quarters in the back." Flavia squeezed her cousin's hand. "Paradiso Vinto will have a personal pastry chef."

"Don't forget Villa Urbino," Agostino cut in. "Mari will be working with me too. With wedding receptions and birthday parties, she will be very busy."

"What about your pastry shop in Turin?" I asked her.

"Carla, my manager will run it, and I will be back and forth for a while. It may be someone else's turn to own it. I feel it is time for my life to take a new direction."

"Wow. This is definitely cause for celebration," I said, taking a sip of my wine and turning to Mari. "The Wilsons have some news too. We paid a visit to Pepina and Brunetta's *palazzo* the other day. I told them about our trip to Turin and your mother's letters. I hope you don't mind, Mari, but Pepina being

Dr. Sabatini's daughter, I thought she might be interested in the story."

"*My* story," Agostino reminded me.

I looked at him. "Yes, your story—and your birth mother's. I was hoping Dr. Sabatini might have told Pepina something about that night."

Agostino's eyes widened. "And . . . ?"

I shook my head. "She said she didn't know what I was talking about."

Terry spoke up. "She was lying. No doubt about it."

He shifted his gaze. "How do you know?"

"*Lingua del corpo*. Body language never lies."

Agostino looked less certain. "So, based on *body language,* you think she knows who my mother is?"

"There's more," Terry continued. "Anna, tell him about the woman and the grave."

I explained about the photo we had all seen in Dr. Sabatini's old room and the same picture in the cemetery. "Angelina Lallo died the year you were born, and she was most probably a patient of Alessandro's."

Agostino sat back. "But this is hardly proof she was my mother."

"That's what *I* said." Tino glared at Terry and me. "It's not fair to get his hopes up . . ."

I glared back. "What other leads do we have? I think another visit to Pepina's house is in order—this time with Agostino."

Agostino shot me a grateful look. "I would appreciate a chance to speak with her if you could arrange it."

"Don't get too excited. She may not want to see either of us."

Agostino nodded. "It is something to think about anyway. How did you find the cemetery? I'm surprised Pepina told you about it."

"Sergei showed it to us after our lunch on Monteluco," Tino answered.

Agostino's eyes narrowed. "You had lunch with Sergei up there?"

"After the hike," Terry added, a twinkle in her eye.

I gave my siblings a dirty look. "I asked Sergei to take me on the Via di San Francesco trail to see the sacred wood and the monastery," I explained quickly.

Agostino stared at me. "I wanted to take you there. It is one of my favorite trails."

"What's the big deal?" I said. "We can go there again."

"There is nothing like going there for the first time. It is magical. *I* wanted to be the one to show it to you." He spit the last words out and threw down his napkin. "My excuses to all of you, but my appetite is ruined." He got to his feet and walked out of the room. A moment later, I heard a door slam.

"He's acting like an ass," I said.

Terry corrected me. "No, he's acting like a jealous Italian man *and* an ass. Given your antics on stage the other night, you can hardly blame him."

"Jealousy is a trait that is rarely attractive, even if it is justified," I shot back. "Acting like a mature person instead of a schoolboy would serve him better. After all, going on a hike with a new friend is not exactly a breach of romantic etiquette. And as far as I'm concerned, I am still a free woman."

Everyone was silent. Recalling Sabrina's eyes on me that morning with my heels in my hand, I realized for the first time how my behavior on stage might have raised eyebrows in the village.

Terry seemed to read my thoughts. "Small town theatrics are to be expected here. My advice to you is to do some serious thinking about your feelings. Don't string Agostino along if you don't love him."

"You are right, of course," I said, feeling properly chastised. "In the meantime, how should I behave toward him?"

Mari patted my hand. "Like a good friend. One who cares about his future. Helping him find his parents may be the best thing for you both. It will bring you two together again."

I looked at her gratefully. "I can do that."

Tino reached for a slice of pizza. "Well, I for one, don't see how anyone could turn down a meal like this for something as silly as jealousy. On second thought, I'll take two."

We all followed suit, and in no time, the pizza and tiramisu were history. While we were clearing the table, Mari turned to me.

"You mentioned the woman in the cemetery's last name was Lallo. I remember Mama talked about a dentist with that name who came to visit the royal family. It was in the last years before the exile, 1947, I think."

"Sergei told me Arrigo's clients included the Savoias. Did your mother meet him?" I asked her.

"Yes. He made quite an impression on her. He was old, already in his late eighties, but capable. The king was in need of dentures, and this dentist made the best in the world. Another man came with him, his nephew, I think, and a young girl of sixteen or so. I remember because Mama entertained her, at Princess Maria-Jose's request, for the week they were at the Palace. That girl may have been Angelina."

"What a coincidence," I said. "Did your mother ever say what Angelina was like?"

"I remember Mama saying the teenager was shy and withdrawn, but when she was introduced to Her Royal Highness's little ones, she became a different person. Her shyness disappeared, and she spent the entire week she was there taking them on outings and inventing games for them. It was obvious she loved children. Mama said she knew she would make a great mother one day."

Chapter 12

Cinderella Gets a Correction

"TRY TO stay out of trouble . . . if that's possible," Tino said as he lifted the luggage out of the trunk and set it on the curb in front of Leonardo Da Vinci International Airport.

Terry gave me a quick hug before stepping out of the car. "I wish I was staying for the jousting match."

"Jousting match?"

"Two knights fighting for the hand of the American princess. Just remember, in the end, you can pick only one."

My eyes widened. "So, you think Sergei might be interested in me?"

Terry thought for a moment. "It's hard to tell what his intentions toward you are. But if he was . . . ?"

"Who would you pick?" I asked her.

"My bet is on the one who fights to win."

On the drive back to Rome from the airport, I thought about what Terry said. I knew she was joking—no gauntlet had been thrown down—but at least one contender had made his feelings clear right from the start. It would have been admirable and flattering except for the whole macho jealous boyfriend thing—and I wasn't sure I liked the life Agostino had so blithely chosen for me. Slinging hash for hotel guests or catering to spoiled brides and their entourage was not what I had planned for my golden years. Life was passing me by quick enough without my having to take orders or be kept under lock and key.

On the other hand, apart from some cheesy stage moves, Sergei had not demonstrated any real romantic interest in me. It was true that the few times we had been together—just the two of us—I had felt a special connection. I even harbored the secret thought that, given half a chance, we could be more. Was I imagining this because I wanted to believe it was true? I also got the feeling he was holding something back—that there was a part of him he didn't want me to know about. For a woman who lived for intrigue, I found it irresistible.

I pulled into the parking garage off Via Sistina and walked the two blocks to the hotel. I glanced at my watch. Five o'clock. I figured I had another hour before it began to get dark. There was plenty of time to check in, shower, and have a glass of prosecco at the corner bar.

The Hotel Metropolitan was not fancy, but it had two amenities I required when visiting the Eternal City: proximity to the Via Corso—the main drag of central Rome—and a 24-hour concierge. For a woman traveling alone, having a live person at the reservation counter was more important than room service.

The area where the hotel was located had been popular in the 1960s when nightclubs dotted the Via Veneto and crowds spilled out into the streets at all hours listening to the sounds of American jazz. The bar on the corner, with its nicked wood counter and mismatched chairs, had a similar throwback vibe even if the clientele sported tattoos instead of sideburns. I checked myself out in the mirror as I walked in: off the shoulder sweater dress, ankle boots, beanie angled jauntily to one side. Give or take a decade or three—I fit right in. With a nod to the man with the nose ring behind the bar, I ordered my *calice* of prosecco and strolled outside to find a table.

I closed my eyes and took a sip. *Absolute bliss.* Apart from the dining alone thing, being unencumbered in one of the world's greatest cities had its advantages. I didn't have to listen to the endless chatter of tour guides or drag bored friends to yet another art-filled church.

"Fancy meeting you here."

My eyes popped open. Sergei was standing on the sidewalk in front of my table. He was wearing washed out jeans, a pink shirt, and a European-cut turquoise jacket slung over one shoulder. *Only in Italy can a man get away with a color scheme like that.*

I touched my beanie to make sure it was still angled. "What the . . . ? How did you know I was here?"

Sergei laughed. "Actually, I didn't. Piazza Barberini is a favorite hangout of mine. In the decadent years, this bar was where my band came to unwind after we finished playing. It was the only place open until 4 a.m. May I sit down?"

"Oh . . . of course . . . may I offer you a prosecco?" I said, finding my manners.

Sergei eased his long torso into the tiny bistro chair. "A Schweppes, if you don't mind."

I signaled the waiter and gave him the order. "You don't drink?" I asked my companion after the waiter had left.

"I haven't touched alcohol in three years."

I waited for the AA sob story that was sure to follow, but Sergei remained silent.

After his drink arrived, I ventured another question. "What brings you to Rome?"

Sergei did not speak right away, as if he were considering how he would answer. "I am taking classes," he finally said.

I raised an eyebrow. "What subject?"

"Philosophy."

Again, I waited for a more detailed explanation.

"Ever hear of Saint Thomas Aquinas?"

I just stared at him.

"He was a Dominican friar," Sergei said. "He was also known as Doctor Angelicus. His teachings revolutionized the world in the thirteenth century and continue to do so today."

"What teachings?"

"That reason can lead the mind to a better understanding of the problems of human existence. And if you search hard enough, his teachings will reveal how our capacity for reason can lead us to God." Sergei laughed when he saw my face. "I know, not exactly what you expected to hear from a man who spent the better part of his life trying to get women into bed with his instrument, right?"

I smiled weakly.

He downed his Schweppes and stood up. "Finish your drink. If you would like, we can walk down the Via Babuino to Santa Maria del Popolo. *My* favorite Caravaggio is the one with the horse."

As we passed the Spanish steps, the lampposts began to come on, the diffused light lending a warmth to the faces crowding the piazza. The shop windows beckoned in the gathering twilight, their magic displays enticing the curious to look, even if they couldn't afford to buy. Ferragamo, Gucci, Swarovski—the illustrious names promised exquisite delights and exorbitant prices.

"The fashion industry's great seduction," I said, pointing to a ridiculous-looking outfit in one of the shops. "If someone were wearing that on this side of the glass, the average person would think they were crazy *and* had no taste. Sometimes I think we are all just sheep waiting for someone to tell us how to think."

Sergei kept his eyes on the people passing by. "If that were true, originality would not exist. You may not like that polka dot smock but it is an original creation."

"An *imperfect* original creation," I answered.

Sergei stopped and looked at me. "Have you ever considered the thought that the imperfection of man is proof that a higher being exists?"

"I'm sorry, I don't follow . . ." I began.

"Do you think that there are perfect people?"

"Of course not," I answered.

"Neither do I. But it is precisely their imperfection that proves there is a more perfect being somewhere in the universe."

"How so?"

"Natural beings could not have intelligence unless it was granted to them."

"By whom? God?" I asked him.

"Yes, or by the higher power you believe in."

"If you're asking me about my beliefs . . ."

Sergei stopped and looked at me. "I'm not. If it is a subject you wish to discuss with me that's fine, but I am not here to convert you."

Contemplating his statement, I asked myself: Did I want to go there? My less-than-traditional ideas concerning my place in the universe might not go over very well. "I have a problem with the inflexibility of the Catholic doctrine," I finally said.

"For example?"

"That we are to believe the Bible as fact."

Sergei turned to me, his face intent. "Maybe you are focusing on the sources of Catholic theology rather than their relevance to everyday life."

I stared at him. "So, you don't believe the Bible is the word of God?"

"I believe it is the word of God *as interpreted* by man. The teachings of Jesus—how he lived his life on earth—those are the important lessons."

"The teachings . . ." I asked, inviting him to elaborate.

"To practice forgiveness, temperance, compassion, and to have the courage to maintain these virtues in the face of temptation."

"What kind of temptation?"

Sergei paused to consider. "To indulge in behavior that is destructive to yourself or others. Dishonesty, avarice, infidelity . . ."

"Cheating on a spouse, you mean," I suggested.

"Or any one you have pledged an emotional commitment to," Sergei clarified.

Thoughts of the first night I had spent with Agostino sprang to my mind. I knew if I was developing feelings for Sergei, it was only right to let Agostino know.

"Your words are thought-provoking, I have to admit," I said, "but a daunting task to live up to. I'm not sure I could do it."

"I prefer to look at it as a journey. One day at a time," Sergei said gently. "And remember, having an open mind and an open heart makes the path easier to follow."

We had come to the end of the Via Babuino. The shops stopped abruptly, and outdoor tables fanned out in front of a huge piazza with a stone obelisk in its center. Crowds were crossing back and forth under a massive arch that had marked the edge of the city many centuries ago. Next to the arch was Santa Maria del Popolo, one of the oldest churches in Rome. We climbed the steps and passed a prostrate woman in ragged clothing holding out her hand. Sergei reached into his jacket pocket and pressed a few coins into her palm. She bowed her head in humble gratitude.

"You know, she probably has a little flat nearby," I said under my breath as we moved on. "Once when I was here, I saw a beggar buying toiletries in a grocery store. Begging is like a job for them."

Sergei turned on me. "And what's wrong with that? If this is her job, then I am helping her be successful at it."

"I guess that's one way to look at it," I muttered.

We entered the church just as the doors opened. Swirls of marble outlined the floor in geometric shapes—Arabic and Byzantine influences dating back to before Christ. If one knew where to look, they were still decorating floors of churches throughout Rome.

We made our way to the Cerasi Chapel where Caravaggio's paintings "The Crucifixion of Saint Peter" and "The Conversion of Saint Paul" drew art lovers from all over the world. Seeing Saint Paul's horse with one leg suspended over his master and a concerned look in his eyes captured my heart every time. For me, it was one of the most original depictions of the subject matter ever conceived, and knowing Sergei felt the same way was a revelation. We kept putting our euros in the box to see the canvases light up until we had no coins left.

Slowly, we made our way to the exit, stopping every once in a while to read the names on the covers of crypts embedded in the floor.

"We were talking about imperfection earlier," I said as we walked out into a night sky and a spotlighted obelisk. "Caravaggio was as imperfect as they come."

"And a genius," Sergei reminded me. "He gave the art world a vision that had never been seen before. He painted religious subjects as if they were living and breathing people—dressing them in sixteenth-century garb with dirty hands and feet. When I see his paintings, I can picture life in those times."

"I agree. I always wondered how such a twisted mind could paint such depth of feeling on a person's face. I still get chills when I see Saint Peter's face as they are pounding the nails in."

"I believe he was inspired by God to paint like that," Sergei said.

I stared at him. "Caravaggio was a murderer. How can a killer be inspired by God?"

"Free will exists in God's universe," Sergei said quietly. "We are free to live as we wish, whether it is to produce works of beauty or acts of depravity. Saint Paul was a murderer too. And clearly inspired by God."

"Caravaggio had a little trouble in that department," I said. "From what I've read, his inspiration came from his own imagination. He never gave God credit for giving it to him."

We crossed the piazza and headed for the Via Corso. Pedestrians had taken over the street, walking down the center in groups so large cars could not get through. We joined in. Young couples strolled by, kissing each other with pierced tongues while thirty-somethings held the hands of toddlers or negotiated baby carriages sandwiched between them. The old walked hand in hand, just happy to be part of the mix.

"Hungry?" I asked Sergei, eyeballing outdoor tables where people were tucking into plates of pasta.

"Starved. I know a great street off the main drag where the prices are good and the food even better. Yes?"

"Yes!"

Sergei grabbed my hand and pushed through the crowd until we came to a narrow side street twinkling with lights. There must have been a dozen tiny restaurants, all with covered trellises and outdoor tables.

"Pick one—they are all good."

The fire that was coursing through my body had begun with the touch of his hand. It was tender and sensual at the same time, and I wanted to hold on to it forever. I felt like Cinderella at the ball with her prince—except this was Rome, the music was Neapolitan, and the evening did not have to end at midnight.

I took his hand and traced my finger along the inside of his palm. "Your life is about to take a new direction," I said teasingly.

Suddenly his manner changed, and he withdrew his hand. "Anna, I need to tell you something . . . I probably should have done it sooner."

I was only half listening. My focus was on the speck of red sauce I wanted to lick from the corner of his mouth.

"At the end of the year, I will be entering the Bachelor of Sacred Theology program at the University of Saint Thomas Aquinas."

My eyes refocused. "Wait, what did you just say?"

"I have been preparing for this for three years with celibacy and prayer. If everything goes as planned, in a year I will be an ordained priest."

My ballroom fantasy vanished in a puff of smoke. My prince was now looking at me with something that looked suspiciously like pity.

The walk back to the hotel was a blur. I half expected him to burst out laughing and tell me it was a joke, that we had the rest of the night—if not the rest of our lives—to be together. But he didn't.

Outside the revolving doors, Sergei, looking the picture of sincerity, took my hands. "I'm sorry if this is a shock. My stage persona can sometimes give people the wrong impression. I would hate to mislead anyone—especially a beautiful woman like yourself."

I was doing okay until he said the last four words. Instead of placating me, they made me realize only too well what I would be missing. A man who knew how to say just the right thing to make a woman fall in love with him.

A sarcastic comment rose to my lips, but I forced it down. I wanted to walk away with some dignity. Besides, I didn't think I could stomach his sanctimonious answer.

I smiled the sweetest smile I could muster. "There will be a lot of disappointed ladies in Scheggino when they hear the news." I stepped quickly through the revolving doors into the lobby before he could see the tear rolling down my cheek.

Once inside, an angry voice stopped me in my tracks. "I'll fucking kill him if he laid a hand on you."

I wiped my face with the back of my sleeve and looked up. Agostino was standing in front of me, his face livid and both hands clenched into fists.

I gave a short laugh through my tears. "Not much chance of that."

He took a step toward me when he saw my tears. Instinctively, he opened his arms, and I came into them. "Why are you crying . . . did he hurt you?" He whispered into my hair.

Not physically I wanted to say. I suddenly dropped my arms and stepped back. I was not going to go from the frying pan into the fire. "I'm fine. It was just a shock, that's all."

"What is a shock?" Agostino searched my face. "Did he follow you to Rome?"

"No. We met by accident. He is here studying . . ." I stopped and eyed Agostino skeptically. "I could ask you the same question . . . standing in my hotel like a stalker."

Agostino looked hurt. "When I found out you were both in Rome, I panicked. I thought he was going to try and seduce you . . ."

A mirthless chuckle escaped my lips. "Sergei is not after me, Agostino. Far from it." I looked around the lobby and then led him to a seating area in a back corner near the bar. "I think we need to have a little talk."

The concierge of the hotel came hurrying over to us with a concerned look on his face. "*Signora,* this gentleman—is there a problem?"

"No problem," I assured him. "Can you find us a waiter? We'd like to order a couple of very strong grappas."

Agostino's agitated manner subsided as I told him of Sergei's future plans. He had the look of a man who had won the damsel—even if it was by default. What he didn't realize was that the American princess wasn't settling for the winner this time. If Agostino thought he could just pick up where we left off now that the competition was gone, he had another think coming. I decided right then and there to opt out of the game altogether.

When the grappas arrived, I knocked half of mine back in one gulp.

"Agostino," I said, patting him on the back like an old chum, "let's go visit that aunt of mine. If we are going to get serious about finding your birth mother, I think we should start with Pepina."

Agostino looked confused. "But what about us?"

Avoiding the question, I stood up and yawned. "*Buona notte.* See you in the morning." I headed for the elevator without a backward glance.

Chapter 13

Family Secrets

THE DOOR of the *palazzo* opened, and a tall, burly man with a scowl on his face stared back at us. Powerful arms hung from broad shoulders, and his thick neck supported a shaved head shaped like a bullet. Peeping out of his rolled-up work sleeve was a skull and crossbones tattoo. *Brunetta's husband, Vito*, I realized instantly.

"I don't think I've had the pleasure," I said in my best Italian. I held out my hand and waited to see if he would shake it. He didn't. Vito glared at my companion for a moment before stepping aside. I assumed it was an invitation to enter.

After we crossed the threshold, Vito turned on Agostino. "So, you are the one who wants to dig this all up again."

I tried to explain. "Agostino is searching for information about his mother. We were hoping Pepina might be able to help him."

Vito's voice rose a notch. "She's an old woman. Her memory is not what it used to be."

"I beg your pardon," a voice from another room rang out. "There's nothing wrong with my memory."

Or your hearing, I said to myself.

When we entered the living room, Pepina was on the sofa, surrounded by blankets and a half-eaten breakfast. I could hear Brunetta bustling about in the adjoining kitchen. "*Caffè?*" she called out.

I looked at Agostino for confirmation. He nodded.

"*Due caffè, grazie*," I called back.

Agostino stood, waiting to be introduced.

I bent down and kissed Pepina on both cheeks. "Zia, this is Agostino Urbino, the man I told you about."

"Piacere," Agostino said.

Standing next to him, I could sense a nervous energy, his eyes reflecting the turmoil going on inside. He held his hands behind his back in an effort to hide the tension. I could only imagine how important it was for him to appear calm and not frighten or alienate the woman sitting before him. Getting her to open up meant he had to approach her in just the right way. *If I could only help . . .*

"Pepina," I began, "there is a very important question Agostino needs to ask you."

Her keen eyes gave him the once over. "You've come looking for your birth mother. What makes you think I can help you?"

Agostino didn't hesitate to answer. "Your father was her doctor. Giulia's letters and Gabriella's testimony tell me that much. I have searched the records of the *comune* and the hospital in Spoleto and have found nothing. You are my last hope."

Pepina twitched.

Agostino drew in a shaky breath and sat down next to her. "I know it must be a shock—me coming here like this. I would like to try and explain how I feel." Agostino began slowly, struggling with the words and the emotions welling up inside of him. "Can you imagine what it would be like to grow up without a mother? I had relatives who cared for me, but it was not the same. I never knew the comfort and warmth of those loving arms . . . that guiding voice in my ear . . . that watchful eye keeping me from harm. No one ever sang a lullaby to me as I drifted off to sleep. Being motherless can leave a void that can never be filled by anyone else. Ever since I found out I was adopted, I have felt this incredible need to know the woman who gave me life."

Pepina stared past him to a framed picture on the mantel of a woman and a baby. When she spoke, her voice was quiet, almost reverent. "I *do* know how you feel. My real mother died when I was five. When my father married Anna's great aunt two years later, he hoped she would fill that void. Teresina did her best, but . . ." A tear rolled down the old lady's face, and her eyes came back to Agostino. "A mother is the one person who, having given you life, would gladly give up hers to save you. That's how deep her love is."

Brunetta had entered the room and was listening. When Pepina finished speaking, she rushed over to her. "Mama, that's enough."

"I told you this would upset her," Vito said. He had positioned himself near the doorway during the conversation, but now he crossed the room and stood in front of us. "I think it is time for you to go."

Agostino tried to let go of Pepina's hand, but she held on.

"No!" She said firmly. "He deserves to know the truth—at least what we know of it. Brunetta, go find the file and bring it to me."

A few minutes later, Brunetta came back into the room with a thick manila folder in her hands. She crossed the room and sat down on the edge of the sofa next to Agostino. The folder she was holding was frayed, as if it had been handled many times. On the inside flap were the words "Angelina Lallo" written in precise script. Brunetta opened the folder and extracted two yellowed sheets of paper. The first sheet bore the heading "*Ospidale di Spoleto.*"

"Give it to him," Pepina instructed her.

Agostino reached for it with trembling hands and unfolded it. "It is a birth record from the hospital in Spoleto."

He scanned the information quickly. "*Data: 15 aprile 1963. Bambino: maschio, peso: 3 chilogammi Nome della madre:* Angelina Lallo. *Medico curante: Dottore* Sabatini."

Agostino put down the paper and looked at Pepina. "This is me, isn't it?"

Pepina nodded. "Angelina Lallo was your mother. Read the comments at the bottom of the page."

Agostino read out loud in Italian: "On April 15, at 1:15 a.m., Angelina Lallo gave birth to a baby boy. The child was carried to full term. Difficult birth due to mother's illness and weakened condition. Baby appears normal and healthy. Mother has allowed me complete authorization to handle adoption proceedings but wishes to remain anonymous. Urbino family has consented to terms."

Brunetta handed him the second piece of paper.

He continued reading: "Death certificate: Angelina Lallo. April 20, 1963. Cause of death determined to be acute lymphoma carcinoma." He let the paper fall from his hands. "My mother died of breast cancer five days after giving birth to me."

Brunetta retrieved the document quickly and put it back in the folder.

Pepina looked at Agostino tenderly. "I remember Papa telling me she knew the dangers of carrying a child with such an illness—that it could complicate the pregnancy. She didn't care. She said she wanted to give birth to that child even if it killed her."

Agostino stifled a sob. Instinctively, I put my arm around him.

"It sounds like there was a relationship between your father and Angelina that went beyond doctor and patient. Were they close?" I asked Pepina.

"We took care of her in the last months of her pregnancy," Brunetta said.

"Here? At your *palazzo?*" I asked her.

"Angelina had an aversion to hospitals and refused to stay there even though she was terminally ill. Then there was the issue with her father."

Pepina shot her a warning look. Brunetta added quickly: "Given the circumstances, Papa decided the best place for her was with us."

"Gabriella told us that Agostino's mother was unmarried. A bastard child can be an embarrassment to a family. Was that the issue?" I was thinking of Agatha, my grandfather's mistress.

Pepina was noncommittal. "Let's just say it was complicated."

"Please tell me about my mother," Agostino pleaded. "What was she like?"

Pepina's eye's brightened, and I noticed spots of color on both her cheeks.

"It would give me great pleasure."

"Another time, perhaps," Brunetta said. "I think Mama has had enough excitement for today."

"Maybe *Mama* can decide for herself," the old lady piped up. "At my age, boredom can kill you just as easily as too much excitement."

Brunetta pretended not to hear her. She rose from the couch, pressing the folder to her chest and started to walk away.

"Wait." Agostino put a hand on her arm to stop her. "What about the father's name on the birth record? I forgot to look."

Brunetta glanced at Pepina and Vito.

Pepina spoke first. "Yes, his name is there, but remember her state at the time. She was very ill and had been heavily sedated. Angelina's father was the one who filled out the paperwork."

"I want to know who my father is." Agostino's voice was firm.

Pepina sighed and nodded to her daughter.

Brunetta opened the folder again and handed the hospital record over to him.

Agostino ran his finger down to the line that said, "*Nome di padre.*" He sucked in his breath, and his face went white.

"Now you know why we had to keep it a secret," Pepina said.

PART II

Chapter 14

The Guest

Monteluco, Umbria, 1962

ANGELINA stepped into the clearing just as the sun inched past the rim of the mountain. She breathed in the cool, crisp air and then exhaled. The sacred wood at sunrise was always magical. She pulled her jacket closer around her thin frame and sat on the low stone wall that separated the sanctuary from the forest. The walk had been harder this time. Her fingers reached inside the jacket, and she felt the lump under her arm. She knew she should tell Papa— he would want her to see someone. Then there would be tests. Endless tests. Too much precious time away from the wood and the sanctuary. She knew getting poked and prodded by doctors was not how she wanted to spend the little of it she had left.

Would God punish her for her what she had done? She had thought about it many times in the early hours before dawn when sleep eluded her. The urgency of the disease had driven her to commit those acts of depravity—all that pain and humiliation and then, a month later, the blood had come anyway. She knew it was wrong, but it had seemed like the only way. The voices in her head had become more insistent. *Time was running out.*

The sun had already climbed to the tops of the trees. She stood up and started back down the trail. Papa would be needing her to tend to the new guest.

From her bedroom window late last night she had seen the big black car drive through the gates and stop in front of the house. Outlined against the moonlight, a stocky middle-aged figure had emerged, a simple duffel bag slung over his shoulder. She had watched him as he stood quietly waiting for the front door to open.

"He is coming for solitude and spiritual reflection," Papa had told her a few days before. "Whatever you do, don't pester him with endless questions . . . especially about religion."

She pushed open the iron gate and hurried up the dirt road, hoping no one had missed her yet.

"Angie, *dove stai*?" An angry voice rang out. "The eggs! We need them for breakfast."

Doctor Pio Lallo stood in the middle of the courtyard, chickens squawking and fluttering all around him. He ran a manicured hand through his slicked back hair and looked anxiously at the chicken coop "I would have collected them myself but . . ."

Angelina wanted to laugh. She knew why he didn't want to go in there. *He is afraid of them, and they know it.*

"I'm off to the laboratory. I've made coffee. Make sure our guest has everything he needs *and leave him alone,*" he reminded her. He brushed off his custom-made suit and glanced at his spotlessly shined shoes before heading for the garage at the rear of the property. As soon as he left, the chickens settled down.

Angelina found her basket and stepped into the little enclosure. A dozen cubicles lined with hay were lined up against the wall. In each one sat a wild-eyed hen. Angelina made cooing noises as she approached the first nest, gently holding the small body with one hand and reaching underneath the downy feathers with the other. A second later, her hand emerged with two brown eggs.

Angelina heard a chuckle behind her. "What your father doesn't realize is hens can't be rushed."

She whirled around. *The guest.*

The eyes staring back at her were kind. "Since I will be staying here for a while, we might as well get acquainted," he said. "My friends call me Wojo."

She grasped his outstretched hand. It felt warm and comforting. "Angelina," she said shyly and turned quickly back to gather the eggs. "Papa says the hens won't lay for him."

"Perhaps it's because he makes them nervous. I'm guessing they prefer the calm and nurturing touch of the owner's daughter."

Angelina laughed. Her guest's insight surprised her. In a short time, he had picked up on the strict, controlling personality of her father. Had they known each other before? Perhaps he and her grandfather, Arrigo, had been friends. She glanced at his profile again. He had a broad pleasant face and the clean manicured hands of a medic or scholar. It was a pity she wasn't allowed to get to know him better. It would have helped alleviate the hours of loneliness.

"If you will allow me," her guest said, "it would give me great pleasure to help you gather the eggs."

Angelina gave him a warning glance. "Be careful. They don't take to just anyone. Sometimes they even give me a hard time." She showed him the scars on her knuckles as proof.

"I'll take my chances," Wojo said, petting a fat hen and gently reaching underneath her with this other hand. He held the bird until his hand was well away from her beak before letting go. "Aha!" he said, turning his wrist and opening his fingers. In his upturned palm lay a large brown egg.

Angelina grinned. "I see you are not a novice at this."

"It's all in the touch. Unlike humans, an animal can always sense if they are in danger." Wojo laid the egg in Angelina's basket and moved on to the next cubbyhole.

When her basket was full, they walked together across the courtyard toward the kitchen entrance.

❦

Remembering her father's words, Angelina did not make an effort to get to know the new guest. She had noticed, however, that, instead of seeking solitude, he appeared to welcome human interaction. Every morning, he met her at the chicken coup and insisted on helping her with the egg gathering. The hens had taken to him immediately. Even Pio had commented on their increased productivity. The guest made himself useful in other ways as well, with little repair projects that never seemed to get done like shoring up the walls of the pigpen or patching the ceiling leak in the downstairs bath. One morning, he even asked for a needle and thread to darn his socks.

Slowly, cautiously, in the hours when Pio was at work, Angelina began to open up. She told Wojo about her solitary life on the mountain, her father's reluctance in allowing her to have friends or to socialize. She even confided in him about her belief that being immersed in nature was her pathway to God.

A couple of weeks after he had arrived, they met, by accident, near the sanctuary. He was coming out of the chapel as she passed by.

"I see you have found our mountaintop treasure," Angelina said. "Saint Francis of Assisi and his followers stayed here for a time and built this beautiful place. Have you seen the friars' cells?"

"The cells are a bit too spartan for my tastes," Wojo said. "I admit I like my creature comforts."

"Hot coffee, fresh eggs for breakfast. Maybe a pillow or two?" Angelina's eyes twinkled. "I agree with you, but I also respect their commitment to living the simplest of lives. That is why they created the sacred wood. Legend has it that a dense forest existed here before they came. The friars cleared the brush, made fire rings and seating areas to worship outside. The friars believed that being in nature is when you feel closest to God."

"I have noticed you here on more than one occasion," Wojo said. "Do you feel His presence here too?"

Angelina smiled. "You are observant. Yes, I come here to reflect . . . and pray. I always feel better afterwards."

"It has that effect on me also. I am at peace here."

Angelina wanted to ask him why he had come—if there were memories that haunted him—doubts about the decisions he had made in his life. Did he have moments, like she did, where reality and fantasy coincided? There were times, in the cemetery, she had curled up by her mother's grave and lain there in a dream-like sleep. The images that had come to her had sometimes felt so real. She longed to unburden herself to this kind, understanding man. Maybe he could help her find her way back to the world that she had once cherished—a world that now seemed to be slipping away from her.

Then she remembered her father's words. *Leave him alone.* "If we hurry, we can catch the sunset," she said instead.

They made their way to the low wall where she sat every morning, this time facing west, toward the setting sun.

"Monteluco has always been a place of spiritual refuge," she said, "Beginning with the Syrian hermits looking for religious asylum. Then Cardinal Cybo owned it in the 1600s—you are staying in his sleeping quarters. We even had a pope stay here. Pope Pius XII had some dental work done by my grandfather and recuperated at the hermitage after the war. 1945, I think."

"Nineteen forty-six." Wojo corrected her then stopped.

Angelina looked surprised. "How did you know?"

"I have heard of your grandfather," he stammered. "Arrigo Lallo was well known throughout Italy."

Angelina laughed softly. "He made the best dentures in the world some said. His handmade porcelain dentures looked like real teeth. He worked on some very famous people in his day."

"Were you close to him?"

"Not very. He wasn't exactly a warm and fuzzy person—always obsessed with work—like someone else I know."

"You mean your father," Wojo suggested.

Angelina nodded. "Days go by when we hardly speak to each other."

"A medical doctor is an important job . . ."

"Papa is a pharmacologist," Angelina said coldly. "He designs drugs that make people feel better. Our family moved here when I was eight. *Nonno* was getting on and needed help running the hermitage. At first, Mama and I were happy, but then the loneliness crept in. We hardly ever did anything together as a family; the men were always working. Then sixteen years ago, when I was fifteen, Mama died. After that, I was left pretty much on my own."

"Your mother died young. Did she have an illness?"

Angelina smiled sadly. "You could say that. All I have left of her is a box of her things under my bed. My life changed after she died. Papa withdrew from me, and I became little more than a servant to him and my grandfather. Cooking their meals . . . cleaning . . ."

Wojo looked at her, concerned. "It doesn't sound like much of a life for a young woman. Didn't you have any friends?"

"The families from Rome that came to spend the summers at Monteluco thought I was too odd to play with their children, and Papa didn't like me socializing with them. I rarely left the hermitage. With one exception. I remember a trip we took together to the Royal Palace in Turin. The king wanted a new set of teeth before he left for Portugal. My grandfather was adamant about doing the work himself even though he was getting too old to travel. These were clients too important to entrust to anyone else, he had said. Papa insisted on accompanying him, and I came too. It was right before the abolishment of the monarchy. I think the king knew he was never coming back to Italy."

"It sounds like quite an adventure, especially in that difficult time. Did you meet the Royal family?" Wojo asked gently.

Angelina's eyes lit up at the memory. "I did! The Princess Jose-Marie was a genuine person and a good mother, but the thing I remember most was the woman who entertained me while I was there. Giulia was a servant but treated very much like a member of the family. She had a small child of her own—about two or three—the result of a love affair that had not worked out. Even though having the child altered the course of her life, she wasn't bitter. In a way, she seemed glad that circumstances had forced her to find a life of her own."

"And she kept the child," Wojo said. "Even in those times, she could have made another choice."

"You mean abortion?" Angelina said abruptly.

Wojo's jaw tightened. "Yes. I am glad she did not choose that."

"Given how much love she showed toward that child, I'm sure she never even considered it. I think that was when I realized how much I wanted to be a mother myself." Angelina's voice trailed off, and she pushed herself off the stone wall and walked toward the trail.

Her companion caught up with her, and they walked back to the hermitage in silence. When they reached the iron gates, Wojo paused. "I hope you find someone you can feel that kind of love for. I am sure you would be a wonderful mother."

Angelina wiped her tear-stained face and looked at him wonderingly. Was he trying to tell her something? All she could think of doing was to open the door for him. "If it is part of God's plan for me, I would be the happiest of women."

Wojo looked up at the sunset now beginning to fade and then back at her. "I have a request. The first nice day we have I would like to propose an outing. Pio says there is a beautiful valley on the other side of the mountain and a river . . ."

"The river is called the Nera." Angelina smiled, feeling encouraged. "It runs along the bottom of the Valnerina for more than a hundred kilometers. In Scheggino, you can rent kayaks and follow it as far as you want. People bring food and stop along the way to picnic. Then they turn around and go back upstream. Quite a workout I'm told."

Wojo's face brightened. "I want to do it! Perhaps you could take me there?"

"And brave the rapids?" Angelina laughed. "I've never done that before."

Wojo smiled uneasily. "I meant you could drop me off in Scheggino and meet me at a spot downstream with the lunch—somewhere where there aren't a lot of people."

"I know just the place," Angelina said. "Do you like waterfalls?"

Chapter 15

An Ordinary Man

THE FOLLOWING morning, it rained with a vengeance. Wojo hitched a ride into Spoleto with Pio to do some much-needed personal shopping. With everyone out of the house, Angelina took the opportunity to clean rooms and do laundry. Their guest had assured them he could clean his own room, but her father had taken her aside and insisted she give the bathroom a good scrub while they were gone.

The guest's bedroom evoked an air of military precision. The bed was neatly made, and the few clothes he had were hung up in the tiny closet. The only items in disarray were the books stacked on the nightstand. The bathroom was spotless, but she made sure she scrubbed the shower stall, sink, and tub anyway. Papa would no doubt require proof. Preparing to leave, she stopped for a moment to check out the reading material by the bed. The titles jumped out at her: *The Works of Marcus Aurelius. Plato and Socrates. The Teachings of Saint Thomas Aquinas. The Complete Works of Shakespeare.* She pulled the last one out and opened it to where the bookmarker was. *Romeo and Juliet. A romantic,* she thought, surprised. Quickly she put the marker back in, closed the book, and adjusted everything back to the way it was. Walking toward the door, she saw his duffel bag half open on a chair. *Don't do it,* she told herself. *These are his private things.* Her hand hovered over the open bag, her willpower wavering. Unable to resist, she pushed back the flap a tiny bit and looked inside. Her breath caught, and she snatched her hand back. Two ecclesiastical collars were folded one on top of the other next to a purple altar sash. *He's a priest!* There was something else in the bag: a drawstring purse, like the kind you would put jewelry in. Her heart fluttered inside her chest. She had gone this far . . .

She drew out the bag, opened the ties, and turned it upside down into her palm. A thick gold ring fell out. It was engraved with a dove, its wings spread over a Greek cross. She had seen a ring like this before, but where? Trembling, she placed the ring back in the purse and returned it to the duffel bag. She took one careful look around and closed the door behind her.

She leaned against the closed door, breathing hard. She remembered where she had seen the ring. It had been on the hand of a bishop.

It took three more days for the weather to clear up. During that time, Angelina had kept her conversations with her guest to a minimum. She was afraid he would see in her eyes the liberty she had taken with his belongings. She felt ashamed—like she had violated his privacy. The knowledge of who he really was and why he had come to the hermitage began to absorb her thoughts.

On the fourth day, Angelina looked out her window to a clear sky. Wojo met her at breakfast already dressed.

"Today's the day," he said smiling. "I'll help you pack the lunch."

The sun had cleared the mountains by the time Angelina's car dropped down into the Valnerina. Castello San Felice was up ahead, its high stone walls built to protect the tiny town nestled inside it. As the sun climbed and the morning fog dissipated, a cool breeze whipped up, signaling a farewell to summer and a yielding to autumn waiting in the wings.

Angelina took Wojo up the back way, along the old Roman road that connected the adjoining towns. He was entranced with the beauty of the landscape and the villages that seemed frozen in time. They drove through San Anatolia, a sleepy one-bar town where a stray cat eyed them suspiciously from under a crooked *ferma* sign. A few minutes later the rocky road turned into asphalt, and an iron gate came into view. A glimpse of a villa beyond it caught Wojo's eye. "Who lives there?" he asked.

"A branch of the Urbino family."

"Urbino," Wojo repeated. "I think I have heard of them. They make the truffles don't they?"

Angelina nodded. "The Urbinos who live here are relatives of the family who run the entire operation. Claudio lives in town—in an even *bigger* villa."

They drove another two kilometers where grazing sheep dotted fields of green. Turning a corner, Wojo saw the castle, its stone façade a dazzling white in the bright sun. Below it, a gently flowing sliver of water wound through the town of Scheggino.

Wojo let out a contented sigh. "What a stunning view. My heart rate dropped just looking at it."

Angelina smiled.

They crossed the bridge that straddled the river and parked on the strip of grass that led to the kayak sheds.

"Just let me out here," Wojo said, looking around. Except for the men inside the shed, there was no one in sight.

"I will be waiting just beyond the next bridge, four kilometers down," she told him. "When you see me, pull the boat up the edge of the bank. We will walk to the waterfall." Angelina put the car in reverse, crossed the piazza, and started driving south toward Ceselli.

Ever since she had discovered the ring in his room, she had seen Wojo in a different light. He was no longer an ordinary man trying to work out a problem in his life. This was a member of the church—an important member. Who *was* he, and why had he chosen the hermitage? She knew priests had visited here from time to time, drawn by the religious history of Monteluco, but they had always arrived wearing clerical clothes and using their official titles. They didn't come dressed as a layman in the dark of night with only a duffel bag. It was then that the idea came to her. Her bedside prayers for the one thing that would give her life meaning had not been ignored. Her breath quickened, and she heard the voices whispering: *This man has been sent by God to help you fulfill your dream of being a mother.*

She rounded the bend and saw the bridge where she was to meet him.

She parked the car and walked the short distance to the bank of the river where she had a good view northward. In less than an hour, Wojo would be popping out of the trees and heading toward her. Her side had begun to throb. She found a dry spot and lay down, her hand under her arm.

The sky had grown dark when she opened her eyes. Wojo was standing over her, blocking the sun. He had a concerned look on his face.

"Angelina, are you okay?"

She moved her hand away from her side and sat up. "I must have fallen asleep," she explained quickly. "I didn't hear you."

Wojo put a hand on her shoulder. "You stay here, I'll go get the lunch."

"But the waterfall is through the woods," Angelina said, trying to get up.

Wojo had a worried look on his face. "I am too tired and hungry to walk. This is the perfect spot."

She watched him walk to the car and open the trunk. She felt a stab and clutched her side. The pain was back. *He must not see it,* she told herself. *It will ruin everything if he finds out.*

The *panini con prosciutto* and pecorino cheese lay unwrapped in her lap. She was not hungry, but she knew she must try to eat. She tore off a corner and started chewing. "Did you know we are in the path of the Via di San Francesco? It winds down from the mountain, here, at Ceselli and runs along the Old Roman Road all the way to Rome."

Wojo looked at her hard. "What is wrong with you?"

Angelina blanched. "What do you mean?"

"Are you ill?"

Angelina considered how to answer him. Denying it was out of the question—it would be like lying to God. She settled for a half-truth. "It's just a touch of anemia. I get it from time to time when I forget to take my iron pills. She extracted an unmarked bottle from her jacket and shook out two pills. *He doesn't need to know its aspirin.* "Ferrous gluconate," she said, popping them into her mouth.

Wojo didn't look convinced. He reached inside the hamper and brought out an apple and started peeling it. "Living up there in the mountains, isolated, a person can lose track of reality. Pretending there is nothing wrong when you feel pain, ignoring symptoms. Is there something you are not telling me?"

"I could ask you the same question," Angelina replied.

Wojo looked up sharply.

"I mean isn't that why people go to Monteluco in the first place?" Angelina was eyeing him intently now. "A place to reflect without distractions. When the rest of the world is far away you can see things more clearly."

Wojo laughed. "Very clever, answering a question with a question. Fair enough. I will tell you why I am here. Maybe confiding in another person—besides God—will help."

Wojo gave half of the cut apple to Angelina and settled himself against the sycamore tree. "I knew from a young age that I was different from others in my village. Where I grew up, life was predictable. You had a few years of schooling and then took over your father's line of work—in my case, that would have been farming. Then you got married, had children, and, if you were lucky, died of a ripe old age. Being born with this incredible zest for life and an insatiable thirst for knowledge, I knew I wanted more. I discovered that one of the few places a boy could find books was the church rectory. I made friends with the parish priest, and he let me borrow as many as I liked. I studied the Roman poets Virgil and Horace and philosophers such as Epictetus and Saint Thomas Aquinas—even the writings of Shakespeare. *Romeo and Juliet* was my favorite. A whole new world beyond my village began to open up. As a result, I no longer wanted the life my parents had planned for me. At the age of sixteen, I left home."

"Where did you go?"

"My life took another direction," Wojo said simply.

Angelina waited for him to continue.

"Unfortunately, the thing that gave my life purpose, this thirst for knowledge, sometimes got in the way of my vocation. I had trouble accepting the limits it demanded." Wojo's eyes followed the water rushing along the riverbank past the abandoned kayak. "I wanted to do it all."

Angelina was getting frustrated with the evasive answers. It was clear he was not going to tell her everything. She tried again.

"Did the 'all' include marriage?"

Wojo chuckled. "You aren't afraid to ask, are you? I admire that. To answer your question, yes, even the idea of sharing my life with someone—having children and teaching them what we believed in—was something I thought about." He looked over at the sleepy town of Ceselli as if envisioning the lives of its inhabitants. "A union between two soulmates can be a sacred thing in the eyes of God."

"Did you ever have feelings for a woman?" Angelina's voice was tentative as if she were treading on forbidden ground.

Wojo was quiet for a while. When he spoke again, his voice sounded very far away. "Yes, I did."

Angelina knew her question could reveal her knowledge of his secret, but she needed to ask it. "Did it make you question your faith?"

Wojo shifted his gaze back to her. "Are you asking me if that is the reason I came here?"

Angelina nodded her head.

Wojo answered without hesitation. "My faith in God has never wavered. It is how I can best serve him that I struggle with."

Angelina whispered the question, "Have you found the answer?"

Wojo smiled. "I think so."

The sound of a car coming around the bend broke the stillness of the afternoon. It slowed as it approached the bridge, and a head leaned out of the window. "Is this the way to Terni?"

Wojo quickly brought his hand up to shield his face. Angelina rose and stepped out from under the tree. "Yes. Another twenty kilometers. Watch the signs."

As soon as the motorist had gone, he started gathering up the remains of their lunch and putting everything in the hamper. "It's time to get back," he said, heading for the car.

"But your kayak . . ." Angelina protested.

Just then, another boat with two men in it came into view. Wojo hung his head a little. "They are coming to take it back. I wasn't sure I had the strength to row upstream."

<hr>

Driving through the overpass toward Spoleto and Monteluco, they were quiet, taking in the magic of the Umbrian countryside as the sun inched toward the western horizon. It was only when they stopped in front of the gates of the hermitage that Wojo turned to face Angelina. "You, young lady, need to promise me you will make an appointment for a full medical check-up."

"I told you, it's just a touch of anemia . . ." Her voice trailed off when she saw his face.

"I may not be a doctor, but I know ferrous gluconate pills are brown, not white."

Angelina tried not to flinch. "I will do it right away. I promise. Don't say anything to Papa. He will just overreact."

"As any good father would." Wojo looked at her sternly. "Tomorrow."

"Tomorrow," Angelina said, avoiding his eyes, "I promise."

Chapter 16

The Burden

"YOU SEEM to be spending a lot of time with our guest," Dr. Lallo said irritably as he sat down to breakfast a few mornings later. "I've seen you together when you thought I wasn't looking. I thought I told you to stay out of his way."

"He likes my company," Angelina said, setting the plate of eggs down in front of him. "Sometimes he comes to find *me*."

Pio's eyes narrowed. "What do you do together?"

Angelina regarded her father coolly. "We talk."

"Talk." Pio said the words facetiously. "About what?"

"Everything." Angelina lifted the pot off the stove, walked over to the table, and poured his coffee. "What are you afraid of? You make it sound like I'm going to contaminate him." Her tone was light, but her eyes were challenging.

Pio looked up from his plate. "Considering how you two are alone here all day, I can't help wondering that maybe you're doing a lot more than talking. This man came here for some peace and quiet—not to be seduced by a religious fanatic."

Angelina felt the nausea starting. Religious fanatic," she repeated. "Is that what you think I am?"

"I think you have odd thoughts—seeing God in trees and bugs and who knows where else—that you have some kind of special relationship with Him that no one else has. Just like your mother, you imagine things that aren't there." Pio hesitated and then added, "You see where that led her."

Angelina's stomach lurched. The nausea was stronger now. "It didn't help that you left us alone all the time. You were always gone. She had a small child—she needed help, someone to talk to." Angelina paused, then added quietly, "There were things she couldn't live with."

Pio's head jerked up sharply. "What things?"

Angelina's eyes darkened. "What was said that night . . . the night you let that terrible thing happen. I heard the whole thing from the top of the stairs."

Pio interrupted her. "Angie, you were a child. You couldn't have understood . . ."

Angelina resented his dismissive attitude—as if it was a subject he did not want to discuss with her. They rarely mentioned her mother, and never talked about the events leading up to her suicide. Suddenly, Angelina was tired of keeping it bottled up inside of her. It was time to get it out in the open. "Mama said this family has blood on its hands. She killed herself because it haunted her."

Pio shook his head. "You don't know that. Your mother's problems began long before that night. She had trouble connecting to the real world. She was delusional."

Angelina turned on him. "Is that what you tell yourself so you can sleep at night? After Mama died, I found medical books in *Nonno*'s room and started reading them. She suffered from depression. How could you not recognize the symptoms? I thought that's what you do for a living—diagnose illnesses and treat them."

"She was *mentally* ill, Angie." Her father's tone was patronizing, like he was talking to a little child. "I always knew it—I was even drawn to it in the beginning. I thought I could help her."

"With medication, you mean."

"That is how you treat the insane," Pio stated matter-of-factly. "I just hope the condition is not hereditary."

I'm going to be sick. Angelina put down the pot and bolted for the bathroom. Reaching it, she knelt over the toilet bowl and vomited.

"Have you seen the doctor yet?" Wojo was standing in the doorway watching her.

Angelina wiped her mouth and stood up. "I haven't . . ."

Without answering, Wojo strode down the hall to the kitchen. Angelina heard two voices in earnest conversation as she moved quickly to the door that led to the outside. Her only thought was to get to the sacred wood—where she would be safe. She was halfway down the driveway when she heard the crunch of gravel behind her. She turned and saw Pio striding toward her.

"Get your things. We are going to Dr. Sabatini's office. *Now*."

❧ ⌒ ☙

Pio's car crossed Via Flaminia at the bottom of the mountain, heading toward the center of Spoleto. Wojo was in the front passenger seat next to Pio, and Angelina lay curled up in the back with her eyes closed. She heard the two men talking.

"She never told me anything about being anemic," Pio was saying, as if trying to absolve himself of any wrongdoing. "How was I supposed to know?"

"Of course, of course," Wojo said calmly. "No one blames you. I just hope Dr. Sabatini will see her on such short notice."

Pio snickered. "Oh, he'll see her all right. With the amount of business I give him, he wouldn't dare turn her away."

Wojo kept silent.

Angelina shuddered. *They will find the lump now, and the horror will begin. They will stick me in a hospital bed, and I will never get out.*

Pio pulled into the underground parking structure and found an empty spot. Wojo got out and pushed the seat back, gently holding on to Angelina's thin arm as he helped her exit the car. She was trembling, and there was a look of fear in her eyes. As they led her toward the stairs, Dr. Lallo kept looking at his watch as if he were late for an appointment.

"I'll stay with her," Wojo told him. "You go on to work."

Pio looked relieved. "My lab is walking distance from here." He handed Wojo the keys. "Have Sabatini call me at my office afterwards . . . then take her back to the hermitage. One of my colleagues will take me home." He pointed a finger at his daughter. "Do whatever Alessandro tells you . . . and be honest about your symptoms."

Dr. Sabatini's office was packed. All the chairs were taken, and there was a line extending all the way down the hall. Angelina saw mothers holding their flushed, sniveling babies; youngsters with scraped knees; and old men gasping for breath still holding cigarettes between nicotine-stained fingers. In each one of their faces, she saw something she had lost a long time ago: courage and a reason to live.

Angelina looked at Wojo. "This isn't fair. Some of these people have been waiting for hours. I can't just walk in and demand to be seen. Let's come back tomorrow."

"We can't afford to wait . . ." she heard him say before everything went black.

The next thing Angelina heard was the sound of Dr. Sabatini calling her name.

"Angelina! Can you hear me?"

Angelina opened her eyes. She looked confused for a moment then she struggled to sit up as if remembering where she was. She saw Wojo looking at her skirt. She looked down. There was blood on it.

"Get a stretcher," the doctor yelled, "and some towels."

Wojo helped her onto the stretcher when it arrived and followed her into a well-equipped operating room. The assistant and Dr. Sabatini transferred her to an exam table and covered her with a blanket.

"I'm fine," Angelina protested as the doctor examined her. "Clinics make me nervous." It embarrassed her to say it, but she needed an excuse. "With all the excitement, I . . . I guess my period started."

"I'm sure you are right," Dr. Sabatini said reassuringly. "We just have to make sure." He felt her abdomen. "Does this hurt?"

She gripped the side of the exam table. "No," she said quickly.

The doctor eyed her face with skepticism. "Why are you here?"

"My father insisted . . ." her voice trailed off.

Dr. Sabatini glanced around for Wojo, who had taken a seat at the edge of the room. "Did she have an appointment today? I don't remember seeing her name."

"We just came in. Dr Lallo thought she needed to get checked out."

Dr Sabatini nodded his approval. "You did the right thing. Now, please go back to the waiting room. We'll take it from here."

An hour and a half later, feeling very tired, Angelina walked into the waiting room. Wojo jumped up and rushed over to her.

She handed him a slip of paper. "Drugs," she said.

Wojo examined it. "This looks like a prescription sedative." He looked up. "What did they find?"

Angelina sighed. "They asked questions, took blood, urine, prodded me like a piece of meat. They were careful not to tell me anything specific, I noticed." *Afraid to scare me*, she almost said. The doctor said he would contact Papa." She touched Wojo's arm. "Can we just go home now?"

"Of course, as soon as we get this filled." Wojo put his arm around her waist to support her as they walked to the parking garage. When they got to the car, he unlocked it and gently helped her into the passenger seat. She lay back and closed her eyes.

"I'm sorry to be such a burden," she whispered.

Wojo's jaw tightened. "Don't think that way. You are not a burden—no matter what anyone else says."

Angelina didn't answer.

Angelina sat in a chair in her room. Wojo entered with a glass of water from the kitchen and took two pills from the bottle and left them on the nightstand.

"These are strong. The instructions say only two every six hours."

Angelina nodded, her eyes closed.

When Wojo walked into the bathroom, Angelina turned her head and opened her eyes. She watched him place the bottle on the top shelf of the medicine cabinet, hiding it behind the face creams. When he closed the cabinet door and turned to go back into the room, she shut her eyes again.

"Where are your pajamas?" he asked her.

"In the dresser." She heard him take something out of the drawer and lay it on the bed.

The bell on the nightstand jingled. "Ring this if you need anything at all. I will hear it," he said. A moment later, Angelina heard the sound of the door closing.

Angelina opened her eyes, pushed herself out of the chair, and walked into the bathroom. She opened the cabinet, and after a bit of searching, found the bottle of pills and walked back to the bed. She unscrewed the lid and turned it upside down into her hand. Eight. *It should be enough*. She took one at a time, following each swallow with enough water to make it go down. Then she undressed, slipped the nightgown over her head, and climbed between the sheets.

Chapter 17

The Dream

A MAN and a woman walked among the graves, the ground under their feet wet from an unexpected midsummer shower. The early morning mist hung in the shadows and filled up the space like a presence.

"I feel like an unwanted guest at a very exclusive gathering," the woman said to her companion. "I could swear the spirits are watching us."

The man smiled and took her hand. "You will be fine. Spirits like me."

They stopped in front of a huge boulder with a crypt cut into it. She ran her fingers along the grooves carved into the rock. "Arrigo Lallo, my grandfather," she said.

Her companion read the inscription out loud. "'In the shadow of the mountain my soul is at peace.' What a lovely sentiment." He pointed to a single carved rose under the name "Elena De Glielci Lallo." "Your mother?"

The woman nodded. "People say I look just like her."

"You don't remember her, then."

"All I have is a memory of a beautiful woman with haunted eyes and a box of treasured things she gave me. Just a sapphire ring and a few seashells— not much help to a young girl who needed to remember her mother. I was fifteen when she died, but because of her illness, she was never here long enough for me to get close to her. Every time she came back, she seemed more like a visitor than the woman who gave birth to me. I always knew it was only a matter of time before she went back to the asylum."

"What was wrong with her?"

"She just couldn't live in this world. Papa thought having a child would help, but it only made her feel guilty that she couldn't love me enough. She wanted to go to God, and, finally, she did."

"How did she die?"

"She overdosed on pills. Pills my father prescribed for her."

The man looked shocked. "I am so sorry . . ."

The woman faced him suddenly. "I have not told you this, but I know I'm going to die . . . soon."

"What is wrong? Please tell me."

"I found a lump . . . it may be cancer."

The man paled. "You have to tell someone . . . there are treatments . . ."

The woman laughed softly.

"Don't you want to live?"

"Going under those machines . . . burning it . . . and then the waiting, the living with the fear that every time I get checked, it might be back. Or being in a hospital bed, staring out the window, far away from the places I love. That isn't living," she said.

He started to protest, but the woman stopped him. "No, let me say this. I've known for a while now that there was something wrong inside me. It's given me time to think about death. I'm not afraid. I believe in an afterlife. There is only one thing I will regret not having done."

He looked at her. "What is it?"

"Bringing a child into this world . . . and all that comes with it. Being able to give and receive unconditional love—even if only for a little while. It is something I needed and never had."

"God can give you unconditional love . . . now . . . if you ask him for it. And think about the child. It would be alone . . . after . . ." The man's voice trailed off.

"If God decides experiencing motherhood is not to be for me, then I would find a place for him, or her. A family that would love him as much as I would have. It would be something I could leave behind, someone who would go on to live in this world after I am gone."

The man spoke gently. "What are you saying?"

"If I could fulfill my dream, I would feel that there had been some meaning to my life—that it had not been in vain." She looked up at him. "I think you know what I want to ask . . ."

The man put a finger to her lips to stop the words. Silently, he took her hand, and they walked out of the cemetery and down the path toward the hermitage.

Chapter 18

A Prayer Is Answered

ANGELINA opened her eyes. She knew immediately where she was. The starched white sheets, the blinding florescent lights—*the smell*. She tried to sit up and felt a jab of pain under her arm.

Wojo glanced up from his seat at the far end of the room. When Angelina moved, he dropped the rosary he had been holding and rushed to the bedside. He smoothed the damp hair away from her brow and pressed the button, alerting the nurse's station. A few minutes later, a nurse joined him, and they gently coaxed the frail figure back down against the pillows.

"There, there," the nurse said lifting her wrist and taking a pulse. "Welcome back to the real world."

After the nurse left, Angelina's eyes slid over to him. "So, who found me?" She did not feel grateful.

"I did. Luckily, I came in to check on you in the night. I could tell right away something was wrong. Then I found the bottle."

"Excuse me for not thanking you for saving my life," Angelina said sarcastically. "How did Papa take the news?"

"Well, he was concerned . . ." Wojo started to say.

Angelina laughed. "Never mind. I can just hear it. 'Crazy, like her mother,' right?"

Wojo avoided the question. "We have all had a scare. You have been unresponsive for four days. You owe your life to both of us, so a little gratitude would be appreciated. After I found you, Doctor Lallo had you down the mountain and into emergency in record time. Maybe you don't value your life, but there are others who do."

There was the sound of a door opening, and the tall, gaunt figure of Dr. Sabatini entered the room. He had a medical folder under one arm. "The nurses told me you were awake." The eyes behind the rimless spectacles looked sad.

Wojo got up and offered him his chair. Dr. Sabatini sat and regarded his patient.

"I don't have to tell you how concerned your father . . . all of us . . . have been. Given your weakened state, you might never have come out of that coma. What you did was not only self-destructive, but it was hurtful to others." He paused and added more softly, "Your actions were motivated by ignorant fear, no doubt." When his patient did not answer, he pulled his chair closer. "I am here to discuss the situation and help alleviate those fears."

Angelina stared at the ceiling.

Alessandro Sabatini cleared his throat and opened the folder. "According to the results of the X-rays we took, there are several masses in the . . ."

"Spare me the technical jargon, doctor, "Angelina said,. "What you mean is that I have breast cancer."

Alessandro answered quickly. "It is a treatable condition. We can begin radiation treatments immediately. Methotrexate has proven very effective for this type of cancer." He hesitated. "However, there is a complication."

Angelina took her eyes off the ceiling and looked at him. "What complication?"

"Your urine sample shows traces of human chorionic gonadotropin, or hCG."

"HCG," Angelina said, "What is that?"

Alessandro looked her straight in the eye. "A hormone present in the trophoblast cells. To put it simply, I am 95 percent sure you are pregnant."

The room was silent. Wojo stepped back to the edge of the room.

"Did you hear what I said, Angelina?" Alessandro finally asked.

"It's not possible," she whispered, almost to herself. "The blood . . . I have had a cycle . . ."

The doctor took a pen out of his jacket pocket and clicked it. "When did you last menstruate?"

Angelina drew in a shaky breath. "That day, at your office . . ."

Alessandro shook his head. "That was not a period. Spotting can be a symptom of the diseased cells. When you said you had a cycle, was it like a regular period?"

"Yes . . . no . . . it was different. It only lasted a few days."

"How long ago was it?"

Angelina thought back. "Maybe a month . . . no two months. I can't remember," she said evasively.

Alessandro wrote something in his folder. "We did the urine sample yesterday and then again today to make sure there wasn't a mistake. Both came out positive for hCG."

"How far along am I?"

"Because of the spotting, it is almost impossible to determine. We can use the date of your last cycle—if it was a cycle—as a tentative conception date. That would make you approximately five to six weeks pregnant."

Angelina lay back and closed her eyes. *How can this be? Have you answered my prayers?*

Alessandro spoke up. "As your doctor, I need to tell you that treatment will be more difficult if you decide to continue the pregnancy."

Angelina's eyes fluttered open, and she tried to sit up. "What do you mean *if?* There can be no question . . ."

Alessandro put his hand over hers. "This is not a decision you can make without a great deal of thought. If we suspend treatment for the cancer, you could die before giving birth . . . or during . . ." he said.

A little warmth had returned to Angelina's face, and her eyes were focused. "I don't need to think about it for even one second. If what you say is true, this news could give me more of a reason to live than I have felt in a very long time."

Alessandro nodded his head gravely and patted her hand. "I have to get back to the clinic. Promise me you will think this through."

Angelina stared back at him. "I have. My mind is made up."

Alessandro hesitated for a moment by the bedside before leaving. "Is there someone you want us to notify—someone who might want to participate in this decision?"

"You mean like the father of her baby?" an angry voice rang out. Pio Lallo was standing in the doorway. "He's in this room. Why don't you ask him, Angie?"

Angelina widened her eyes in horror.

Pio pointed an accusing finger at the man standing against the wall. "After all, he and my daughter have been inseparable for over a month now. Perhaps he has an opinion to offer about all this."

Alessandro turned and looked at Wojo.

"No! You don't understand . . ." Angelina shouted.

"Of course, you *would* try to protect him," Pio sneered, "considering who he is."

Wojo stood still, his eyes on Angelina.

"No!" The cry came again, heart wrenching and full of pain. Angelina collapsed back on the bed, clutching her side. Pio rushed to the bedside as Alessandro held her down and buzzed for the nurse's station. Two nurses rushed in a moment later.

"Sedate her," Dr. Sabatini told them.

Angelina fought the two men, pushing their arms away, her eyes wildly searching the room beyond them.

Wojo was gone.

The afternoon light was waning. A lone figure crossed the highway and began climbing the steep hill toward the Via di San Francesco. Inside the forest, the setting sun glinted through the trees and lit up the white stones marking the trail. The man zipped up his jacket as the late August wind whipped around him. He moved purposefully, his face set with the determination of someone who has made up his mind. Even though the incline was steep, and he was no longer young, he did not stop until he reached the hermitage. He pushed open the iron gates and headed toward a side entrance at the back of the property. Once inside, he walked to the hallway and picked up the phone.

Sometime later, he set down his duffel bag and opened the door to Angelina's room. He quickly crossed to the bed, knelt down, and reached under it. He pulled out a small metal box with the name "Angelina" written on the top. Inserted in the lock was a tiny key. Wojo turned the key, and the box sprung open. He took out an envelope from his jacket pocket and placed it inside. He closed the lid and locked it. He held the key there for a moment, then withdrew it and slid the box under the bed. As he stood and looked around the room; his eye caught a string of rosary beads on the nightstand. He gathered them up, looking closely at the gold heart that connected the two strands. He fit the key through the same loop as the heart, letting the crucifix hang from a single separate strand. He placed the beads back on the nightstand and walked out of the room.

Standing outside the gates, he pulled the hood of his jacket over his head and waited. In a few minutes, the sound of wheels crunching on gravel penetrated the stillness of the forest, and a large black car came into view. The driver stopped, got out, and opened the rear door. Wojo turned and looked back at the hermitage. The light from the lamppost shone down on a gold ring he wore on his hand—a dove with outstretched wings. He fingered the ring, his lips moving, before he turned away and climbed into the back seat of the car. With a slight nod to his passenger, the driver closed the door and got back in the driver's seat. The car made a sharp U-turn and continued down the mountain, turning left onto the highway toward Rome.

PART III

Chapter 19

By Any Other Name

Spoleto, Umbria, 2016

"IS THIS the same man Angelina referred to as Wojo? I asked, pointing to the name written under "*Nome di padre*" on the birth certificate.

"Papa said 'Wojo' is the name he gave everyone there at the hermitage. I suspect it was to hide his identity," Pepina answered.

I looked at Agostino's shocked face. "I'm sorry, but I seem to be missing something. How come I'm the only one who doesn't recognize the name on this document?"

Brunetta raised an eyebrow. "You must be kidding. Have you been living under a rock for the last thirty-five years?"

I was still clueless.

"Google it," she finally said.

I started typing the first name, and my screen filled instantly. I sucked in my breath and looked at Agostino. "Holy crap."

Agostino wiped the beads of sweat beginning to form on his brow. "I think you need to tell us the rest of the story, Pepina. The part you can vouch for anyway."

Brunetta picked up the tray and started walking toward the kitchen. "I'm making more coffee." She glanced at the figure standing in the doorway. "Vito, you're making everyone nervous. Pull up a chair and join us."

The big man lumbered to an armchair and plopped himself into it. "I can't believe we are bringing this all up again," he grumbled.

When Brunetta returned with fresh coffee, I noticed she had included a dish of chocolate *biscotto*. Vito took two pieces.

Brunetta slapped his hand. "Those are for the guests." She gave me one of her long-suffering looks. "Ever since he quit smoking last year, all he does is eat."

Agostino handed Pepina a steaming cup and a napkin. "Please continue with your story. I want to know everything."

"After hearing the news that she was pregnant, Angelina suddenly became a model patient. She requested three meals a day and an array of vitamins that even Papa found bordering on excessive. In her mind, the stronger she became, the better chance her baby would have to survive. But the cancer was growing too. It was a race against time and a battle between her baby's life and her own. Papa said he had never seen a woman so determined to stay alive for the sake of her child. There was only one thing she asked for herself. She wanted to leave the hospital and go home.

"Papa had balked. Her condition demanded constant monitoring, he told her. The hermitage was too isolated to treat her properly. What if there was an emergency? From Monteluco, it would take too long to get her to a hospital. He suggested bringing her to our house. There was an extra bedroom, and he could hire a full-time caregiver."

I cut in. "This seems above and beyond even for Dr. Sabatini."

Brunetta spoke up. "*Nonno* would do anything for his patients . . . even invite them to live with him if necessary. Mama was not consulted in the decision, and neither one of us was particularly happy about it. I was only seven at the time, and I remember that having a very sick pregnant woman in the house was difficult."

"Dr. Lallo's accusation had made everything mysterious," Pepina continued. "Pio was obsessed with the fact that his daughter, a woman with a history of mental illness, had been taken advantage of. This obsession was clouding his ability to make good decisions involving his daughter. Papa thought a new environment would be the best thing for Angelina."

"And Pio agreed?" I asked.

"I think he was relieved that the burden of her care was in someone else's hands. It was a difficult situation for him. He had, in a way, brought Angelina and Wojo together. He felt responsible."

I snuck a glance at Agostino. He seemed withdrawn, as if contemplating what all this meant. It was all well and good to speculate about the details, but we had to understand that it was an intensely personal subject for him. These people we were talking about were his immediate family. I wanted to bring the conversation back to his mother. Agostino deserved to know as much about her as possible.

"You have mentioned Pio's feelings, but what of Angelina's?" I asked the two women. "Did she ever talk about herself?"

Brunetta looked at her mother.

"I spent many hours tending to her while Papa was at the clinic," Pepina said. "She resisted all sedatives except at the very end. She wanted to enjoy every moment of her pregnancy with mental clarity. We talked about life, death, and religion. She believed that God was the cause of everything. If we knew how, she said, we could observe His hand in every aspect of our lives. The magic of how a chrysalis becomes a butterfly, what happens when a bee pollinates a flower, or how a fertilized egg can become a human being."

"It sounds like my mother was an original thinker," Agostino said, his voice almost reverent.

"She also believed in free will," Pepina continued. "How faith could guide reason and prevent mistakes if we chose to accept the existence of God. She told me about the many conversations she had with their guest, the man they called Wojo. They had similar beliefs."

I remembered what Sergei and I had talked about in Rome. "These beliefs are at the core of some of our greatest theological philosophers, Saint Thomas Aquinas for one."

"I don't pretend to understand everything she talked about, but I never doubted her sincerity," Pepina said.

"Did she ever mention what she had wanted to do with her life . . . before the illness?" I asked.

"Other than cook and clean for her father, you mean? She wanted to study philosophy at the University, but Pio never considered she might have dreams of her own." Pepina smirked. "Typical Italian male mentality."

I snuck another glance at Agostino. I hoped he was listening.

"You said that Angelina spoke about Wojo often. It sounds like they had a spiritual connection as well as a personal one," Agostino said.

I shot him a look. "You believe, then, that something physical happened between them? Despite what Angelina started to say at the hospital?"

Agostino looked at Pepina. "Did she ever talk about that?"

Pepina chose her words carefully. "Early on, no. She talked only of their spiritual connection. Later, when the disease progressed, and the pain medication increased, she did allude to it. Some days she called it a dream; other days it seemed she was recounting something that actually happened. It always began with a morning walking through the cemetery of Monteluco." Pepina sighed and sank back into the pillows of the sofa. "I never could tell what part of it was real."

Everyone was silent. The implications of what we had discussed continued to sink in—especially for Agostino. He sat quietly, staring off into the distance. I desperately wanted to reach out, to hold him in my arms but I knew I no longer had that right. In his vulnerable state, and with our future together in doubt, it could damage him further.

"Could I see the room where she stayed?" he asked Pepina. "Just to get a sense of her last days," he added.

"Of course," Pepina said without hesitation. "But she died in the hospital, not here."

"I know. I just want to feel her presence. If that doesn't sound ridiculous."

"It doesn't," Pepina replied. "I have often felt it in this house."

I helped Agostino lift Pepina off the couch and into her wheelchair, and the four of us crossed the room toward the hallway.

When we got to the door, Brunetta turned and eyed the man in the chair. "Are you coming?"

Vito bit into another *biscotto*. "I'll wait here. Ghosts give me the creeps."

Brunetta led the way down the corridor to the small room beyond Pepina's bedroom. The stale odor hit us as soon as she opened the door. Brunetta hurried to the window and started to open it.

"No!" Agostino cried out.

Everyone turned to look at him.

He turned red. "I'm sorry, I just wanted to keep everything the way it was."

Agostino walked around the room, taking in the simple furnishings. There was an armoire, a nightstand, and a single bed made up with a white coverlet. The austerity reminded me of a nun's cell. As he approached the bed, Agostino reached out and lifted a string of rosary beads off the bedpost. He turned to Pepina. "Was this my mother's?"

"It was. She always had it near her, even at the hospital. That and her little box were the only things she requested from the hermitage."

Agostino looked at her sharply. "Box? What box?"

"It was a small metal box filled with keepsakes. She was always looking at things in it, but she never shared them with me."

Agostino's eyes lit up. "I'd like to see that. Do you still have it?"

Pepina shook her head. "It got lost somehow. I remember Papa brought back the rosary, saying Angelina wanted him to have it. Then after . . ."—she dropped her voice—"we didn't see the box in her things."

Agostino sighed. "It's a shame it was lost. It would have been something to remember her by." He fingered the beads. "May I have these?"

Pepina smiled at him. "Of course. They belong to you now."

"Can I see it?" I asked, holding out my hand. The beads were pale blue and made of glass. At the point where the two strands joined the crucifix, there was a tiny gold heart and a key.

"Agostino, did you see this?" I put his fingers on the key. "I have never seen a rosary with a heart and a key before."

"Bring it here," Pepina called out from her wheelchair.

Agostino and I crossed the room, and we all examined it in the light.

"I can't believe I didn't notice this before," Pepina said. "One thing's for sure, this key was not always here. It is not gold like the heart." She turned it in her hand. "See? It's starting to rust."

"I wonder what it opened," Agostino whispered.

"The keepsake box?" I suggested.

Pepina nodded her head slowly. "Yes, it is about the right size. It was a small box."

She handed the rosary back to Agostino. "I'm sorry it never made it back here. The rosary is all we can offer you."

Agostino accepted the rosary gratefully. "Thank you. I will treasure it always."

We wheeled Pepina out of the room, and Brunetta closed the door behind her.

"Can you tell me what happened at the hospital?" Agostino asked Pepina when we were back in the living room.

"You mean Angelina's last days?"

Agostino nodded.

"Per cari da!" Vito wiped his mouth and stood up, a shower of crumbs tumbling off his lap to the floor. "Pepina needs a break."

The old woman ignored her son-in-law. "Come back tomorrow," she said to Agostino and me. "I will be happy to tell you the rest of it."

When we got in the car, we sat for a while in stunned silence.

"It can't be true," he said.

"Hard to believe," I said.

"Then again," Agostino countered, "we have proof he was there. Dr. Sabatini saw him with her twice, once at the clinic and then in the hospital after the overdose." Agostino sat silently, staring beyond the windshield as if in a daze. "What do I do now?" he whispered.

I rubbed his shoulder gently. "You can't change a past you had no control over, but there is an option."

Agostino stared at me. "Go on."

"You have accomplished what you set out to do, namely, to locate the identity of your birth parents. If the information you received is correct—and we have no proof that it isn't—you can set this chapter of your life aside and go on as before. Your future does not have to change."

"My future." Agostino's voice had a bitter edge to it. "Not so long ago, I thought it was going to be *our* future. I actually pictured you there beside me—planning events, catering to the needs of our guests. Having the right person to share it with seemed like a dream come true. Now, all of that seems to be in doubt."

You haven't asked me if I want that too, I said to myself. If he didn't see that he was the one who needed to ask—not I the one to tell him—there was a problem.

My silence seemed to confirm his suspicions.

There was a lost look in his eyes when he spoke again. "I am not sure that what we heard today is the whole story. I need to find out the truth. If I don't, for the rest of my life, I will wonder where I belong."

Chapter 20

A Night Off

CLAIMING fatigue and a raging headache, I asked Agostino to drop me off at the *alimentari* in Scheggino. I felt bad knowing he probably needed a shoulder to cry on, but that was part of the problem. Exploring the possible benefits of sympathy sex did not seem like a wise move for either of us. I was looking forward to making dinner and spending a nice quiet evening, alone, in my apartment. I heard the familiar bell tinkle as I opened the door to the shop.

Sabrina looked up from behind the counter. "How are things going?" Her eyes had a mischievous glint in them. The unspoken words *with Agostino* hung in the air. *They're not, you nosy little bitch,* I wanted to say, but I didn't want to give her the satisfaction.

"*Benissimo,*" I answered instead. *Better not to tell the villagers more than necessary.*

I grabbed a package of pasta, a bottle of ragu, and a bulb of garlic and walked to the white enameled deli counter. It was full of cuts of meat and a variety of cheeses. "*Due salsicce,*" I said, pointing to two sausage links. "*E un po di parmigiano.*"

Sabrina wrapped everything and rung it all up. The four euros was less than I would have paid in the States for similar items, and the quality was far superior. Even the simplest spaghetti sauce had a rich tomato taste I could never find back home. I wished her a *buona sera* and started for the door when I saw the wine. No way was I going home without a bottle. When I doubled back to the counter with it in my hand, Sabrina smiled her little smile again. I could just hear her telling her husband, "*Poor thing, drinking alone again.*"

I carried my groceries up the three long flights of stairs and pushed open the heavy wooden door that led to the enclosed patio. Tonight, of all nights, I had no interest in making small talk with the neighbors.

As soon as I keyed in and set my groceries on the kitchen counter, I walked to the far end of the room and goosed up the thermostat. Even though it was early spring, the temperature could drop severely after the sun went down. I moved to the fireplace and replenished it with newspaper and kindling and a few small logs. I found the small box of fire starters, broke off a chunk, and nestled it into the mix. With a strike of the match, the blaze took off. Only one more thing to do before I started dinner. I reached into my jacket pocket and pulled out my cellphone. The group call to my siblings in San Diego was long overdue.

It wasn't so bad, I said to myself as I uncorked the bottle and poured myself a glass of the hearty Montefalco red. I cut up the vegetables for the pasta sauce and brought the salted water to a boil. I didn't need a man by my side to enjoy a meal in my beautiful little place. This was why I had bought it, after all. To experience the Italian lifestyle and live the way my ancestors did a hundred-plus years ago. And I was happy, damn it! I reached for the glass and took a sip.

After I had eaten and washed the dishes, I took the considerably lighter bottle and trudged up the stairs, eager to reward myself with a nice hot bath. I was lucky the apartment came with a tub—not all of them did—and I was determined to take advantage of it. I ran the water using a liberal amount of the fragrant mineral salts we had bought at the truffle festival and stepped in.

Sliding down into the sudsy water, I thought about what Terry and I discussed after Tino had signed off on the group call. How were things with Sergei? When I told her the startling news that he was studying for the priesthood, she cracked up. "Well, it's obvious he had no interest in you, then—you imagined the whole thing." I was mulling that over when she dropped the next bombshell. "You wanted to believe there was something between you two so you could get out of your commitment to Agostino."

Ouch. Was it possible—even subconsciously—that I would allow myself to play with Agostino's feelings like that?

And what *about* Agostino? She had asked next. Was it on or off?

That was the annoying thing about heart-to-hearts with siblings. They got right to the point and weren't always delicate about it. The truth was, I didn't have an answer for her. On my last trip, four months ago, everything had looked promising. Then the reality of a sink full of dirty dishes and dealing with hostile guests had set in. I thought about what kind of life that would be for me. Would I have to decline any entertainment opportunities because Agostino disapproved? Festival activities, including dancing, were a regular part of Scheggino's social life. And that raised the bigger question: Would I need to ask "permission" to do the things I wanted?

That was not why I had come here.

My thoughts wandered back to the day I saw the apartment for the first time. To the sliver of stone with the dead plant on the doorstep. Apart from its connection to my family's past, Scheggino had been the promise of a new beginning, a symbol of my independence. I could live the life I wanted here, and that included not having to accept someone else's idea of what that might be.

Terry said getting physical with Agostino before our compatibility was tested had been a mistake. I agreed with her, but for me, that first night had been an exercise in self exploration. Sex could be liberating if entered into with the same expectations. Mine had been different than Agostino's. I had been looking for an experience that could lead to a serious relationship. He was making love to the person he wanted to spend the rest of his life with. Unfortunately, as I learned later, *his* life was all he seemed to be concerned about.

I poured myself a little more wine and slid deeper into the bubbles. It was all my fault. If I hadn't coaxed SJ to go on that trip to Turin, Agostino never would have found out he was adopted. And if I hadn't come into his life, he would still be that happy-go-lucky hotelier making a good living helping unsuspecting newlyweds enjoy a few hours of wedded bliss before real life set in.

I pictured Agostino, all alone in his big house, contemplating what he had learned about his parents. I had been careful not to tell my siblings everything. The story of Angelina was news enough without getting into the detail of the name written under *"nome di padre."* Opening that can of worms was Agostino's decision, not mine.

Then I remembered the day he had asked me to help him find his real family. "I will be there every step of the way," I had promised. And I would be, I decided, no matter how things ended up between us.

The water had turned cold, the bottle was nearly empty, and tears were spilling down my already wet cheeks. Maybe it was the effects of the wine, but instead of feeling brave and independent, I felt lost and alone—with no answers to my questions and no one to comfort me.

It made no sense, and I couldn't explain it—even to myself—but all I wanted was to have Agostino hold me in his arms and tell me it was going to be okay.

Chapter 21

Revelations

TOWARD morning, I opened one eye and peered at the patch of pre-dawn gray beyond my bedroom window. I opened my other eye and saw the empty bottle on the nightstand. *Did I really drink all that last night?*

With a groan, I sat up and swung my legs off the bed. Groping for my running clothes, I knew the best way to get over my hangover was to do it cold turkey.

My pounding head had established a harmonious rhythm with my pounding feet by the time I reached Ceselli, and when the roosters announced my arrival back in Scheggino an hour later, I was ready to take on the world again.

Approaching Sergei's house, I saw him standing outside his front door, watering the pots in his herb garden. My first impulse was to turn around and run the other way, but then I remembered what Terry had said. His intentions had never been romantic toward me, so for him, there was no conflict in seeing me again. *I* was the one who was embarrassed. Determined not to be a wimp, I slowed my pace and walked toward him. When I got closer, something about him looked different. I sucked in my breath. The scraggly rock-star locks were gone. The back of his head was razored up, and the barely there forgot-to-shave beard had been replaced by the smooth cheeks of a newborn babe.

"Sergei," I called out, "I hardly recognized you. You look positively ecclesiastical!"

He laughed and blushed at the same time. "I have been accepted into the Istituto Superiore of the Largo Angelicum."

"I am so happy for you," I replied. It was *almost* true.

I felt his eyes scrutinizing me. "You look like you could use a double cappuccino."

"Is it that obvious?"

"Don't forget, I've been there a few times myself." His gaze was more penetrating this time. "Come in. Let us talk."

"Yes, *Father*," I said jokingly.

He laughed again and held the door open.

While he busied himself in the kitchen, I put a few more logs on the already blazing fire and settled on the enormous bench lining the wall. His house was so unique—like the man himself. He could have chosen any walk of life after his music career. He could have built furniture, become an interior designer, or married some rich widow and traveled the world. Instead, he had chosen to withdraw into an exclusive club and devote his life to God. Listening to him firing up the cappuccino machine, I realized how unfair that sounded. Choosing to become a priest was a calling. It required a unique commitment—celibacy—and an understanding of why it was still a necessary vocation in our modern world. He had that understanding. I needed to respect that choice and the sacrifices that went with it.

The glass and steel table in front of me was covered with a variety of papers and books. It looked like Sergei was preparing for an entrance exam.

"What is all this?" I asked him as he brought the two steaming mugs in from the kitchen.

"My entrance composition. All seminarians who enter the Angelicum have to give an account of why we feel we have been called. We also have to name someone specific who has influenced us to make that decision." He gave me a wry smile. "Its main purpose, I suspect, is to weed out the flakes."

"So what you're saying is, even with the dearth of applicants these days, they don't take just anybody."

"Surprised me too." Sergei chuckled.

"Who did you choose as your mentor?"

He handed over the coffee and sat down next to me. He sorted through the books and slid one over. It had a benevolent looking man with a broad face on the cover.

I set the cup down hard.

Sergei frowned. "*Stai attenta.* That table's made of glass."

"I am *so* sorry," I said, recovering my composure.

"He was an alumni of the Angelicum, you know, and an advocate of the teachings of Saint Thomas Aquinas."

"Very clever," I said, trying to keep it light, "Considering the seminary's focus on his teachings, the faculty will no doubt appreciate the coincidence."

"I didn't just choose him for that reason," Sergei was quick to point out. "He really did influence me greatly. I have studied his life for many years now—from his ordination to his priesthood, to his appointment as bishop. And also, in October 1962, when he distinguished himself at the second Vatican Council in Rome. I am reading about that right now. Something happened in his life at that time that changed him. His contribution at the Council—the sentiments he expressed and the conviction he showed toward change within the church—were radical. It made him stand out. Many believe his suggestions to open up dialogue to all people, laymen as well as the clergy, brought the church into the modern world. He was the one who encouraged friendship with other denominations and offered the idea of using regional language in masses instead of Latin." Sergei paused. "I see I've lost you. Sometimes I get carried away ..."

"No, I'm just thinking." My voice sounded strained. "Does the book mention any names he went by in his youth or college years? A nickname perhaps?"

"As a matter of fact, it does." Sergei leafed through the pages and put his finger on a chapter entitled "The Theatre Years." "This was before he was ordained, of course, while he was in the seminary. He organized a theatre group there and even acted in some of the productions. They were mostly of a religious nature and written by the students themselves. It says: "At the end of the academic year, he took on the role of Sagittarius in a fantasy-fable called *The Moonlight Cavalier*. It was at that time he became associated with the nickname Wojo."

I gripped the coffee cup more tightly. "So, his theatre group called him 'Wojo.'"

Sergei stopped reading and looked up. "Yes. Is this important?"

I took a deep breath and faced him. "It may be a little early to be requesting your ecumenical services, but I have come across some news that puzzles me. Since you seem to be well informed on the subject, I could use a little divine guidance."

Sergei set the book down. "I'm all ears."

"Considering you are not yet ordained, I must request that this remain just between us."

"Of course," Sergei said.

"The day we hiked up to the sacred wood and you took us to the cemetery, we had a conversation. Do you remember it?"

Sergei seemed to steel himself. "I remember it."

"You had a strong reaction to the area—and the graves. I asked you if you recognized any of them. Tino interrupted us, so I never got your answer. I'm going out on a limb here, but did you know Angelina Lallo?"

Sergei dropped his eyes. "I did know her. I was unaware that she had died. It was a shock."

I waited for the rest of the story, but he remained silent.

I continued. "The subject is a delicate one, but because you knew her, you may be able to shed light on some information I have received."

Recounting the bizarre story Pepina had told us, I tried not to leave anything out. If he was to counsel me properly, he needed to know all the details.

When I got to the part about Angelina finding out she was pregnant, his eyes darkened, and his face composed itself into set lines. He looked like he was trying to keep his emotions in check and concentrate on the facts presented. He asked a few questions: the date and time of year, the physical description of the hermitage's guest, and what kind of relationship Pio had with his daughter. He also asked if I thought Pepina still had the presence of mind to remember something that had happened over fifty years ago.

"She's as sharp as a tack," I assured him. "But don't forget, Brunetta was also present. She corroborated everything."

"And you have no reason to suspect Pio of an ulterior motive in making such an accusation against his guest?" Sergei asked.

"Ulterior motive? Like what?"

"Needing someone to take the fall for his daughter's condition," Sergei said.

"For Angelina's getting pregnant you mean."

Sergei nodded. "Pio's guest never admitted to being the father of her baby, did he?"

"No, but he didn't stick around to explain himself either," I replied. "According to what Pio told Dr. Sabatini, Wojo left the hospital and walked back to the hermitage that night, packed a bag, and was driven away by someone. Another big black car maybe?" I didn't mean to sound challenging, just fair. There was more than one viewpoint to be considered here.

Sergei spoke quietly, his brow more furrowed than before. "There are a lot of unknowns in this story. For example, just because Pio's guest was there during the approximate time of conception doesn't mean it was him. She could have gotten pregnant by someone else."

"True," I countered, "but unlikely. Monteluco is isolated, and Angelina led a very sheltered life. Plus, she was hardly the promiscuous type. It wouldn't be the first time something like this happened in the history of the Catholic Church. Don't forget who Lucretia Borgia's father was."

Sergei cut in. "It was different back then. Strict adherence to celibacy was often overlooked among the clergy. Especially if the Pope came from a powerful family."

"Even so, it is common knowledge that . . ."

Sergei stopped me. "I don't think you are seeing the big picture here. You have to understand how damaging a story like this could be for this man's reputation—and his legacy. You are aware that there already exists speculation about friendships he has had with women—some of it documented in letters. He never hid the existence of these relationships, always maintaining they were of a platonic nature and based on mutual interests. If this story of yours becomes known, it could cast doubt on this issue and his credibility. Think of what a tragedy that would be to mankind. In the years since his death, he has become a symbol of goodness and a role model to many throughout the world. Men of his caliber are getting harder and harder to find, and we are in sore need of them."

We stared at each other in silence.

"What are you going to do with this information?" He finally asked.

"It is not up to me." I answered. "It is up to . . ." Before I could continue, my cellphone rang. I reached into my jacket pocket and picked up.

I listened for a few minutes. "Of course I will. Meet you at the piazza in ten minutes." I hung up the phone and turned to Sergei.

"That was Agostino. He received word Gabriella is asking for him. They think this may be the end."

Chapter 22

A Change of Heart

AN ALFA ROMEO Giulietta and a Maserati were parked along the driveway in front of Gabriella's villa. As the gates rolled open and we drove in, I saw the driver of a Mercedes leaning against the hood, smoking a cigarette.

"It looks like all the Urbinos are here," Agostino said. "They are hoping Gabriella will make a last-minute change to her will, no doubt."

"Agostino! Aren't you being a little *cavaliere* about all this? Gabriella is your grandmother. You two have been close all your lives."

"*Nonna* has been doing the deathbed thing for more than a few years now. Every time she feels neglected, she says she's dying."

"Maybe this time it's true," I countered. "After all, she's almost a hundred."

Agostino laughed. "That woman will outlive half the people here. Mark my words." He opened the car door. "Let's go humor her a little."

"Maybe it's better if I don't go in," I said uneasily. "She probably doesn't want to see me anyway."

Agostino turned to me, his face anxious. "Believe it or not, I am scared shitless to walk into this house. I do not know what to expect or how I will be treated, and I need an ally. Someone who is looking out for me. Whatever else is going on with us, I know where your loyalties lie."

I sat quietly, waiting for more.

The words came haltingly, as if they were difficult to admit. "Look, I know things aren't right between us. I have a feeling I've disappointed you, and I'm trying to understand how. My jealous nature can sometimes get the better of me. Can you give me another chance to make it right?"

I opened my door. "I appreciate your honesty, and you are right about my loyalty. I will defend you to the death. All I need is a sword and some flattering armor." Hearing my words, I wanted to slap myself. Levity was always the easy way out. I touched his face with the back of my hand. "What I mean is I will always be there if you need me."

Agostino turned my hand around and laid it against his cheek. Then he brought my fingers to his lips and kissed them. "I was hoping you would say that." He took a deep breath. "Remember, all those people inside know I am not one of them. By now, Beniamino will have told them the story about my past. I'm pretty sure I will not be welcomed with open arms, and because you are with me, neither will you."

"I was expecting that," I replied. "Before we go in, can you at least prepare me a little? Which one of the Urbinos owns the Mercedes?"

"Giovanni. Ben's only son. He stands to inherit the truffle business. And Pamela, the mayor, is his wife. She might be here too." Agostino's jaw clenched. "She's been waiting a long time for this."

I stared at Agostino. "Wow, *that* was cold."

"This family lives and breathes money. I would like to think Pamela married for love, but I doubt it." Agostino got out and walked around to my side. Helping me out of the car, he cracked a smile. "I hope your armor is bullet proof."

As soon as we walked up the steps, a tough little man with a swarthy complexion stepped into the doorway, blocking our way.

"*Ciao,* Tulio," Agostino said, his voice clipped.

Tulio dipped his head slightly but didn't move. "Giovanni! Agostino *sta qui,*" he called over his shoulder.

Clearly annoyed, Agostino brushed him aside and started walking through the hallway. I was right on his heels.

"Is Tulio an Urbino?" I whispered.

"That little turd?" Agostino scoffed. "He's a distant cousin of Ben's wife.

Always shadowing Giovanni like some sort of bodyguard. It's ridiculous."

"I've never met Beniamino's wife."

"A piece of work, that one. Donatella comes from one of the wealthiest families in Milan. Up there with the Guccis. Ben's father put those two together. Good for business." Agostino looked at me knowingly.

As we walked into the living room, I saw a familiar-looking man poring over a stack of papers at a table by the fire. He didn't even look up. Giovanni was seated on the sofa, legs sprawled out with a glass of what looked like whiskey in his hand. His tie was askew, and his expensive Italian suit was a wrinkled mess. His wife was talking *sotto voce* with a middle-aged blonde woman.

"I've got to get back to the *comune*. I hope this doesn't last all night," she said.

The blonde nodded. "You and me both."

Pamela turned, putting on her public smile when she saw Agostino. *"Ciao, caro.* It is good of you to come." She crossed the room and kissed him on both cheeks.

"Anna," she said coolly, her eyes sweeping over me for a nanosecond.

Agostino addressed her. "How is *Nonna?* I was told she was asking for me."

Before she could answer, Giovanni got off the couch and staggered toward them. *"Nonna?"* he sneered. "Are you still calling her that?" He stumbled, and some of his drink slopped onto the rug. Pamela grabbed his arm and steered him away from us. *"Sta zitta!"* she said, holding her index finger next to his face and pushing him back down on the couch.

"Oh, boy," I said under my breath. I was getting a rare glimpse of how the high and mighty Urbino family behaved when the rest of the world wasn't watching.

"Agostino!" A shrill voice called out. The blonde woman was eyeing us, her suit jacket unbuttoned to display a fleshy cleavage. *"Vieni qui.* I have not seen you for ages. Give your auntie a big hug." She opened her arms and stretched her puffy lips into a big grin, a smear of red lipstick all over her front teeth. I glanced at the empty glass by her elbow. *I guess everyone has been dipping into the sauce.*

Agostino met her halfway. "Donatella, *come stai?*"

Her plump arms enveloped him as she nuzzled his neck and giggled. I watched Giovanni turn away in disgust.

Agostino gently pried himself away and helped her to a chair. He turned to Pamela. "Where is Beniamino?"

"He's with her now. She has had her turn with all of us but keeps asking for you." Pamela gave Agostino a concerned look. "Something feels different. She may not be faking this time."

Agostino grabbed my hand, and we hurried down the hall to Gabriella's room. As I stood in the doorway, I could see Beniamino by the old lady's bedside, holding a sheaf of papers in his hand. The last time I had seen him was when he met Terry at the truffle festival. Then, he had seemed vital, full of the self-confidence befitting the CEO of one of the largest truffle-exporting businesses in the world. Now, his seventy-plus years seemed to weigh heavily on his shoulders. I could hardly believe it was the same man.

As we walked into the room, he quickly shoved the papers into a briefcase on the floor by the bed.

"Why didn't you tell me about her condition?" Agostino glared at Beniamino. "Why did I have to find out from Flavia?"

"I wasn't sure you could tear yourself away from your *new life*," Beniamino said sarcastically.

The implication didn't escape me. I could only imagine how the Urbinos felt about Agostino taking up with the granddaughter of the man who killed one of their kin.

Agostino flushed with anger. "Me? What about you? You never come here unless you want something. Always talking her into transferring more of her shares to your *son*." Agostino glanced at the briefcase and back at Ben.

"Stop!" A tremulous voice cried out. Gabriella's eyes were open, and she was staring at them. "Look at the two of you, duking it out like a couple of prizefighters past their prime. It's pathetic." She turned her face to Beniamino. "You just don't see it, do you?"

"See what?" Beniamino's eyes had turned cold.

She put a hand on her nephew's arm. "I want to speak to Agostino alone."

Beniamino seemed surprised. *"Zia,* it isn't wise, considering . . ."

"I haven't got all day," she reminded him. "Now go."

He cocked his head in my direction. "What about *her*?"

"She can stay," Gabriella said.

After Beniamino left, Agostino pulled a chair up to the bedside and sat. Standing behind him, I took in Gabriella's shriveled features, the blue veins of her hands standing out against the bones as if her skin were already disappearing. Her face was motionless, like a marble slab, and a thin layer of moisture was forming at her temples and above her parched lips. I couldn't help thinking that, if this was a plea for attention, Gabriella was a better actress than I thought.

"I'm not faking this time," she whispered, as if reading my mind. "There is something I need to get off my chest. Listen good because I don't want to have to repeat it."

Agostino and I leaned in closer.

"There is something you don't know about the Foundation, something I have put off telling you . . ."

"Nonna," Agostino interrupted, "I have news too. Let me tell you mine first. I have found my birth certificate—the real one."

"How on earth?" Her eyes opened wider, and she pushed against the bed. "I need to sit up. Help me."

We added a few more pillows and scooted her against them. There were two spots of color on her cheeks now.

Agostino continued. "After my mother's death, Dr. Sabatini took all the hospital's documents to his home for safekeeping."

"What documents?"

"My birth certificate and my mother's death certificate. She died five days after giving birth to me. Her name was Angelina Lallo."

Gabriella did not speak right away, and I sensed she was holding something back. Finally, she let out a sigh. "What a mess we made. There is part of your story that I never told you . . . or anyone in this family. The night you were born, I got a call from Dr. Sabatini in the hospital. Cecilia's second baby had died minutes before, and Cecilia and her firstborn were down in the morgue. He asked me to break the news to my son.

"'*You* do it!' I demanded. 'If I tell him, he will kill himself.'

"Alessandro said he needed to get back to a patient of his, an unwed mother who had just given birth. She wanted someone to adopt her baby, and he had to help her fill out the paperwork.

"That is when the idea came to me. *I* was the one that suggested he make the switch. An unwed mother's baby for a dead one."

Agostino was silent for a moment. Then, he reached out and took her hand. "You did a good thing, *Nonna*. Angelina was not going to live long enough to be a mother to me, and who knows what family I would have ended up with." He glanced at me as if he needed permission to go on.

"Tell her the whole story," I said.

Gabriella sat up straighter. "And just what do you mean by the 'whole story'?"

She listened in silence as Agostino told her of the brave woman who fought to bring a child into this world despite incredible odds.

"And what about the father? Did you happen to see a name on the birth certificate?" she asked.

Agostino shot me another glance and raised an eyebrow. I gave him an almost imperceptible shake of the head.

"I'm afraid not," he said.

Gabriella seemed to relax a little. She squeezed Agostino's hand. "I think I have a little unfinished business here still. A bit of brandy will do quite nicely. Can you pour me a glass?"

After the brandy, Gabriella requested a small bowl of minestrone. The nurse who brought it in had a surprised look on her face. I could tell she had not expected to see her charge looking so perky. I helped spoon the fragrant liquid into the old lady's open mouth. "Swallow carefully," I told her. "When those reflexes get tired, it goes down the wrong side and infects the lungs. That's when you can get pneumonia."

She looked at me with renewed interest. "It sounds like you took care of someone as old as me."

"My mother. She was just shy of one hundred when she . . . uh . . ."

Gabriella waved her hand dismissively. "I'm not afraid of the word dying . . . when the time comes, of course." Agostino and I cracked up.

She glanced surreptitiously at the closed door. "I am going to offer a word of advice. It might be in your best interest to do a little research before someone else does. I am talking about the cemetery. When Dr. Sabatini brought the corpses here that night, he brought something with him. Something that belonged to your mother."

Agostino's eyes lit up. "What was it?"

"A keepsake box. It was locked, and the key was lost. For some reason, he wanted me to have it."

I sucked in my breath. "Is it here? We would give anything to see what's inside."

Gabriella leaned toward us and whispered, "I put it in the coffin." She glanced again at the door. "I didn't want it to fall into the wrong hands."

Just then, I heard a noise outside the door and footsteps walking away.

"You'd better get a move on," Gabriella told us. "My nephew, old flannel ears, might have heard this entire conversation."

Chapter 23

Cradle Robbers

"ARE WE doing what I think we're doing?" I asked Agostino as he peeled out of Gabriella's driveway into the bright sunlight and up the old Roman road to the cemetery.

"We are." He reached for his cellphone.

He dialed quickly, and after a few rings, someone picked up.

"GP, what are you doing right now?" Agostino listened a minute. "Save the bottle, we may need it later. I need your help. Get off your *culo* and meet me at the cemetery with a crowbar."

I knew the gnome-like plumber was Agostino's right-hand man, but I was still surprised he had called him. "Are you sure you want to bring GP into this mess? Isn't grave robbing illegal in Italy?"

"Not if it's a family member you're robbing," Agostino answered. "I'm not proud of what we're about to do, but the fact that Gabriella thinks this is important enough to postpone her welcoming party in heaven means something. Besides, why was Beniamino eavesdropping like some clandestine character in a spy movie?"

"You might have a point," I said. "Did you see the faces of the crowd in the living room on our way out? They couldn't figure out what was going on. One minute they're planning a funeral, and the next . . . it looks like they will have to wait for those extra shares a little longer."

Agostino banged his hand on the steering wheel. "Those greedy little bastards. As if they don't have enough."

"Is money the only thing that motivates them?"

"Money and the power it brings. They are all obsessed with it."

I was skeptical. "Even Pamela?"

"*Especially* Pamela. Being mayor of Scheggino is just the first rung on a very high political ladder for her. Then there's Giovanni, whimpering at the feet of his father like a well-trained puppy dog, all the while waiting for his chance to take over. Beniamino runs that company like a dictator—not even his son can make a decision without his approval. That kind of system never works for long. Look at what happened to Mussolini. Strung up like a . . ."

"Okay, okay," I said, "No need to get too descriptive here."

"And don't even let me get started on Donatella. She isn't happy unless she's shopping on Via Condotti or flat on her back in the plastic surgeon's office."

I was shocked. "Agostino, I had no idea you felt this way about your relatives."

"*Former relatives*," he reminded me.

A thought came to me. "Did you harbor this animosity toward Ben's side of the family before you knew about the adoption?"

"I think I told you . . . my grandfather and my father wanted to be farmers. The truffle business was Ben's grandfather's idea, not ours. Don't get me wrong. My uncle Claudio worked hard to continue the legacy his father had started, but it consumed him. I never saw him stop and enjoy life. That's not the way I wanted to live." Agostino glanced at me as he crunched up the rocky path that followed the asphalt. "It's funny. I never felt my personality meshed with the rest of the Urbinos, and now I know why."

"I noticed a man sitting in the corner going over papers," I said. "Massimo Ladro, if I'm not mistaken."

Agostino nodded his head. "I remember you had a run-in with him. What was it again?"

"The *comune* had hired him to oversee the documents when I bought the apartment. He tried to hit me up for a *tip* afterward. What was he doing at Gabriella's house?"

"He is the Urbino Truffle Foundation's personal lawyer."

"That explains why he pretended not to recognize me."

Agostino turned off the road and into the gravel apron fronting the tiny cemetery. We got out and stood looking over the edge of the cliff, the clay tile roofs of the Villa Urbino in the distance. "I hope my ancestors can forgive this sacrilege, but it isn't just the box I'm looking for," Agostino informed me. "The only way to know if this story is true is to open Cecelia's coffin."

I stared at him. "So, you aren't entirely convinced Gabriella is telling the truth?"

"I believe she is, but, it would help if there was corroborating physical evidence."

"And what if there is only one infant skeleton in there?" I asked him.

"We will have to rethink this entire thing."

The iron gate marking the entrance to the cemetery was unlocked and shoved open into the dirt. There was nothing to stop anyone from walking right in. The grass rose untamed between the graves, leaving the impression that the living had better things to do than visit their relatives.

"It's amazing," I commented. "In the States, this would be manned twenty-four hours a day."

"In the big cities it is different," Agostino explained, "But in tiny villages like Scheggino, vandalism is practically nonexistent."

I shot him a look. "Not counting family members, of course."

Inside the cemetery, the miniature villas of the Claudio Urbino clan rose up on our left. High-end real estate for the dearly departed. I stopped in front of a steel door with a wrought-iron window and looked inside. Claudio and Olivia, the Truffle Foundation's founders were stacked on the left, and Agatha, Santo, and his wife were on the right. *My relatives,* I thought to myself. We walked a little farther to a small headstone where my great grandfather was buried. Above his name was my great aunt, her husband, and their daughter. Next to Teresina's picture was the gaunt face of Dr. Sabatini. *"Beneficando sempre tutti"* it said next to his name. The more I knew of this man the more I was amazed at his generosity. There wasn't a family in Scheggino he hadn't been willing to help. Now, Agostino could say the same thing.

We stopped in front of a white marble slab laid into the ground between my family's plot and where Agatha and Santo were housed. The words "Spirito Altarocca. *Nato 1923. Morto 2015.*" were carved in simple letters on its surface.

"Is this the first time you've seen it?" Agostino asked, gently, seeing the expression on my face.

I nodded. *So like you, uncle SJ, not wanting to be with either family. Even in death you wanted to carve out a space of your own.* I knelt down and put my hand on the surface of the marble and whispered: "I would say, 'Rest in peace,' but I know you aren't—resting that is. Off on some wild celestial adventure, no doubt."

"No doubt," Agostino said, helping me up.

Finally, we came to two small buildings that housed Agostino's branch of the family. Agostino's great grandparents Angelo and Mariella and their offspring. The second crypt was newer. Marina Urbino, Agostino's aunt, was on one side with Gabriella's husband. Above his tomb there was an empty space.

"For Gabriella?" I suggested.

Agostino nodded and cracked a smile. "She won't be needing it just yet."

Across the aisle below Agostino's father was the tomb of Cecilia. On the back wall, there was another empty space.

"My future digs," Agostino pointed out. "We are in luck. Because I'm not dead yet, we have better access to Cecilia's tomb."

I put a hand on Agostino's arm. "Look, not a lot of people know about this, but I get queasy around dead bodies. Even eighty-year-old dead bodies. So, if it's all the same to you . . ."—I pointed to a stone bench on the far side of the cemetery—"I'll be over there."

Before I could make my escape, I heard the cemetery gate scraping on the gravel followed by a loud *"Cazzo!"* GP was coming toward us with a crowbar balanced on one shoulder and a tool bag slung over the other. When he got close, he fixed his eyes on Agostino and the open door to the crypt. *"Ma come, sei pazzo?"* he growled.

Agostino cleared his throat. "GP, we have been friends for half our lives, and I have never asked you to do anything that didn't absolutely need to be done. Am I right?" He waited in the uncomfortable silence.

GP's eyes were still on the tomb. "Not until now," he said. He handed his friend the crowbar and extracted a chisel and a hammer from his tool bag. He laid them on the floor of the crypt and started to walk away.

"I'm going to do this with or without your help," Agostino called out to the retreating figure. I could hear the desperation in his voice.

GP stopped and turned around. "Why in God's name would you want to dig up your own family?"

Agostino sighed. "I've got some news for you, but I have limited time. I will fill you in as we work, but If I don't get to this first, I have a sneaking suspicion someone else will finish the job for me."

The two men began removing the connecting grout from the heavy marble lid. Working side by side, GP hammered the chisel in, then Agostino used the crowbar to pry it open. The noise echoed through the quiet cemetery. With every tap of the hammer, I cringed, fighting the urge to run. Agostino's eerie background monologue recounting the series of events that had led us here only added to my mounting hysteria. Then came the screech of the marble lid as it scraped across the opening and the grunts of the two men as they lifted it off and placed it on the ground.

"Ora apriamo la bara," GP said. *Now we open the coffin.* I felt the bile rising in my throat, and I covered my mouth with my hand.

"Let's do it," Agostino replied.

I bolted for the iron gate. As I hurried through the tall grass, my hand over my mouth, I could hear the crowbar and the creaking of rotted wood. Once outside the cemetery, I emptied the contents of my stomach onto the gravel. *Wimp*, I said to myself. *They haven't even opened the coffin and you're bailing.*

At the sound of a car, I looked up. The Alpha Romeo I had seen at Gabriella's was slowly cruising by the road that led to the cemetery. I could see Giovanni's head poking out of the passenger side. When he saw me, the car backed up and turned into the gravel apron.

I ran back through the gate. "Agostino, we have company."

When I got there, GP and Agostino were standing over the tomb. I could see the lid of the open coffin and a bashed-in lock hanging from it.

Agostino looked over at me. "You need to take a look—as my witness."

"I can't!" I whimpered. The bile was rising again.

"Anna, there is just a bunch of bones," GP said. He glanced quickly in Agostino's direction. "Sorry. I didn't mean to sound disrespectful."

I took a deep breath, stepped into the crypt, and peered over the edge of the coffin. Fragments of a nightdress, yellowed with age, clung to the skeleton. There were bits of hair still attached to the skull, but the flesh and eyes were long gone. "That's Cecilia, isn't it?" I whispered.

Agostino nodded.

In her arms were two tiny skeletons , bits of cloth still clinging to their bones.

Agostino reached for me suddenly, burying his face in my hair. "It's true, it's all true."

GP gently touched his arm. "There is something in here." He pulled out a rusted metal box with the name "Angelina" scratched into the lid.

"What is going on here?" A voice behind us said.

The three of us turned. Beniamino and Giovanni were standing a couple of feet away, their faces grim.

"I hope you have permission from the *comune* to do this," Beniamino barked. "Otherwise, you are committing an act of vandalism."

"Come off it," Agostino shot back. "That law doesn't apply to family members, and you know it."

I heard the sound of the cemetery gate being shoved farther open and footsteps. Tulio and another man were coming toward us, equipped with the same tools we had brought with us.

"Looks like we got here first," Agostino said, his eyes glinting.

Beniamino turned and put a hand up to stop them. *"Tulio, fermati. Non è più necessario."* The two men looked surprised to see us.

"Vai, go!" Beniamino commanded them.

After they had left, Beniamino took a step forward, his eyes on the box. "Did you find something in there?"

As I watched him, I couldn't help thinking that he seemed more focused on the box than on the open coffin. *Was he worried about what it might reveal?*

Agostino gripped the box tightly. "Close the coffin," he said to GP.

Beniamino took another step. "May I have a look?"

Agostino frowned.

"It wouldn't be a bad idea," I said. "Just so there is no question . . ."

"I'm taking photos," GP announced, whipping out his cellphone. The angle of his shots looked like they included everyone present.

As Beniamino entered the tiny space, I noticed his hands were shaking. He gripped the edge of the tomb and stared down into the open coffin. He started, as if visibly moved at what he saw, then stepped back and shoved his hands into his pockets. Without saying a word, he exited the crypt.

"Giovanni, it is time for us to go," he said, taking his son's arm and leading him away. He seemed strangely subdued.

They were halfway to the gate when Giovanni stopped and turned. His eyes were on Agostino.

"This proves once and for all you are not one of us."

Beniamino looked away, as if embarrassed, and kept walking.

After Agostino and GP closed the crypt, we walked out of the cemetery and stood for a moment in the late afternoon sunshine. I could see the tension in Agostino's hands as he held the rusted box. GP got in his Ape.

Agostino laid a hand on GP's arm. "Thanks, my friend. I owe you one."

"And I intend to collect," GP said before he drove away.

It was just the two of us now.

"What are you going to do?" I asked him.

Agostino seemed anxious. "I don't know. Before, all I was thinking about was getting this"—he gripped the box tightly—"before Beniamino did. Now, I'm afraid of what it will tell me . . . how it will change my future."

"Do you need time alone?"

Agostino glanced at me apologetically. "I think I do. Just to sort out my feelings. Can I call you later?"

I put my hand on his arm. "Of course."

"I can take you down to the village," Agostino offered.

"I shook my head. "I'd like to walk."

I watched him drive the short distance from the cemetery through the open iron gates and down the long drive toward his villa.

I looked at the sun sliding west toward the mountains. If I hurried, I could reach Beniamino's residence before dark.

Chapter 24

Urbino Powwow

THE IDEA had come to me when I saw Beniamino's preoccupation with the box. And then how the two tiny skeletons had affected him—like he had seen proof of something. I had to know what it was, and the only way was to confront him . . . alone.

As I walked down the old Roman road, I remembered my decision last night to be there if Agostino needed me but to let him take the lead in uncovering more about his past. Yet here I was, entering enemy territory with just that intention. Like my sister had said: I just couldn't help myself.

At the entrance to the village, I crossed the bridge skirting the river. On the other side was Highway S55 and the big *palazzos* of the Urbinos. Approaching a pair of ancient wooden gates fronting the street, I saw a sign that read, "Cardinal Fausto Poli. Circa XVI." I remembered Agostino had told me about the history of this villa. In the 1600s, a Vatican bigwig had built it for his pregnant mistress. Agostino had explained that it was common back then for high-level clergy to have illegitimate offspring tucked away in pockets of rural Umbria where they would not be noticed. Cardinal Poli was no exception. Before Beniamino had acquired the property, descendants of the cardinal's mistress had lived there for generations.

One of the gates was slightly ajar, the hinge no longer holding it closed. With little effort, I slipped through and found myself in a courtyard in front of a large three-story estate. Moments later, the gates began to creak open, and I ran toward a series of garage doors that annexed one section of the main house. I ducked under an arched portico and flattened myself against it.

In a single file, two high-performance cars entered the large courtyard and parked in the haphazard manner that indicated a familiarity with the property and its owner.

The driver's side door of the Maserati GranCabrio swung open. A solid-looking woman I recognized as Beniamino's wife, Donatella, heaved herself out of it. "This better be good," she growled. "I had to cancel a wine-tasting event I was supposed to attend this evening in Tuscany. Francesca Banfi was not happy."

Giovanni hopped over his Spider convertible. "If you paid more attention to what is going on you would know how important this meeting is. Papa doesn't call unexpected meetings unless it is urgent. You aren't the only one who had to change plans. Pamela and I were on our way to the Teatro Nuovo tonight to see Domingo. Those tickets cost a fortune."

"Who's Domingo?" Donatella asked.

"*Plácido* Domingo. He's only the greatest tenor since Pavarotti. Don't tell me you've never heard of him."

Donatella scrunched up her face. "You know I don't like opera."

The Spider passenger door opened, and Pamela stepped out.

Donatella's eyes swept over her daughter-in-law's outfit. The high-waisted silver gaucho pants and short jacket accentuated her long legs and tiny waist. "No wonder I don't have a grandchild yet," she smirked. "You're never home long enough to have sex."

Pamela's face darkened, but she kept silent.

Giovanni glared at his mother. "Delicately put, as usual, mother. I don't know what you're whining about. With your busy social life, you wouldn't have time to be a proper grandmother anyway."

A black Mercedes turned into the courtyard and parked.

I peered past the stone column to get a better look.

"Massimo's here," Pamela said. "You all go inside. I want to ask him something."

Donatella stood her ground. "If it's something about this meeting, I'd like to hear it . . . if you don't mind."

Giovanni laughed. "So *now* you're interested."

Massimo got out of his car and walked toward them, briefcase under one arm. He inclined his head. "Donatella, thank you for canceling your trip. I know you were headed up north tonight and weren't due home until tomorrow. Giovanni, good of you to come." He turned to Pamela. "You brought it?"

"Brought what?" Donatella asked.

"Something from the *comune* I wanted to show Beniamino," Pamela said. "Let's go in."

The four of them walked through the manicured garden to the side entrance of Beniamino and Donatella's residence. From my vantage point under the portico, I saw a heavy-set woman with graying hair meet them at the door.

"*Signore* is in the study," she said. "He asked if you could join him there."

As soon as they entered the villa, I considered my next move. My original intention coming here had been to ring the doorbell, but when I saw the half-open gates, my impulsive nature had gotten the better of me. Then when the two cars entered, I was stuck. I knew I could just walk out right now, but then I would miss what looked like a very important meeting. Maybe I could find a way in and learn something that would help Agostino. The prospect was irresistible. I looked around for a back door and, spying one, walked over and turned the knob. It was unlocked. A set of service stairs led up to what was probably the kitchen and pantry. I passed the closed door on the first level and climbed up cautiously to the *piano nobile*. Listening, I thought I heard voices. I kept climbing until I reached the third floor. I carefully opened the door and looked out. A corridor accessing the bedrooms with a railing on one side ran the length of the second floor. A few feet from where I was standing was a staircase leading to the lower level. The space below me was gigantic, with a twenty-foot frescoed ceiling and lined on three sides with books. At one end of the room, centered between two arched windows, a fire blazed in the hearth. Beniamino stood nearby, behind a heavy mahogany desk where four empty chairs were drawn up close. To one side were a decanter and five crystal glasses. I was directly above him, hidden from sight, but I could see and hear everything.

Beniamino looked at the group taking their seats. "Our Grappa del Re is very good this year. Would you care for any?"

"Please," Giovanni said a little too quickly.

Pamela frowned. "Half a glass only for him, Ben,"

Beniamino poured, and everyone sat down.

"I know you are all wondering why I called this unscheduled board meeting," he began. "It has to do with some information I recently received. Information that puts the future of the Foundation in jeopardy. As major shareholders, you all need to have a say in how we go forward."

Donatella swung her crossed leg back and forth, looking bored. "Spare us the chairman-of-the-board speech, Ben. Just tell us what's going on."

"Gabriella is the problem. She is refusing to sign the transfer of assets that we agreed to a few months ago. Massimo had everything drawn up—it was all set to go—then today, she just cancelled the whole thing. Without her signature and approval, the entire Foundation stays in her name."

"This is all your fault, mama," Giovanni sneered. "We wouldn't be in this predicament if it weren't for your family's shady business deals."

Massimo cut in. "We've been over this a thousand times, Giovanni. Because of the investigation into Donatella's family's business, and her connection to us through marriage, we thought it a safe move to transfer the Foundation into Gabriella's name. All of you voted to do that."

"If we hadn't, we would all be sitting behind bars," Giovanni muttered.

Donatella stopped swinging her leg. "What happened today, anyway? I thought the old lady was going to croak, and the next thing I know, she's having a brandy and minestrone."

"Agostino and that American woman happened," Giovanni said. "After they talked to her, she made a miraculous recovery."

"It's not entirely a bad thing," Pamela said. "Now we have more time to persuade her. Everything felt so rushed today because we thought she was going to . . ." her voice trailed off. "This has to be her decision too. It can't look coerced."

Beniamino spoke again. "After everyone left, she told me she would be willing to sign something that stipulated that her shares be equally divided among her heirs and that the Foundation be put in their names."

"That sounds good to me," Donatella said to Ben. "That would mean you, Giovanni, and Agostino . . . that reminds me . . . where is the paperwork on Agostino's adoption? Have you ever seen it?"

Beniamino ignored the question. "I am excluding myself from the inheritance."

"So, the Foundation would be in Giovanni's name?" Pamela asked.

"Gabriella wants the language to read 'heirs.'"

Pamela looked confused. "But Giovanni is your only heir. Does she want Agostino included as part owner of the Foundation? His family never was part of it. Why now?"

"I can't answer that," Beniamino said.

"And why are you excluding yourself?" Donatella demanded to know.

"It will make things much simpler for this family later," Beniamino said.

"Where does that leave me?" Donatella asked.

"You have your dividends, your trust fund. You will be fine," Beniamino told her.

"What about this house?"

"When I die, it will belong to Giovanni. I am sure if you are still alive, he will let you stay here." Beniamino avoided looking at his son.

"You can't do this to me!" Donatella slammed her hand on the desk. She rose from her chair and started pacing the room.

I quickly took a step back to make sure she didn't see me.

"My money helped you make those big deals that got us all that attention from America. It helped the Foundation become a worldwide commodity, and now you're cutting me out."

Beniamino laughed at her. "Don't kid yourself. Your money helped you maintain the extravagant lifestyle you have always been accustomed to. Your family never helped us, and after the investigation, it brought us the wrong kind of fame."

Donatella made a noise in her throat and returned to her seat.

Massimo cleared his throat loudly. "Everyone needs to calm down. The Urbinos have worked hard all their lives, and it was unfortunate that the Brambillas' financial problems forced them to put everything in Gabriella's name. It was never meant to be a permanent move. Even Gabriella understood that. If she wants to put it in Giovanni's name, I am in favor of it. At least everything will be back with Claudio's side of the family and not his sister-in-law's. As for Agostino, Donatella's question is important. Do any official adoption papers exist, tying him to Gabriella's estate? If not, it can be argued that he has no claim to the inheritance. Massimo looked at Pamela. "Have you seen anything in the *comune* records?"

As if taking her cue, Pamela extracted a yellowed sheet of paper from her briefcase and slid it across the table to Beniamino.

He examined it for a minute. *"Liber Mortuorum.* Cecilia Urbino. *Il 14 aprile 1963,"* he read out loud. "This is the record of Cecilia's death. Is this from the *comune?"*

"Yes. The births and deaths of Scheggino residents were recorded by hand prior to being transferred to hard drive," Pamela told the group. "The old ledgers are still in the back rooms behind my office. My employee, Ariana Frangipani, told me Agostino and his American friends were there looking for information about his birth some months ago. I had to investigate. That's when I found this." She pointed to the sheet of paper. "You can see beneath Cecilia's records there is a line that reads, "Angelo Urbino. *Nato Morto. Il 14 aprile 1963.* That is the stillborn baby. Below that there is another line. Read it."

"Nato Agosto Urbino. *Il 14 aprile 1963."* Beniamino looked up, a puzzled expression on his face. "That must be Agostino. But I thought . . ."

Pamela pointed to the next two lines. "Someone blocked this part out."

"I can't read it."

"Hold the paper up to the light," Pamela told him.

I took a step into the corridor to see what Beniamino was doing and saw him hold the paper up against the glow of the lamp on his desk. "*Morto 15 aprile 1963. Un giorno in vita,*" he read out loud. "I don't understand. Why is it slashed up with ink?"

"My guess is it was done by someone who didn't want there to be a record of the second baby's death so they could pass the adopted child off as their own," Pamela offered.

"Who would do that?" Donatella asked her.

"Someone from Gabriella's side of the family—her sister, maybe. What do you think, Ben?"

Beniamino took a while to answer. "I want to make clear what I know about this story. I was called to Gabriella's house three months ago. Agostino was present. Gabriella began telling me this whole ghastly tale of the two sisters preparing Cecilia and her two babies for burial and sealing up the coffin. The way she told it, Gabriella and her sister were only trying to protect that poor grieving husband. By letting him think he still had a child, they were giving him a reason to live." He sighed. "You can't blame them for that. The sisters kept the secret all their lives until those Americans found the letters."

Donatella snorted. "If you ask me, there was another reason why Gabriella never told you. The way this ledger reads now, Agostino is her only direct heir. When she dies, he stands to inherit the entire Foundation."

"And now," Giovanni cut in, "thanks to those meddling Americans, we know the story of Agostino's adoption is true. The way I see it, Agostino did us a favor opening Cecilia's tomb."

Donatella jerked her head around to look at her son.

I pulled back into the shadow of the doorway.

"He did *what?*"

"He opened the tomb. We both saw it. There were two baby skeletons in that coffin."

Donatella turned back to Ben. "What were you two . . ." Her voice trailed off, and she started laughing. "He got there first didn't he? Gabriella thought she was dying, so she must have told Agostino something important enough that he rushed over to the cemetery before anyone else got there."

She zeroed in on Beniamino. "We were all in the living room. How did you know what they were talking about?"

Beniamino's eyes skittered away from her face.

"Eavesdropping again?" Donatella sneered. "That little habit of yours is going to get you in trouble someday."

I covered my mouth to stifle a groan.

Massimo's voice rose above Donatella's. "Let's stay focused on the big picture here. The fact that Agostino did the digging actually plays into our hands. If we had been forced to do it to prove Agostino was not an heir, it would have looked bad. Did anyone take photos?"

"Agostino's plumber, GianPietro, did," Giovanni answered.

"Even better. He will have to disclose that should it become necessary."

Giovanni chuckled. "Looks like Agostino just dug his own grave. What a fool."

Beniamino cut him off sharply. "He was only trying to get to the truth. He wasn't calculating every move—like this family does. He just wants to know where he belongs."

The emotion I heard in his voice surprised me.

Massimo held up the yellowed sheet of paper. "So, what do we do with this?"

"Burn it?" Giovanni suggested.

"God, you are such an idiot sometimes," Donatella shouted at him. "We need that as back-up proof that Agostino is *not* one of us. The tampering could also be a criminal offense that could work in our favor. Since there are no other birth records at the *comune,* it must mean Agostino's real mother is from somewhere else. Hang onto that, Ben."

Donatella's right," Massimo said. "Taking it back to the *comune* could result in it being altered again, or worse, stolen."

Giovanni spoke up. "But isn't that exactly what *we* have done?"

Massimo shook his head. "With the document in our possession, Pamela, being the mayor, can always say she was investigating."

I heard shuffling and the sound of a drawer opening. I craned my neck to see Beniamino putting the document into the top drawer of his desk.

Then he rose and faced the group. "If there isn't anything else to discuss, I will adjourn the meeting. I am suddenly very tired. Please see yourselves out."

Everyone filed out of the room except Donatella.

"Ben, darling, we have to talk." She gave him a look and uncrossed her legs.

"Not tonight," he said harshly. He walked over to the fire and put on a new log. "I haven't the energy to deal with you. We will talk tomorrow."

"You'd better believe we will," Donatella said, getting to her feet. "I have a feeling there is more to this story than you are letting on, and I can promise you, I am not someone you want as an enemy. And don't come looking for me tonight. I'm spending the night at Giovanni's house."

Chapter 25

Reflection

AFTER HEARING Donatella's car screech out of the courtyard, I saw Beniamino move to the ancient stone fireplace and run his hand along the mantel and down its marble sides. Although it was blackened with centuries of use, the quality of the workmanship was exquisite. Turning away from the blaze, he walked into the center of the room as if admiring its elegant proportions and furnishings. I could tell how proud he was to be the owner of such a magnificent house. After several moments, he walked back to the desk, poured himself another drink, and slid open the desk drawer. He pulled out the *comune* document and knelt down by the fire.

By the time I reached the bottom of the stairs, Beniamino was holding it high over the flames. A flicker of yellow licked at one of the edges, threatening to envelope it.

"Are you sure you want to do that?"

Beniamino snatched the paper back, scrambled to his feet, and reached into the desk drawer. He pulled out a gun and aimed it at me.

My heart leaped into my throat. *I hadn't considered this.*

Recognizing me, his face registered more shock than fear. I saw his fingers relax slightly, no longer intent on pulling the trigger.

Taking a deep breath, I said in my best Italian, "I am sorry to startle you. I knocked but no one answered. My guess is someone left the door open."

He kept the gun aimed. "I could have you arrested for breaking and entering."

I held my voice steady. "You could, but sitting in a jail cell, I'd have a lot of time to talk to reporters."

Beniamino blanched. "Then you heard . . ."

"I heard," I said, slowly inching my way over to the chair Donatella had vacated. I sat down keeping my eyes on the gun. "Look, Beniamino, it may surprise you to know that we are on the same side."

Beniamino lowered the gun and placed it on the desk. "What side is that?"

I looked at my host intently. "We both want the best for Agostino, don't we? And that includes helping him find out about his past . . . who his mother and father were . . . or are." I waited a minute. "I saw how you reacted when you saw the box with Angelina's name on it. You knew her, didn't you?"

Beniamino walked to the window and looked out. I thought he was going to order me to leave but then he turned. There were tears in his eyes. "I first saw her from my bedroom window when I was seven years old. We lived next door, you see, when I was growing up."

I rose from the chair and walked quickly to him. Side by side we stared at the massive *palazzo* outlined against the gathering twilight.

"Elena De Glielci and her fifteen-year-old daughter were strolling in the garden among the lilacs that evening. Elena's parents owned this villa then, and she had come down from Monteluco to visit. I was fascinated by the delicate-looking girl with the huge brown eyes and the sad smile. She seemed like a vision from another world. There was something tragic about the two of them. They were like ghosts inhabiting a space that was only temporary—two lost souls on their way to somewhere happier. A year later, my father told me Elena had committed suicide with an overdose of drugs."

Ben turned to look at the fireplace. The fire was dying. He crossed the room, took a large log from the wood pile, and placed it in the center of the embers. He poured two fingers of grappa into his glass and walked back to the window.

"God how I wish that had been the last time I saw Angelina," he said.

"Tell me the story, Beniamino, I want to understand."

He looked into my eyes for a second as if gauging the sincerity of my words. Then he led me back to the fireplace where he pulled up another chair and gestured for me to sit down. We sat in silence for a few minutes, and I sensed my host was gathering his courage. Finally, he began speaking.

"By 1960, after the lean war years, my father's business began to expand exponentially. As the demand for his product increased, he turned to more advanced methods to cultivate and extract the truffles that grew so plentifully in the nearby hills. In the past, he had always used pigs, but he found they were slow to obey commands—preferring to eat the truffle before the hunter could get to it. Dogs were much more trainable. They could be taught to wait for the treat that followed. As the future scion of the Foundation, my father encouraged me to get involved in every aspect of the business, including dog training.

"I loved the work and looked forward to taking the dogs up the rocky paths behind the house and through the mountain passes that led to Monteluco. Many times, I passed the shacks built by the inhabitants who had carved out a life raising livestock in the rocky landscape. They got to know me too—often offering refreshment and a bit of conversation in the months before winter set in. It had been on one of these hunting trips with the dogs that I saw Angelina again.

"I recognized her instantly. I was only seven when I had first laid eyes on her, but the memory of a girl strolling with her mother in a cardinal's garden had never left me. The frail, ghostly look was still there—her long dark hair contrasting sharply with the pale translucent skin—but something was different. In the thirteen years that had passed, she had become a woman.

"The dogs had made their introductions first. Even as they bounded up to her, a sight that would have sent any normal girl cowering, she seemed to have no fear. She bent down and let them nuzzle her face. Soon they were demolishing treats that had magically appeared from her pockets. She stood up and smiled.

"She offered her hand shyly. 'My name is Angelina. I live at the old Eremo delle Grazie, the former monastery. It's down the road a bit.' She pointed to the rough trail leading down the west side of the mountain.

"I was going to tell her who I was, but at the last minute, I decided against it.

"'I'm guessing you are a truffle hunter,' she said, petting the dogs who were still nuzzling her fingers. 'I hope I haven't spoiled their appetite. My treats are the best. Dried chicken skins.'

"I laughed, her simple, straight forward admission disarming me.

"It should have ended there, I realize now, but something about her intrigued me. Our conversations were not typical; weather, politics, the latest fashions—none of that interested her. It was ideas and philosophy that made her eyes light up. The big questions, like what happens to us when we die. And how does God decide who goes to heaven and who goes to hell. I found the discussions refreshing. At home, the talk was always about profits. As the days passed, I kept finding excuses to take the dogs up the trail to the mountaintop. Most days, she met me there, always with something special for the dogs and often, a picnic lunch for me. I never told her my name, not even when she told me about her life at the hermitage. She didn't seem to want to know anything about me. I found it strangely liberating—to be away from my structured and disciplined family with a person who didn't care who I was."

Beniamino pulled out a handkerchief from his breast pocket and wiped his forehead.

"There was no question I was falling for her. It had happened without me realizing it—a yearning to be with her when I was not—a warm feeling when she touched me. I held back, knowing that my family would never let me marry her—and I had no right to ruin her life with an affair. I was engaged. Donatella's family and mine had announced the impending nuptials at a gathering the week before.

"I went up there that day to tell her of my engagement—that I would not be coming to see her anymore. I had left the dogs at home to make it easier for both of us. We walked to the old Monteluco cemetery, holding hands, prolonging the inevitable. She had stopped to look at her grandfather's rock crypt when I turned her around to face me.

"Maybe she had sensed it, the cold resolve written on my face as I started to explain. Suddenly she changed. Her manner became bolder—like there was one last thing she wanted to do before she let me go.

"'I know what you want to tell me,' she said. 'I can only imagine the life you have—the life I don't want to know anything about. I just want one thing. Something to remember you by.'"

Beniamino paused and looked into the fire. "Her intentions were clear, and I didn't have the strength or the will to resist her."

"Did anyone see you two together? Her father, perhaps?"

Beniamino shook his head. "Her father came home earlier than expected, but she got me out of there without being seen, guiding me to the trail to Scheggino. No one saw me leave her house."

"Was that the only time you were with her?"

Beniamino nodded. "I never saw her again."

He brought his hands to his face, shielding it. I felt like an unwilling witness to the pain. "If only I had come back . . . asked for her hand in marriage . . . *something* . . ."

He rose abruptly and walked to the window. I followed him. "As much as it hurts to hear this, maybe she didn't want marriage. From what I've been told, she was ill. Telling you would have complicated your life. You did what you thought was right. After all, you had already made a commitment to Donatella . . . and her family."

Beniamino faced me. "You have to understand something. My father was the one who pushed the marriage. The Brambillas were wealthy; their contacts would help him move the company in another direction—worldwide exporting—and that included America. The icing on the cake for me was this house. He had approached Elena's parents and told them he was interested in buying it—a wedding present for his son. Unlike our family, the De Glielcis had fallen on hard times. They liked the idea of their next-door neighbors owning the home they had lived in for generations. Elena's parents had been present at our wedding ceremony that May . . ." Beniamino's voice faltered, his face showing a mix of raw emotions, guilt the most prominent. He looked out the window. The sky had relinquished its light to darkness, and the garden where he had first seen Angelina was now an indistinguishable black mass.

When he resumed speaking, he was under control again. "My love for Angelina was real. I know that now. I can blame my marriage on my father, but the truth is, I let it happen. I wanted the house, and my father had made buying it conditional. 'I will buy it if you marry her' was how he put it." Beniamino smiled sadly. "He was thinking of Brambilla money—not his son's happiness. I knew Donatella was spoiled and shallow, but at twenty-one, I found it easy to overlook her less attractive qualities in favor of a splendid house and the approval of my father. If only I had seen how superficial all that was in the face of what really mattered in life."

"The past cannot be altered, but there is still time to amend the consequences," I said.

Beniamino looked at me intently. "You mean where Agostino is concerned."

I blurted out the question I had wanted to ask since our conversation started. "Do you think you are Agostino's father?"

Beniamino held my gaze unflinchingly. "I do. I have thought about nothing else for hours now. My encounter with Angelina, Agostino's birth date. It all fits."

"What do you want to do about it?"

Beniamino looked startled. "What *can* I do?"

"Tell your wife. Acknowledge openly that he is your son. Then there will be no conflict with sharing the Foundation ownership with Giovanni."

Beniamino shook his head vehemently. "No, Donatella will crucify me. She'll try to take everything. How will that help Agostino?"

"You weren't married yet. A one-time affair before you took your vows is not exactly grounds for divorce."

Beniamino was silent. My mind was trying to digest the information too. I hadn't really thought this thing out before going to Beniamino's.

"Has Agostino opened the box?" Beniamino finally asked.

"He wanted to be alone tonight. I'm guessing he has opened it by now." A thought occurred to me. "Do you think there is something in there that ties you to him?"

"Perhaps."

"That's why you wanted to get at it first. Does Gabriella suspect you are his father?"

Beniamino considered this. "I think she does. Earlier, when Agostino and I were arguing, she said, "You don't see it do you?" I didn't understand the comment then, but she must have been talking about that."

I stepped away from the window and headed for the front door. "I have to get back to Agostino. I want to be there when he opens the box . . . if I'm not already too late."

"Are you going to tell him?" Beniamino called out after me.

I stopped and turned toward the fireplace, glancing at the piece of paper on the desk. "Are you going to burn the ledger?"

Beniamino's jaw clenched. "I'm not going to burn it."

"Then I won't tell Agostino what we discussed tonight." I walked to the front door, opened it, and let myself out.

Chapter 26

Expectations

I CROSSED the bridge under the artificial glare of the lampposts. The cool night air felt good after the hour I had spent in Beniamino's library. Looking up toward the houses perched against the hillside, I saw that there were no lights on in Agostino's villa. Was he sitting there, in the dark, with the box open beside him? What had he found inside? My first impulse was to go to him, but then I remembered he had wanted to be alone. I needed to respect that. And even though my heart yearned to tell him what I had learned tonight, I knew I couldn't. I had made a promise, and I was determined to keep it. It was up to Beniamino to tell Agostino the truth.

Standing at the edge of the bridge, the wind whipping around my shoulders, I tried to come to a decision. Suddenly I thought of Agostino shouldering the burden of his past with no one there to support him. I started up the road to Villa Urbino.

Thirty minutes later, I passed through the open gates and down the long drive to the kitchen entrance. The outside door was unlocked. I pushed it open and walked through the empty kitchen into the dining area. The room was dark, but because of the lighted patio and the French doors, I could see a figure seated in a chair, legs propped on the table, head bowed.

Agostino was asleep.

My eye went to the sideboard where I could make out a metal box next to a string of pale blue rosary beads. Had he opened it yet? Just as I was trying to decide if I should wake him, a man walked up the steps from the pool area and entered the dining room. I stepped quickly back into the kitchen.

"GP!" Agostino said, jerking his head up and swinging his legs off the table. "It is late. I did not expect you."

"No guests?" GP asked.

"Not until Saturday. A big group is coming in from Terni. Bride's parents are loaded." Agostino rolled his eyes. "Can't wait. Lots of whining."

GP produced a bottle from inside his jacket. Remember you told me to save it for later?" He set the whiskey on the table. "Well, later is now."

Agostino chuckled. He walked over to the sideboard, found two shot glasses from inside the cabinet, and brought them to the table.

GP poured the dark brown liquid all the way to the rim. "I was on my way home and thought you might like a bit of company . . . all alone with so many big decisions." He handed a glass to Agostino and pointed to the box. "Have you opened it yet?"

Agostino shook his head. He tilted his head back and let the liquid roll down his throat. "Working up my nerve. It has occurred to me I may find out something I don't want to know."

GP downed his in one gulp. "You can't live your life that way. Some surprises can make your life better."

"Name one."

"Meeting Anna."

Agostino snorted. "If I hadn't met Anna, none of this would have happened."

Just inside the kitchen doorway, I could see and hear both men . . . even if I didn't want to. The last thing I wanted to do was eavesdrop on another conversation. Still . . .

GP refilled both their glasses. "Would you rather not have discovered who your real mother was? You don't *have* to open the box, you know."

Agostino glanced at his friend. "And stare at it every night wondering? No, I'm glad I found out about her. I have a better understanding of who I am now—even if there are still some unanswered questions."

"You mean like who your father is?" GP ventured.

Agostino nodded. "I have a feeling the answer to that question may be inside that box."

The two men were silent, drinking their thoughts.

"So, do you think it's true?" GP finally asked.

"That Wojo was my father, you mean?"

GP grunted an affirmative.

"I have to consider it a possibility. Why would Lallo write that name on the birth certificate if it wasn't true?" Agostino asked him.

"Maybe he didn't know his daughter very well—what kind of life she led. A doctor is a busy man." GP cleared his throat uncomfortably. "Angelina might have had other lovers—lovers her father didn't know about."

Agostino's brows furrowed. "Even if it is true, I need to know everything . . . including what kind of woman my mother was."

"And if you *do* find out that Wojo was your father," GP paused to let the words sink in, "what will you do then?"

"I don't know."

"What does Anna say?"

"Anna! How do I know what she thinks! Hot one minute and cold the next. Don't get me started."

GP grunted again. "Are we talking about something else now?"

Did I want to hear this or not? I considered making a quick exit, and then I heard the next sentence.

Agostino sighed. "I guess I can tell you—just between us, you understand."

I held my breath and took a step closer.

"We had this incredible night—right when she got back to Scheggino. I was head over heels, I guess, and I started in about our future. I even talked about marriage."

"The first night?" GP sounded incredulous. *"Ma sei pazzo?* That is crazy."

"I guess she thought so too. She cooled off pretty quick after that. Then, the night I asked her to wait on tables she almost dumped an entire plate on a customer's lap . . ."

"*Dio mio!*" GP hit his head with the palm of his hand. "You threw her into a crowd of hungry Italians? No wonder. Maybe being a waitress in a hotel was not the future she had in mind."

Agostino looked annoyed. "So is that what I did wrong? What about *her*? You think it was fun for me to watch her on that stage with Sergei? I was never so embarrassed . . ."

"Why?"

"She made a spectacle of herself in front of the whole town!"

"A spectacle?" GP raised an eyebrow. "My wife was in the audience that night. She thought the performance was fantastic. Didn't you hear the applause?"

Agostino sighed. "I heard it all right." He emptied the glass in one gulp.

"It was a *performance,* Agostino. They are entertainers. That's what they do."

Agostino was silent.

GP looked at his friend. "Tell me something. What is it about Anna that you like?"

"She's different . . . exciting. Life sizzles when she's around."

GP waited for more.

"She's not a spectator . . . she's a participant."

"Exactly."

Agostino stared at him as if realizing something for the first time. "Are you saying she's not right for me?"

GP chose his words carefully. "Anna is not like the women in this town. American women are independent. Many of them—like Anna—don't need a man to support them. You have to offer her something she *wants.* Something she doesn't already have."

"I thought that's what I did the first night," Agostino said quietly.

"*Mamma mia!* I'm not talking about sex. She can get that in America."

GP was sounding exasperated. "Have you even asked her what her dreams are?"

Agostino fingered the glass, thinking. GP refilled it.

"That's the problem, right there. You don't know because you never asked her. You were just thinking how she could fit into *your* dreams. If you want her to be part of your life, you have to try to be a part of hers."

Agostino looked at his friend anxiously. "I've totally blown it, haven't I?"

GP smiled. "If it's any help, I think she's here searching for something. Something she hasn't found in America. Maybe it has to do with her family's past—I don't know—but it's here. In Scheggino. Why don't you help her figure it out?"

Agostino lifted the glass to his lips and downed the contents. He gestured for GP to refill it. "How do I do that?"

GP flung up his hands. "I have to do all your work? Try asking her to share *this* with you." He pointed to the box. "Asking her to be there when you open it shows you value her opinion. She knows your future is in that box. If she wants to be part of it, she will say yes."

Agostino stared at his friend for a long time. "I'll do it."

He whipped out his phone and stopped. "What if she says no?"

GP chuckled and refilled his own glass. "That's a chance you have to take."

Agostino dialed the number. After half a ring I picked up.

"Pronto?"

"Can you come over? I'm here with GP. We are discussing things, and I . . ."—he glanced at his friend—"I need you here."

GP nodded his head encouragingly.

Agostino took a deep breath. "I value your opinion."

I stepped out of the shadows and walked into the room. Both men's eyes widened.

"How long have you been listening?" Agostino asked. He looked embarrassed.

"I just walked in," I said.

"I didn't hear your car," Agostino said.

"I walked."

"I left you at the cemetery more than two hours ago. You have been walking all this time?"

"I like to walk," I answered.

Agostino's brows furrowed. "I don't like it. A woman walking alone at night..."

I laughed. "It's been dark less than an hour."

"I don't care..." Agostino started to say then I saw him jerk as if someone had kicked him under the table.

GP refilled their glasses. They both downed them and stared at me.

I waited. "Can you dig up another glass?" I finally said.

Agostino got up, walked over to the sideboard and took out a shot glass. He glanced at the metal box before returning to the table.

I accepted the glass and poured myself two fingers from the half-full bottle. The two men's eyes were on me as I took my first sip. I grabbed my throat and coughed, the kick almost knocking me off my chair.

"Jack Daniels is not a drink for ladies," Agostino said.

"It's delicious," I countered. "An American product, I believe?"

Both men nodded.

Silence.

GP cleared his throat and winked at Agostino. "Well, I've got to get home. The wife made lasagna." As he rose to go, Agostino grabbed him by the arm. "Have another drink."

I wanted to laugh out loud. Agostino was afraid he would have to have a certain conversation without GP's help.

"Anna, Agostino has something he wants to ask you," GP said in English.

Agostino looked clueless.

"Dreams," GP prompted.

"Right." Agostino looked at GP gratefully. "Uh...Anna...do you have dreams?"

"Dreams?" I said innocently. "You mean like nightmares?" I wasn't making this easy for him.

"No, no . . . I mean things you want to do . . ."

I pretended sudden clarity. "Ah. You mean something I want to accomplish in life."

Agostino nodded vigorously.

I sat back, savoring the moment. "Well, yes, as a matter of fact. I have always wanted to open a ballet school."

GP refilled their glasses.

"Ballet school," Agostino repeated. "You want to teach?"

"And put on performances."

"For children?" Agostino said hopefully.

"For everyone. Adults too. If we could find a space here, it could also be a place to rehearse for community events."

Agostino swallowed hard. "A dance school in Scheggino." He said the words slowly as if he were trying them out. "And you would run it?"

"Why not?"

My heart went out to him as I watched him struggle with this new revelation. I knew he was trying to bridge the gap, not only between our respective goals but also between the differences in our cultures and the way we had both been raised. In the history of the Urbino women, Agatha Altarocca had been the only woman who had had successfully managed a professional career. Could Agostino accept my need to do something on my own? I knew it wouldn't be easy for either of us to adapt, but if we could meet each other halfway . . .

I thought about the words he had used earlier. *I value your opinion . . . I need you . . .* For the first time in a while, I felt hopeful. The thought that he needed me didn't scare me anymore. I was ready to share Agostino's discovery—if he wanted me to.

I looked at the nearly empty bottle and flushed faces of the two men. If this conversation lasted much longer, neither one of them would be able to focus much less open a rusty metal box.

"Agostino, is there something you wanted to ask me? You started to mention it on the phone . . ."

Agostino stood up. "Yes," he said, walking toward the sideboard. GP's strong arms grabbed him a second before he fell.

GP held Agostino up under the arms and looked at me apologetically. "*Colpa mia.* I bring the whiskey. I thought it would help."

GP was going back and forth from Italian to English for some reason. Maybe he wanted to make sure nothing important got lost in translation. What he didn't realize was that, with the amount of alcohol he'd consumed, things were getting murkier. "You thought it would help what?"

"Loosen *la lingua*," He pointed to his tongue and grinned.

Agostino shook himself loose from GP's grasp. "We were having heart-to-man discussion."

"That's man-to-man," I said. "Sounds fascinating, tell me more." I crossed my arms and regarded the two men. GP burped and Agostino hiccupped. Both men started laughing.

"Agostino, why did you invite me over?"

Agostino wiped his eyes. "We were going to open the box. I wanted you here."

"You said you *needed* me here. And that you valued my opinion, remember?"

Agostino managed a lopsided grin. "I most shertainly do." He swayed, and, before GP could catch him, pitched forward and landed facedown on the floor.

GP and I put him back on his feet, and with an arm on each shoulder, we got him up the stairs to his bedroom. He was snoring before we even got him into bed.

GP glanced at me cautiously. "I guess plans have changed."

"I guess so. I'm taking you home."

GP glared at me. "What do you mean? My Ape is the only car here. You walked."

I looked into his bloodshot eyes. "That's right, and I'm driving you home in it. My apartment is barely a kilometer from there."

GP stuttered. "But no one—not even my wife—drive my truck."

"There's a first time for everything," I answered.

Chapter 27

Conspiracy Theories

"MAKE MINE a double, Emilio," I called out to the man behind the bar. He nodded and turned to start the cappuccino machine behind him. I picked my favorite table, the one with the view of the piazza, and sat down.

The town was waking up. Businessmen on their way to Perugia hurried to their parked cars, collars turned up against the brisk morning air. Two ladies with empty shopping bags on their arms crossed the bridge to Sabrina's *alimentari,* anxious to be first in line at the meat counter. Outside the bar, a group of older men gathered to share greetings and their first cigarettes of the day.

I was a little surprised Agostino hadn't called yet. Last night, before he pitched over onto the floor, things were looking hopeful. He had even said he valued me—words I had been waiting to hear for a while now. What still remained to be seen was if he valued the real me . . . not the image he had of a subservient woman doling out pleasantries and plates of pasta. I had seen the effort he had made—with GP's prodding—to ask the important questions I needed him to ask. It was a shame man-to-man talks over glasses of whiskey usually ended up with at least one of the participants unconscious. Today, we would have to start all over.

The conversation about teaching ballet classes had been more of a test to see how Agostino would react than a serious plan. But now, the more I thought about it, the more I liked the idea. The old truffle headquarters off the main piazza would make a great space, but it would need work. A wood floor, barres and mirrors on the walls—and Beniamino's permission. With the current friction between the two families, that was not likely to happen.

I saw a striking woman wearing a puffy jacket, jeans, and knee-high boots walking down the strip of sidewalk between the castle and the river. Entering the bar, she pushed a length of dark hair over her shoulder and flashed a smile at Emilio. He smiled back. *"Buon giorno,* Renata. The usual?"

"Sì, un Americano."

"Renata! *Dove sei stata?* I haven't seen you for days! Come sit with me."

She pulled up a chair. A few minutes later, Emilio hurried over with a glass of steaming black coffee.

"Perfetto," She said.

I gave the coffee a swift glance. "I've often heard it ordered in the States. What is it?"

"Diluted espresso. Italians are obsessed with all things American at the moment. I'm guessing." She reached for two sugar packets and stirred them into her glass. She raised the glass to her lips. "Worked for me."

"How is Georgio?" I asked, remembering my manners.

"For an eighty-four-year-old with a history of heart disease, Papa is doing great. Still goes to his garden every morning and putters around. He doesn't hunt for truffles anymore. We may have to get rid of the dogs."

I winced. Italians, especially those living in rural villages, have a different mentality when it comes to canines. They let them sleep under flimsy sheds in the gardens outside the village even in winter. They are considered working animals, and in Scheggino the work is hunting for truffles. I had given up trying to convince the residents that keeping an animal near starving just so they would hunt better was heartless if not barbaric. When I told them my Labrador slept on my bed back home and got his nails clipped, they looked at me like I was crazy. Lately, mortified at seeing their forlorn faces, I had gotten in the habit of sneaking bits of pasta and chicken to the howling dogs I passed on my morning run. I knew it ruined the owner's training regime—treats were given out only as rewards—and if they ever caught me, I would probably be shot.

"Tell me what is going on with you and Sergei?" Renata's eyes were twinkling over the rim of her glass. "Rumors were flying after that concert. The whole town is wondering if you two are an item."

I laughed. "I'm afraid they are all going to be very disappointed." I looked at Renata's puzzled face. "I think I'll let him tell you about it."

I signaled Emilio for another cappuccino. "That is old news anyway. There have been a lot of new developments since I saw you last . . . concerning Agostino."

Renata scooted her chair closer to mine.

I brought her up to date on what we had learned at Pepina's house, being careful to leave out the little detail of the father's name on the birth certificate. I was mindful of what Sergei had said about spreading gossip that might not be true and the damage it could cause.

Renata looked shocked when I started talking about the Lallo family. "Are you telling me that Angelina Lallo is Agostino's mother?" She asked.

"I said it's *possible*. Do you know who she is?"

"Papa knew the De Glielcis." She pointed across the piazza to Ben's house. "Angelina's mother was a De Glielci. They were related to Cardinal Poli, you know."

I almost mentioned Beniamino had told me this story, but then I remembered my promise. "Tell me more."

"Angelina's mother, Elena, married Dr. Lallo and moved to his place, the former monastery, up in Monteluco. Papa lost track of her after that. Then there were reports she had a child, and then we heard she spent time in an asylum. Poor thing, all alone up there. No wonder she had mental problems."

"Did you ever know Angelina?"

"No, I was eight when she died. I think she's buried up there with the rest of the Lallos. The doctor died a few years ago—he was almost a hundred." Suddenly Renata's eyes widened. "You said there is a birth certificate claiming Agostino is Angelina's son, right? If it holds up, he stands to inherit the monastery."

I stared at her. "I hadn't thought of that until now. I hiked up there last week. You know it's for sale. I wonder who put it on the market."

"It must be the doctor's distant relatives," Renata said, digging into her purse. "I know how we can find out. I have a very good friend in the business." She pulled out her cellphone and dialed.

"Francesca? Renata. Who's got the listing for the Eremo Delle Grazie? I see. Congratulations. I have someone interested in the property. Can we meet you there tomorrow . . . say 2 p.m.? Good." She hung up the phone and looked at me. "Francesca has the listing. We are all going up there, you, me and Agostino—with the birth certificate."

"Did you find out what family member put it on the market?"

Renata's eyes glinted. "Francesca is a good friend. I will get the whole scoop. There will be a fight, you know." Her eyes were glowing. "Dr. Lallo's relatives will not take this lying down. Any claims of ownership Agostino makes will be contested."

She grabbed my arm. "Let's go talk to Papa. He knows a lot more than me."

We paid for our coffees and headed up to her compound.

Renata continued the conversation as we climbed. "If the doctor had siblings, Agostino could be faced with a court battle even if he *didn't* want to keep the monastery. As an heir, even an illegitimate one, he could receive a portion of the proceeds when it is sold."

"I'm not sure of his intentions," I said evasively.

As we approached the iron gate, I saw Georgio in the courtyard bending over his geraniums. Besides Renata, Georgio was my last link to my great grandfather's brother, Fernando. I would always be grateful for the inheritance my great uncle had given our side of the family. It had helped us gain a foothold in America. Georgio looked up when we walked into the courtyard—a little round man with a head as bald as a billiard ball. His startling blue eyes reminded me immediately of my grandfather Spirito.

"*Zio,* you look better every time I see you."

"Fatter, you mean." He laughed, patting his belly.

Renata gestured to the metal bistro set in the courtyard. "Everybody sit. I will get a notebook and a pencil." She disappeared into the house.

"What's this about?" Georgio asked me.

I filled him in, then asked, "Do you know Doctor Lallo's relatives?"

"I know *of* them," he answered carefully. "Old political family from Rome. Supporters of *Il Duce*. I would think twice about tangling with them."

I raised a skeptical eyebrow. Georgio was talking like we were in the 1940s. His claims seemed a little far-fetched given fascism had been dead and buried for more that seventy years.

Georgio leaned in and dropped his voice to a whisper. "I'm talking about Pio's father, the dentist. He was a high-level fascist operative. People say he had Mussolini up there to the Eremo on a number of occasions. The Savoias too."

"Pepina said he worked on their teeth."

"A cover. He held important meetings there during the war. I am convinced of it." Georgio crossed his arms and winked at me.

I stifled a chuckle. I was having a hard time taking what he said seriously. Georgio seemed prone to exaggeration when it came to stories from the past. After all, he had single-handedly kept the tale of "Spirito's Revenge" alive for years.

Renata appeared with a notebook under one arm. "We have to get all of this down." She took the pencil from behind her ear and started scribbling down notes.

"Renata . . . do you really believe the fascist thing?" I looked at her skeptically.

Her eyes narrowed, and she put down her pencil. "Why wouldn't it be true?"

"Pepina never said . . ."

"Of course she didn't. Pepina and her father were fascists. They were all in it together," Renata snapped.

I sat looking at the two of them. It was obvious that an enthusiasm for conspiracy theories ran in the family. I was outnumbered.

"Then there's no way I want you involved in this Eremo *caper*," I said to Renata, trying to keep a straight face.

Renata looked crushed. "Why not?"

"Too dangerous."

Renata seemed to consider this seriously. "I can handle it," she said firmly. "I'm going to ask Francesca who the owners are." She reached for her phone.

"Wait," I said. "Don't you think we need to discuss it with Agostino? This is his decision to make, and given what you just told me, he may not want to get involved."

Renata was determined. "Not even to take a look? The place has probably been vacant since the doctor died. There may still be some of Angelina's things in there."

She had a point. If the Eremo sold, Agostino would not get another chance.

Georgio and Renata were both staring at me now, conspiracists unleashed, practically salivating at the possibilities.

I took a firm stance. "Before you mention anything about Agostino's connection to the Lallo family, let me find out what his intentions are concerning the property."

My relatives looked disappointed. Promising to meet Renata at the Eremo the next day, I hastened down to the bar to call Agostino.

He picked up on the first ring.

"I was just about to call you," Agostino rasped then cleared his throat. "I got up late."

A sarcastic comment sprang to mind, but I considered it beneath me. I waited for him to continue.

"I've been thinking. I'd like to have Flavia there when I open the box. You know, a neutral witness in case we turn up something monumental. What do you think?"

"Are you asking for my *valued* opinion? If so, I think it is an excellent idea," I answered.

Agostino laughed. "Meet me at Paradiso Vinto at six. I am cooking dinner."

Chapter 28

Family

MARI MET me at the door with a warm hug.

"I didn't know you were here!" I exclaimed. "When did you get in?"

She brimmed with excitement, and little crinkles formed in the corners of her eyes. "I drove from Turin yesterday; the car is still packed with kitchen supplies. If I can clear out Agatha's shed and start ordering the counter and baking appliances, the pastry shop could be up and running by summer."

"It sounds wonderful. I am so happy for you."

Mari's face turned serious. "Flavia told me about the box. If this is a private matter, and you and Agostino would rather I not be present . . ."

"This is Agostino's show. I am only here to lend support or a comforting shoulder depending on what we find. Have you discussed this with him?"

"He says I should be here . . . because . . . I am family." Mari blushed, and her crinkles got deeper.

I squeezed her hand. "You are."

"Thank you. It certainly feels like home." She glanced toward the kitchen and back to me. "You are in for a treat tonight. I am making *zuppa Inglese*. It is a dessert that has its origins up north, in the Emilia-Romagna."

English soup, I translated silently. *I hope it tastes better than it sounds.*

We walked through the vast living space to the dining room and kitchen area.

Flavia greeted me with half a hug, the other arm holding up a pile of wood with her apron. "Anna, make yourself useful. Tend to the fire."

Instead of being put off by her brusque, no-nonsense manner, I felt a warmth come over me. When you are among family, formalities are not necessary. I took the logs from her and got to work.

"You are here," a voice behind me said. I looked up. Agostino was standing over me with a tray of dressed pork chops. He had an uneasy look in his eyes. "I am so nervous I may burn the *filettos*."

I scooted over and made a place for him by the fire. "We will do it together," I told him. I noticed his hands were trembling as he placed the meat on the rack inside the flames.

"Have you tried the key?" I asked him quietly. "If it doesn't fit, we will have to break the lock."

"A well-aimed chop with the axe is the least of our problems," he replied.

"*Un calice di vino?*" Flavia appeared holding two glasses of red wine.

I accepted them and held one out to Agostino.

He shook his head. "I'm not drinking anything until we see what's inside that box."

As we sat down to eat, I reached for Agostino's hand on one side and Flavia's on the other. Mari understood immediately, connecting the circle of hands.

"A small word of thanks might be in order?" I asked—the impulsive gesture surprising even me.

We all bowed our heads.

"This has been a journey for all of us, but I have a feeling fate and your divine guidance had something to do with it. Thank you for bringing us all together." I looked up at the faces surrounding me. "I feel honored to be included at this table."

"I, too, am honored," Mari said.

"*L'onore è tutto mio*," Flavia answered, then broke into a gap-toothed grin. "*Mangiamo!*"

Agostino speared the perfectly roasted fillets onto plates, his eyes occasionally glancing in my direction—intent and searching—but hopeful. Flavia ladled the minestrone into bowls while discussing future plans for the *pasticceria,* and Mari looked like a proper *maestra della casa* serving up the layered custard. There was an unspoken feeling of acceptance at that table, a feeling that, even though we had all come from somewhere else, we had found what we were looking for and that we were home.

◦────⌒────◦

After dinner, we gathered around the coffee table in the living room, the box in front of us. Agostino took a deep breath and inserted the tiny key attached to the rosary into the box's keyhole. Its rusted edges, long unused, resisted, but Agostino was patient. He worked it back and forth, drew it out, and tried again. After a few attempts, the key went all the way in and turned. The box jerked as if waking from a long sleep, but the lid, still clamped shut, needed additional persuasion. With the aid of a little Urbino olive oil, Agostino pried it open.

A single strand of pearls and a sapphire ring lay at the bottom along with a collection of seashells and a bunch of withered flowers held together with ribbon. An envelope with the name *"Angelina"* written on the front was nestled in their midst. The writing was in a female hand, and there was a drawing of a rose beneath it.

"Angelina's mother?" I asked.

Agostino gently opened the envelope, withdrew the letter, and began reading:

> *Mia Carissima Bambina*
>
> *When you find this letter, I will already be gone. Even as I write this, I pray God will forgive me for leaving you alone in this world. A world I can no longer stand to live in. There is something that happened in this house that I cannot forget or forgive, and it haunts me every day. You know what it is. I saw you hiding that night when she came. He could have saved her... we could have saved her, but we were weak. Please forgive me. I love you more than you know.*
>
> *Your mama, Elena.*

When Agostino looked up, there were tears in his eyes. "This must have been written right before she overdosed. What was it that haunted her? What happened at the Eremo?"

I shook my head. "I'm not sure we will ever know." I looked into the box again and saw another envelope. I lifted it out and handed it to him.

Agostino turned the envelope over and read the printed words on the flap: *"Eremo delle Grazie. Monteluco, Italia."* He looked at me. "The writing is very different but also written by someone using the stationary at the hermitage."

My eyes widened. "Could it be from Wojo?" I put a hand on his arm. "There is someone who needs to see this at the same time we open it. May I call him?"

"You mean Sergei," Agostino said.

"As a person who has studied the writings of this man, maybe he can help us determine if Wojo wrote it."

"Call him."

Sergei picked up on the second ring. *Thank God he was home.*

I got right to the point. "We found a letter addressed to Angelina. We think it's from Wojo. Can you meet us at Paradiso Vinto?"

"I'll be there in ten minutes," came the immediate reply.

Mari spoke up while we waited. "By the way everyone is behaving, I'm guessing Wojo is someone you all know."

Flavia looked at Agostino. "If this is something you want to keep private . . ."

Agostino shook his head. "I want no secrets. I consider you and Mari part of my family. He looked at the two women. "There is something I haven't told you. I think now might be a good time."

⁕ ⁓ ⁕

Fifteen minutes later, the doorbell rang. Agostino got up to answer it. I heard the heavy wooden door open and Agostino's voice echoing in the foyer. "Sergei, thank you for coming."

I turned my head just in time to see Sergei clasp the outstretched hand of his host. "I will give you all the help I can," he said, placing his other hand on Agostino's shoulder. I blinked twice. It was a moment I could not have envisioned a week ago.

The two men walked toward the living room and joined us on the sectional. Agostino slid in next to me, and Sergei sat to my right.

Agostino's hands shook a little as he broke the seal, withdrew two brittle pages yellowed with age, and read:

Cara Angelina,

Please forgive me. I hope one day you will understand why I chose this moment to say goodbye. Although it may seem like I am abandoning you in your hour of need, I am convinced it is the sincere love and affection of your father and the capable care of your physician that must guide you on this journey. My presence would only serve to undermine those relationships.

I want you to know that the issues that brought me here have been resolved—in large part because of the questions you were not afraid to ask me. You asked if I was doubting my faith in God. My response was my faith had never wavered, but it was the path to serve him that I struggled with. That path has now been revealed to me more fully than ever before. My fulfillment and happiness lie in absolute devotion to the Church in the exclusive manner that Jesus Christ demanded. Given the false accusations by your father of my impropriety and my commitment to act in obedience of my vows, I can no longer remain by your side.

My prayers are with you now and in the months ahead. Whenever you are in need of spiritual guidance, call upon Our Lord and he will help you.

I remain your devoted servant and good friend.

Karol Wojtyla.

Agostino looked up. The faces around him were full of quiet astonishment. The signature at the bottom of the last page came as no surprise to any of us.

"May I?" Sergei asked. Agostino handed over the letter. Sergei reviewed the contents carefully for some minutes before returning the pages to Agostino.

"From what I have read of his published works, this is very consistent with the way he writes and the beliefs he holds dear." Sergei looked Agostino in the eye. "I think you can safely assume that this man is not your father."

Agostino let out a huge sigh of relief.

I glanced at the top of the first page. "Did you notice it is dated *'il 12 settembre?'* Agostino, when were you born?"

"Fourteenth of April," he replied.

I thought back to my conversation with Beniamino. He had made those trips to Monteluco in August, he had said. "I am guessing this letter was written the day Wojo left the hermitage. The same day Angelina woke from her coma. He had been there a month according to Pio Lallo. Even if Wojo and Angelina had been intimate the day he arrived, it would still make her less than eight months pregnant by April. Dr. Sabatini's comments on the birth certificate say she carried the child to full term. Wojo *couldn't* have been your father."

Agostino stared at me with admiration. "You are brilliant."

Sergei had grown quiet, his expression unreadable. It was obvious the contents of the letter had affected him deeply. I could only assume he was thinking about how all of this would affect the reputation of his mentor.

Flavia turned to Agostino. "How do you feel about all of this? You seem relieved."

"You have no idea. The responsibility of keeping my birth father's name a secret from the rest of the world is not something I was looking forward to."

Sergei cut in. "And if this letter got out, even with his professed innocence, it could change the way the world regards him. His whole life would be held up for public scrutiny, and he would no longer be considered a man above reproach. Now that we have DNA, I can only imagine what a circus the media could make of this."

"Are you saying they could go so far as to suggest exhuming the body?" I asked incredulously.

"Probably not. But just because he has been canonized doesn't mean he is above scrutiny. The mere suggestion of it by the media would be damaging enough. He would become infamous instead of revered."

Agostino refolded the pages and inserted them into the envelope. Placing the letter in the box, he said, "I can say with all certainty this letter will never see the light of day again."

"Don't throw away the key," Sergei cautioned him. "Because of the information on the birth certificate about Angelina carrying the child to full term, you may need to show the letter to prove you are *not* Wojo's son. Keep the box in a safe place, but remember, if any of this gets into the wrong hands, it could be disastrous."

I thought of Beniamino and our conversation. What Sergei said was true. The Urbinos would have a field day with this.

Agostino paled. "I guess my relief was short lived. Another thing just occurred to me. This journey is not over."

Mari spoke up. "Not over? It is just beginning. I have some experience with this subject, remember. I was lucky that my father came looking for my mother and found *me*. Because of that, I am here today. You may not be so lucky. This letter closes one door, but another is still wide open. You have to consider that your quest to find your father may be one sided. He may not want to be found."

The stars were out by the time Agostino and I left Paradiso Vinto. The ground was wet, a minor shower having penetrated the ground while we were indoors. It had washed the sky clean and left the landscape refreshed.

"What are your thoughts?" I asked Agostino. "This was a momentous occasion . . ."

Agostino's face in the semi-darkness looked untroubled. "Having Sergei there was a great comfort to me. I must confess, when I considered him a rival . . ."

I thought about that disastrous night in Rome. It seemed like a lifetime ago. "Agostino, that was before . . ."

Agostino put a hand up. "Let me finish. I did not give his character the consideration it deserved . . . *before*. Now I see that he is a serious person and truly committed to his calling."

"And an authority on the man who wrote that letter you read tonight," I said quickly. "Maybe you and Sergei have more in common than you think."

Agostino stopped in his tracks and turned to me. "I look forward to getting to know him better."

"And keeping him abreast of whatever happens in your future would please him greatly," I added.

Agostino cracked a smile. "Suggestion noted."

We resumed our pace and started down the newly paved road that led to Villa Urbino.

Gazing out at the fields of faro connecting the villas, I remembered that, when my Uncle SJ was alive, an ugly wire fence had divided the two properties— a physical reminder of the strained relationship between both families. After his death, it had been Flavia's idea to tear it down and create a more direct access for guests who wanted to use the facilities of both hotels. Flavia's villa had the private casitas in the back, and Agostino had the pool. Since they both served delicious regional cuisine, Flavia reasoned, the guests could walk from one villa to another to sample the various dinner entrees during their stay. The plan had been discussed, and in a few months, Agostino and Flavia planned to put it into effect. Now, with the pastry shop going in, there was one more thing to bring the two families together.

"For most of my life, my family never associated with Agatha's sons," Agostino said as we crossed the property line between the two villas. "So many wasted years hating each other because of a secret no one wanted to talk about. You changed all that when you showed SJ how to live a different kind of life. A life with no regrets. That trip to Turin changed all our lives."

"I hope you can forgive me. Yours has changed in ways you never thought possible."

Agostino looked at me tenderly. "I have no regrets, do you?"

I had the feeling we weren't talking about Turin anymore. I was hoping it was too dark for him to see me blush. "No regrets. The path ahead is less certain, though," I said more softly.

"I can relate to that."

We had reached the villa's back entrance. "Nightcap?" Agostino asked holding the door open.

"I'd like that," I said. I walked past the dark kitchen and into the dining area. I tried not to glance at the stairs leading up to Agostino's bedroom.

"I was just thinking about the night you filled in waiting tables." Agostino's eyes were twinkling.

I rolled my eyes. "Don't remind me. The less said about that night the better."

"I acted like an ass," Agostino said.

"A macho Italian ass," I said.

"Okay, okay. I would like to be the one to acknowledge my shortcomings if it's all the same to you."

The tender moment was gone. *My fault this time.*

I put a hand on his arm. "No more sparring, You mentioned a nightcap, I believe?" I moved to the dining room table and sat down. "There is another hurdle to cross, and it involves the Eremo delle Grazie. I hope you don't have plans for tomorrow."

Chapter 29

The Eremo

"THE ONLY reason I am doing this is because I want to look around," Agostino said as we turned off the autostrada and started the climb to Monteluco. "There may be something that belonged to my mother still in there."

"So you're not interested in trying to claim ownership of the Eremo?" I asked him.

"No. It would mean showing proof that I was Angelina's son. If the owners saw Wojo's name on the birth certificate, it could make things more complicated."

"What are we going to say to the realtors?" I asked. "We have to have a valid reason for snooping around."

"I'll just say I'm thinking of buying it to expand my hotel business. That I want to turn it into a B&B."

I frowned. "Destroy the historical ambiance with *amenities?* You wouldn't dare."

"And what would *you* do with it?" he asked me, his tone playful. "It's a bit isolated to attract a museum crowd."

"Find a balance. It could be a retreat, a place where one comes to get away from the hectic life of the city and live like the hermits did five hundred years ago. With certain conveniences, of course."

Agostino seemed amused. "What kind of conveniences?"

"Modern plumbing . . . maybe an in-house cook . . ."

"Wi-Fi?"

I chuckled. "I wouldn't go that far. After all, it isn't a retreat if you bring the noisy world with you."

Agostino regarded me thoughtfully. "It's an idea worth considering."

He turned onto the gravel apron off the main road. The gate was open, and I could see two sets of muddy tire tracks disappearing around a corner.

"It looks like the realtors are already here," I said. "I will let you do the talking."

"Francesca doesn't know my parentage, right?" Agostino asked.

"Not a thing. I made Renata promise."

Agostino gave me a sharp look. *"You told Renata?* She's the biggest blabbermouth in Scheggino."

Crap. He was right. When would I learn to keep my mouth shut? I didn't dare tell him Georgio also had been told. He had a bigger mouth than Renata.

"I only told her the bare minimum. That it was *possible* Angelina was your mother."

Turning the corner, we passed under a tree-shaded lane skirting a cliff. Beyond it, an incredible view of the city of Spoleto opened up. At the end of the lane was a patio and an annex next to a larger stone building. The flat-roofed, ocher-colored structure had a quaint arched doorway and large windows.

"Perfect for registering guests before they enter the Eremo," I pointed out.

Agostino laughed.

As soon as we got out of the car, a woman appeared in the doorway.

Francesca Corti's red lips were already forming a smile as she descended the steps of the annex. Her razor-sharp haircut skimmed her jaw line and her well-tailored suit clung to her body in all the right places. Walking toward us, she staggered a little as her stilettos struggled to gain a footing in the damp gravel.

Her eyes settled on me briefly. "Anna, a pleasure. I see you have settled in well." Her gaze went from me to Agostino and back again.

Without waiting for a response, she sidled up to Agostino. "A quick word with you before my colleague comes out. Are you going to fight the relatives on claiming total ownership, or will you settle for a portion of the proceeds of the sale? The relatives would probably be happy to give you something rather than deal with the cost of a court battle."

I turned on Francesca. "Who told you about Agostino's connection with the property? Renata?"

Francesca regarded me coolly. "She said you wanted to clear it with Agostino first, but really, Anna, this is an opportunity he shouldn't pass up."

"Maybe he doesn't see it that way," I snapped, my anger plainly evident. "I hope to God you didn't let the Lallo family know about this."

"I'm not interested in the villa," Agostino said.

"I'm sure I can get you a nice . . ." She stopped and stared at him. "Surely, you're joking. Even in its present condition it is worth a considerable amount."

"I am here to see if there is something that belongs to my mother."

Francesca's voice lowered conspiratorially. "I understand completely. There are a number of very fine antiques, but we would have to get permission." She looked over his shoulder like she was expecting to see a moving truck in the driveway.

A muscle in Agostino's jaw tightened. "I am talking about a keepsake or two, nothing more."

Francesca brightened. "I'm sure we can manage that." She took his arm and led him through the arched door into the annex. I followed behind, utterly forgotten.

The main building looked far older. Frescoed angels adorned tall ceilings and the walls were covered with religious paintings. Through an arched doorway I glimpsed a kitchen, a dining area, and a terrazzo. At the far end of the salon, a graceful curving staircase led up to a second level.

Francesca's arm made a sweeping gesture. "This building was the original monastery. The monks lived in the ground floor rooms and ate in this salon."

"Are the original hermit cells still on the property?" I asked.

Francesca looked impressed. "So, you know the history of this place. Yes, they are below ground, beneath the building. Remember, they were built in the fifth century. The monastery came later."

"As I understood it, the first inhabitants were Saint Isaac and his followers," I continued. "They came from Syria to escape religious persecution."

An older woman walked into the salon from one of the other rooms. "The Eremo has always been a refuge—a place to escape from the real world." The woman spoke confidently, her intelligent eyes taking us both in. Her clothing was couture, her diamonds discreet, and a rarified, detached air suggested she was equally at home among the famous and the infamous. "I am Ida," she said, extending her hand to Agostino. "I am representing the owners."

My next comment was a guess, but I wanted to see her reaction. "You are referring to Pio's siblings, then."

Ida turned her head sharply in my direction. Her face was expressionless except for the calculated look in her eyes—like she knew we had done our homework.

The two women turned their attention to Agostino, waiting for him to speak.

"As I told Francesca, I have no interest in fighting a long and expensive battle to gain title to the property. I am interested only in seeing the place where my mother grew up."

My eyes shot to Agostino. *He is not going to keep it a secret after all.*

If Ida was surprised at Agostino's words, she didn't let on. She kept her face impassive. "I am not sure who you are referring to, but I can give you a tour of the rooms . . ."

Agostino's eyes met hers. "I am referring to Angelina Lallo."

Ida was the first one to look away. "I will be happy to show you the house . . . including Angelina's room. Follow me, please." As she led the way through the salon to the various rooms, I detected an absence of warmth in them. The house seemed soulless.

"Angelina's room?" Agostino reminded the realtor when we had seen all of the downstairs.

She took us up the staircase to a closed door at the end of the hallway. Ida unlocked the door with a key from a ring she extracted from her pocket, and the door creaked open. Inside, there were sheets covering some of the furniture, and the curtains were drawn. Crossing the threshold, I felt a restless energy in the room—as if someone had been unpleasantly disturbed after a long sleep.

Agostino moved instinctively to the bed and ran his hand along the white eyelet bedspread. I saw him fight back the tears.

Ida must have noticed, too, because a moment later, she closed the door gently behind her. When we heard her footsteps walking away, I went to Agostino's side. "Why did you tell that woman . . ."

He turned suddenly and put his arms around me, burying his face in my hair. "I feel her here," he whispered.

I held him tightly. "So do I. I think she was waiting for you."

I could hear him sobbing quietly, his tears wet and warm against my cheek. "Do you want to be alone?" I asked.

"No." He pulled back and looked at me intently. "I can't think of anyone I want here—in this moment—except you."

For once, I was speechless, stunned by the sincerity of his words. We stared at each other for a beautiful, awkward moment before I stepped back, embarrassed. I quickly walked around the room. "I . . . I'm going to do a bit of snooping," I stammered. "It may be our last chance." I stopped in front of a large mahogany secretary dominating the opposite wall and pulled down the lid. There were two sets of cubby holes with a drawer under each and a larger drawer in between. It had a keyhole but was locked up tight. I slid my hand along the slim space underneath the drawer, hoping to feel a piece of paper, a photo, anything Angelina could have left behind. There was nothing. I was about to close the lid when I saw a raised piece of metal, like a knob, at the back of the desk. I slid it back, and a secret compartment was revealed. Inside was a palm-sized book with a clasp holding the pages together. *A diary.*

I reached in and drew it out. "I found something!" I called out.

Agostino was by my side in an instant. "Open it," he said, his eyes bright with anticipation.

I undid the clasp, opening the book to the first page. "To my darling daughter on her ninth birthday." It was signed "Elena Lallo."

"Here," I said, handing it to Agostino.

He put his arm around me, and we turned the next page together. *"Il 25 maggio 1940"* was scrawled in a childish hand at the top of the page. The first couple of pages were carefully written, like a child's writing assignment, but with each passing day, the writing became more relaxed and natural. At times, the thoughts appeared to be rushing ahead—as if the pen could not keep up.

Agostino flipped to the last page. The date entered was *"giugno 1943."* He sighed.

"Maybe there is another diary . . . a later one," I said, opening the lid again. We did a second examination of the secretary but turned up nothing.

"Try the bed," I told him. "The side slats, the footboard . . . If there was another diary, Angelina would have been making entries in it—maybe even the night she overdosed." We searched the pillows and bed linens but came up emptyhanded.

Agostino remade the bed, careful to make it look like before. I suspected he didn't want the realtors to think we had ransacked the room like common thieves. As he tucked the bottom sheet underneath the mattress, his body froze. Then, he pulled out another hardbound book the size of the first one. This one looked well-handled and had the name "Angelina" inscribed on the cover. He held it up.

"Paydirt!" I said.

Agostino came around from the other side of the bed and took me in his arms. He lifted my chin, looked into my eyes, and kissed me on the lips. It was a spontaneous gesture, but once his lips touched mine, he lingered, unable to break away. A warmth spread through my body and down to my toes. I closed my eyes and let myself savor the moment.

I pulled away, glancing at the door. "We found what we were looking for.

Let's get out of here before they become suspicious." I tucked the first diary into my purse, and Agostino slid the second one into an inside jacket pocket.

We crossed the room, and Agostino started to close the door behind him.

I put a hand on his arm. "You said you wanted a keepsake . . . if you don't take one, they will wonder what you took that you *don't* want them to know about." I looked around and spotted a tiny iron figurine of a bird on the windowsill. "That looks good."

Agostino grabbed it, and we left the room.

The two realtors were standing in the salon when we came down the stairs. Agostino held out the bird. "May I have this?" he asked. "This seems so much like something that belonged to her."

Both Ida and Francesca looked relieved. I'm sure they expected he would want a much more valuable keepsake. "Certainly," Ida said, her voice crisp. She glanced at her watch and back at Agostino. "It has been a pleasure." Her eyes were telling us she had done her duty and now it was time for us to go.

Before Francesca could snag us again, we were out the door and safely inside the car. Agostino started the motor and, tires grinding on gravel, we U-turned in front of the two ladies standing outside. Without looking back, we passed through the open gates and down the road to the bottom of the mountain.

Chapter 30

A Window Opens

"DID YOU check the dates in the second book?" I asked Agostino as we cruised the autostrada toward Scheggino.

"No, I didn't even open it." He reached into his jacket with his right hand and pulled it out. "You take a look."

The second book had no clasp, just a string tying it together to keep the pages from coming loose. I undid the string and opened it to the first page of writing.

"*Il 13 settembre 1943,*" I read out loud.

"Angelina was twelve years old," Agostino said. "What was the date of the last entry?"

"*Il 1 ottobre 1945.*" I said.

"Two days after Mussolini and his mistress were executed," Agostino whispered.

"Wow, good recall," I told him.

"It is a date most Italians remember. Like the assassination of your President Kennedy."

Not exactly a fair comparison, I wanted to say, but given the mixed feelings the Italians have toward the dictator, I decided not to argue the point.

"This second diary is not going to help you find your father, is it?" I asked him.

Agostino sighed. "No. It will help me know my mother, though . . . to understand what it was like for her growing up in that cold, forbidding place."

"Is that how you saw the Eremo? Forbidding?"

Agostino nodded. He turned to me. "I am anxious to start reading these diaries, and I don't want to do it alone. Can you come over tonight?"

I thought about the last time we had tried that. Suddenly, I had a better idea. "Why don't you come to my apartment for a change? I can make a decent meatloaf."

Agostino raised an eyebrow. "You are inviting me over to your house?"

"Why not? You don't have guests until Saturday."

Agostino kept his eyes on the road. I could just hear the questions running through his mind. At the end of the night, would he end up on his ear or in my bed? I waited for his answer.

"*Meatloaf*? Good choice. It's pretty hard to mess that up."

We stopped at the *alimentari* on the way. Sabrina was all smiles when we walked in. Her smile got wider when we started bickering over the ingredients. "My meatloaf, my ingredients," I said shooing Agostino toward the door.

"Just make sure you get *two* bottles of Montefalco red," he said on the way out.

We drove up the long ramp to the top level at the east end of the castle. He parked his Fiat in one of the empty spaces before the arched entrance, and we walked with our groceries up the narrow cobblestone pathway to my apartment.

Keying in, I felt a blast of cold air hit me. I had left the house early that morning, and the coolness of the day had permeated the ground-floor space. It brought home the fact that I was just not spending enough time here. I took the groceries to the kitchen counter and lifted a pan off the wall. "I'm cooking," I announced.

Agostino watched me break up the sausage and quickly moved to my elbow. "Use a little olive oil to coat the pan first."

I shrugged him off. "There is only room for one cook in this kitchen." I pointed to the *camino* on the opposite side of the room. "Can you please see to the fire?"

Reluctantly, Agostino walked to the fireplace and started feeding it newspaper and kindling. A few minutes later, I heard the crackle of a roaring fire. He sat down in one of the cozy armchairs nearby and opened the first book.

I set the pasta water to boil and uncorked the bottle of Montefalco red. I poured two glasses and walked over to the figure bent over the book.

"Anything interesting?" I asked, handing him a glass.

"She was nine and ten when she wrote in the first book. The writings are mostly observations of her surroundings up there in the mountains. She sounds like a sweet but lonely child. She mentions Elena infrequently as if she were a visitor rather than her mother." He shook his head sadly, closed the book, and reached for the second one.

I was back to the kitchen, slicing mushrooms, when I heard a low whistle. "Anna, listen to this."

I turned down the boiling water and joined him.

Agostino cleared his throat. *"Il 13 settembre 1944."*

> *A big car drove up around midnight and a lady and two*
> *men got out.*

"Wait. I want to get some perspective. Angelina is fourteen years old now, right?" I asked.

Agostino gave me a "do try to keep up" look and continued:

There were voices downstairs—Nonno's and Papa's. I tiptoed to the edge of the staircase and crouched down. I could see six people in the salon: two men standing by the doorway and a woman with Nonno and Papa on the couch. Mama was there too, hunched in a corner like she was afraid of being seen. Even from the stairs, I could see the lady on the couch was nervous. As she talked to Nonno, her hands kept moving as if she couldn't sit still. I listened quietly.

"Zio, I cannot thank you enough for letting us rest here. Saro is still many hours away, and my bodyguards think it best that we do not travel farther tonight. We will leave again at dawn."

Nonno seemed upset. "Claretta, you are getting in over your head. This isn't one of your sister's films where you can just walk away after the scene is over. If you are captured with him, they will take you down too. Go back to Rome. I have spoken with your father. He says he will keep you safe."

"Safe?" I heard her raise her voice. "Arrigo, we are not safe anywhere now. The enemy is already in Sicily."

I saw Papa get up and start walking around the room. When he turned to her, his face was all distorted. "We are losing, cousin. You could do the country a favor if you told him to switch sides. That republic he formed is a sham. Everyone knows he has become a puppet for Hitler."

"He could never be anyone's puppet. You know that," the lady shouted back. "He knows what he's doing, and he has asked for me to be at his side. He needs me."

"The question is, do you need him?"

The lady's voice was strong. "I will not desert him now."

Nonno sighed. "Pio, show her to one of the downstairs bedrooms and make sure she is comfortable."

Pio led her out of the salon with her bodyguards.

"Godspeed my brave one," Nonno called after her.

I woke at four and looked out my bedroom window. The car was leaving.

⌒

Agostino put down the diary and looked at me. "The way she writes, it's like a novel, not a diary."

I sat on the arm of the chair next to him. "I was thinking the same thing. She had a gift for bringing a story to life. Do you think it really happened, or was it just a child's imagination?"

Agostino shook his head. "I think this really happened. Even at her age, she sensed the importance of this event and wanted to record it . . . maybe write about it one day."

Agostino looked at the pages again. "The lady she refers to . . . are you thinking what I'm thinking?"

I nodded, fingers already flying over my phone. "Clara Petacci. *Claretta* to those closest to her." I read from my screen. "It says here she fled Rome to be with *Il Duce* sometime around the middle of September 1944. Reports say she was with him the day he spoke to a crowd in Saro on September 23. The day the Italian Socialist Republic was officially announced."

"It all fits," Agostino said. "She called Pio 'cousin' and Arrigo, *'zio.'* Is there anything on Clara's father?"

"Yes." My eyes were on my phone screen. "Francesco Petacci was a prominent physician who had clients who worked at the Vatican." I looked up. "I'm sure he and Arrigo were contemporaries."

"So how were they related?"

"It says here that Francesco had a son, Marcello, who was also a doctor. He married a Vittoria Lallo.

Agostino's eyes lit up. "We found the connection! Arrigo's sister. They are the ones trying to lay claim to the Eremo."

I thought about what I had said to Ida. My intuition had been correct. "Let me get this straight. Angelina's great aunt married the brother of Mussolini's mistress." I looked at Agostino. "No wonder that Ida was careful not to reveal the family name. They probably don't need publicity of *any* kind. In Italy, even now, the association could still be newsworthy."

"I could say the same thing," Agostino said. "Ironic, isn't it? It seems we both have skeletons in our past."

"Is there another entry?" I glanced at the diary in his hands.

He looked down. *"Il 1 maggio 1945.* Two days after . . ."

"I'm keeping up," I said. I got up and walked over to the kitchen, turned off all the burners, and brought over the Montefalco. "It looks like dinner is on hold."

Mama has been home a week, and already she and Papa are arguing. This time they don't even care if I hear them.

"You sent her to her death!" Mama shouted at him. "You could have forbidden her to go . . ."

Papa shouted back. "It was a done deal. She had been summoned. If I detained her, he would have sent his men to get her. Who knows what would have happened to us . . . we could have all been executed. You saw how he treated Galeazzo—his own kin."

Mama slumped back in her chair. The look in her eyes scared me. "And now Francesco is coming here with his whole family. What do they want?"

"They are afraid, Elena, afraid the partigiani will come after them too. I promised them they could stay here for a while."

Mama was crying. "What if the partigiani *do come here? Arrigo is an old man, and Angelina . . ."*

"I told them to watch the roads coming here . . ." Papa said.

Mama raised her voice again. "You spoke on the phone? You know the lines can't be trusted anymore."

"We'll be all right. They won't be looking for them in Monteluco. As soon as the partigiani stop this witch hunt, they will go back to Rome." Papa's voice did not sound confident.

An hour later, two cars pulled up. I watched from my window as a group of people, including a little boy, got out and hurried into the house. The driver unloaded a lot of luggage from the trunk and brought it inside. I ran to the hallway and looked down the staircase. The two women, one old and the other young and beautiful, were holding onto Papa and crying. Nonno *came into the room and hugged the men. I could barely make out the voices. I crept down the stairs and sat in a corner. No one even looked at me.*

The beautiful woman was sobbing. "Did you see what they did to my sister after they strung her up? They didn't care that she was already dead. They ripped her dress . . . they spit on her . . ."

She was shaking so bad Papa had to bring her over to the couch. "I'm going to give her something to settle her nerves," he told everyone and left the room.

The older woman looked like a ghost. She never said a word, only kept holding Mama's hand. No one was paying attention to the little boy. The lost look on his face broke my heart. I held out my arms, and he came running. I held him very close. "It's going to be okay," I told him.

Papa came back with a bottle of pills and a glass of water. He made the younger woman take them.

Nonno *was telling everyone to calm down, that they would be safe here. "This is temporary," he told them. "The Italian people are venting their rage and using* Il Duce *as the scapegoat for losing the war." He shook his head. "A few years ago, they were all mad for him, calling him the savior of Italy—and now look. It's a disgrace." He spit the words out. His face was dark and angry.*

The older man, the one they called Francesco, spoke up. "Claretta refused to leave his side even though it meant certain death for her. As far as I'm concerned, our little girl is a martyr."

"A martyr?" I heard Mama's voice cry out. I saw her rise and walk toward Francesco. "Even now you can't accept that your cause is flawed. A doctrine that believes one race is superior to another can never be honorable. Il Duce *was aligned with a man who was obsessed with that idea, and he allowed himself to be seduced by it because he wanted power. The more he craved it, the more genocide became a means to an end. Your leader accepted it as the price to be paid for achieving world domination."*

Mama stood there in the center of the room, her fists clenched, glaring at all of them. I had never seen her act like that before. The little boy held on to me and buried his face in my shoulder. I could tell Mama's shouting had scared him.

The woman on the couch was sobbing hysterically now. I could barely understand what she was saying. "Claretta was seduced too. I just know it. I doubt she even understood what Hitler was doing."

The room was silent. Papa got up from the couch and walked over to Mama. He grabbed her wrist and put his face close to her ear. I couldn't hear the words, but I saw Mama try to get away. He pushed her in the direction of the door. I knew he was going to inject her with a sedative.

After they left, Francesco took a seat on the couch. He reached out and took the hands of both women. They stayed like that for a while, not saying anything, their heads bowed. Then Francesco started talking. His voice was loud and clear like he was speaking to more than just the people in the room. "When you are fighting for a cause, there are always casualties. I am not ashamed of my daughter. In the years to come, no one will remember our names, but history will never forget her."

Agostino closed the book and looked up.

An eerie sense that we had laid bare a piece of Angelina's life no one had ever seen before stole over me. It felt prophetic, pre-ordained—like someone had guided us to this place.

"That's it?" I said. "That's all she wrote?"

"I'm afraid so. She ran out of room."

"There must be another diary. She wouldn't just stop there."

Agostino shook his head. "Anna, we covered every inch of that room."

"I'm not giving up. Let me think about it. I know this is a big shock and all . . ." I glanced at the pot on the stove. "Are you even hungry?"

Agostino helped me to my feet. "Not really, but we have to eat." He thought for a minute. "We will make *polpettini*. Meatballs. They cook a lot faster."

We were both quiet as we put dinner together. For once, Agostino followed my instructions without complaining.

"Angelina was fifteen when that happened," Agostino said as we sat down to eat. "You can imagine how that must have affected her as she got older."

"It probably affected the whole family. Pio controlled Elena with drugs. That part is obvious now." I pushed away my untouched plate and looked at Agostino. "Your mother saw a lot of tragedy in her life. I think she was very brave putting all that down on paper. If anyone had found it . . ."

"You mean the *partigiani*?"

"Yes. It would have been proof the Lallos were supporters of Mussolini. By letting her spend the night before going on to Saro, Pio protected Mussolini's mistress. The whole family could have been killed. Just having the diary there, in her room, was courageous."

"Foolish, many would say . . . putting her family at risk." Agostino countered. "But she wasn't thinking about the danger when she wrote it down. She wanted to record it for someone else to read . . . in the future."

"Like the children she might have one day?"

Agostino nodded.

Reaching across the table, I put my hand over his. "I wish she could have known the man you have become. She would have been proud."

"It's strange, but these diaries are helping me get to know her in a way I never expected. And sharing it all with you . . ." He interlaced his fingers with mine, and I saw something in his eyes I hadn't let myself see before.

"I feel it too, Agostino. This adventure we are having has made me realize a lot of things . . ." I hesitated.

Suddenly I was up and standing behind his chair, my arms around his neck. He drew me into his lap and held me close. "I want you in my life, Anna." He whispered.

"I am right here."

I stood up and offered him my hand. "Let's go upstairs."

Agostino looked uncertain. "I'm not sure if tonight . . . with all that's happened . . ."

"I'm talking about just holding each other."

Without another word, Agostino rose from the table and followed me up the stairs.

Chapter 31

Intimacy

"THAT WAS nice." A voice said into my hair. Agostino was snuggled up against my back with one arm stretched across my tummy.

"It's called intimacy . . . or so I've been told," I murmured, my eyes still closed.

Agostino chuckled and drew me closer.

I opened one eye. The patch of sky beyond my bedroom window was turning gray, and I felt the familiar restless energy. My morning run was calling me. Something else was calling me too. It was hard and throbbing and pressing against my thigh. I felt soft lips planting kisses on the back of my neck, and when I turned, they found mine. *So much for the run.*

The feeling—like I was floating on a cotton-candy cloud pillowed on all sides by an airy sweetness—was exquisite. When his skin touched mine, his fingers and lips exploring, it felt multi-layered, like flavors reaching beyond the physical to an emotional connection that had not been there before. In a dreamlike state, I closed my eyes and let the sensations take over my body. I was dimly aware that beyond the cloud lay a void, and if I fell, the hard ground beneath me would hurt like hell. I blocked out the thought and let go. The last thing I remembered before I fell asleep was Agostino holding me tenderly and whispering that he loved me.

When I woke, the patch beyond the window had turned to blue, and my cellphone was ringing.

"Don't answer it," Agostino said and snuggled closer.

"I won't."

It rang again.

I sat up. "The world is calling, Agostino." I looked at the screen. "Shit. It's Brunetta. I haven't called them in days."

I spoke into the phone, my voice light. *"Ciao, cara. Come stai?"*

"Don't *'cara'* me," Brunetta barked. "Where have you been? Pepina has been waiting for you for four days now. I thought you were coming back to hear the rest of Angelina's story."

I glanced at Agostino who was hastily pulling on his trousers. "We are. We just got sidetracked." I filled her in on the cemetery discovery, the letter inside the metal box, and the trip to the Eremo.

"You've been busy," Brunetta said after a long pause. "Pepina is waiting. I am out of excuses."

I groaned. "Is this something we want to hear?"

Brunetta let out a deep breath. "How soon can you get here?"

"I don't know if I can take any more surprises," Agostino muttered as we got out of the Cinquecento and walked to Pepina and Brunetta's *palazzo* off Via Flaminia. We buzzed the intercom, and the front door buzzed back. We entered and climbed the stairs to the third floor. Brunetta already had the door open.

"Is Vito here?" I asked anxiously.

"Of course he is." Brunetta gave me a funny look. "I get the feeling you don't like him very much."

"No, no, it's not that. I just think he's not happy about us dredging all this up again." I glanced at Agostino for support.

Agostino tried to explain. "We don't blame him. The more we uncover, the deeper the story gets."

"In the States, we call it a Pandora's box," I added.

Brunetta nodded. *"Sì, il vaso di Pandora."*

I saw a lumbering figure in the hallway coming toward us. "In construction it happens all the time—a small project turns into a big one,"

Vito said, sticking his hand out by way of apology. "I'm sorry if I was cranky last time. Cigarette withdrawal."

Agostino accepted the handshake. "How is that going?"

Vito patted his stomach. "I've traded one vice for another. That's what my wife tells me anyway."

"Anna! *Dove stai?*" A chirpy voice came from the living room.

Brunetta rolled her eyes. "Let's get in there."

Pepina was perched on the edge of her wheelchair near the sofa when we walked in, her fingers moving restlessly over the pages of a small, familiar-looking book.

"*Vieni!* Come, sit down." She gestured to the sofa. "Brunetta told me about the keepsake box. Now I know what happened to it. Your discoveries have made things more complicated." Instead of looking irritated, Pepina's eyes were bright and alive.

Agostino and I sat down and waited.

Brunetta drew up a chair, and Vito assumed his usual position near the doorway.

"Mama," Brunetta began, "I think you have some explaining to do. It's time you gave Agostino the whole story."

Pepina took an annoyingly long time adjusting her shawl and the blanket over her legs before she spoke again.

"The day you were here, when I showed you the birth certificate and the hospital records, I was hoping that your search would end ... that you wouldn't want to go further. I can see now that I was naive. It seems it only made you more determined to find out who your father was."

Agostino leaned toward her, his face intent. "Pepina, you have to understand something. The woman who I always thought of as my grandmother, Gabriella Urbino, *told* me to look in Cecilia's tomb. I had to know if all this was true, and then we found the box and the letter from Wojo. It contradicted what was on the birth certificate. This is not the direction we thought we were going in but it happened." He looked at the book in Pepina's lap. "We all know my mother documented everything. I'm guessing this is the last diary she wrote in before she died. Am I right?"

Pepina smoothed the cover with her hands. "You are. I found it about a month after Angelina passed. Papa had told me to dispose of the mattress. After her months of sickness, he felt it prudent. When I removed it, I found the diary. She must have stashed it underneath to keep it from being found, and when she was transported to the hospital, it got left behind." Pepina looked at Agostino before continuing. "As her son, you are the rightful owner of this book. A word of warning, however. The information inside may not be something you want to know."

"So, you've read it," Agostino asked her.

"I have."

Agostino sighed. "There's no going back now."

Pepina nodded. "Your mother and I grew quite close during the last months of her life. I would sit with her in the long afternoons before Papa came home from seeing his patients. I was only five years older—she was thirty-one and I was thirty-six. I suspected she needed someone to confide in. As she grew sicker, she reached out to me, and we began to talk about her life. That was when she told me about her great need to bear a child—to leave behind something that was hers, 'a living memory that her life had not been in vain,' as she put it. I sensed she needed to unburden herself, and I encouraged her. She broke down and confessed that she had done things she was not proud of to make that dream a reality. I asked her who the father of baby was. She said she didn't know."

Agostino sucked in his breath. "She didn't know because . . ."

"Because she had more than one partner," Pepina said. She flipped through the pages of the book, put her finger on a paragraph, and read aloud: *I am so ashamed. I can't believe I did those things, but I was desperate. After a few weeks when the blood came back, I knew it hadn't worked. I had to try again.*

Agostino covered his face with his hands.

Pepina's voice was softer now. "I know this is hard to hear, but you need to understand something about your mother. It was never the father of her child that was important to her. *It was the child.* I have been waiting for the right moment to tell you this. I think it is now."

Agostino looked up, his eyes wary. He nodded, giving Pepina permission to continue.

"The day after Angelina gave birth, I asked Papa if I could visit her in the hospital . . . to say goodbye. I hadn't seen her in a week, and even though I knew how sick she was, I was shocked by her appearance. Her hollow face and skeletal frame told me she had little time left. She gave me a thin smile as I sat down by the bedside, and then she turned her head toward the bundle in her arms. I will never forget the look of love in her eyes as she gazed down at that scrunched up little face.

"'I have you and Alessandro to thank for this,' she said to me. 'You have helped me fulfill a dream, the dream of being a mother . . . even if only for a little while.'

"I told her it was her strength and her will that made it happen, but she shook her head. 'There were forces at work beyond anything I could have imagined or hoped for. I am just grateful to be given this time with my son.'

"I wanted to tell her the baby would be taken care of, that it would be loved and cherished and grow up to be a man she would be proud of, but I knew my words would be bittersweet. She would not be there to see it happen. Then I heard Angelina's voice. 'I want you to have this,' she said, lifting her arm from under the covers and opening her hand. In her palm rested a string of pale blue rosary beads. As I gathered them up and thanked her, she nodded and turned back to the bundle in her arms. I rose quietly, and reaching the doorway, I turned one last time to look at the figure on the bed. The image of a little boy, calm and content in the arms of his mother, has never left me—even after all these years. It is the way I want to remember her."

Pepina handed the diary to Agostino. "That was the last time I saw your mother alive. I have thought about that day many times. I believe Angelina's actions were motivated by her intense desire to have a child . . . the disease influencing her to make the choices she made. Was she mentally ill or just determined to give her life some meaning? You can judge her as you wish, but I have no doubt she had help achieving her dream of giving birth and living long enough to hold her child in her arms before she died."

Agostino opened the book to the last page.

My darling son, when the time is right, you will know who I am. Please forgive me. I did it for you.

Chapter 32

Two Are Better Than None

AGOSTINO turned from the window and looked at the woman in the wheelchair. *"Nonna,* you seem convinced Beniamino is my father . . . even after reading the diary. Tell me why."

I stood nearby, watching the distant mountains still shadowed in darkness. The morning fog was receding, leaving patches of gray, like giant puffs of smoke, hanging in the valleys. I thought of my conversation with Beniamino and wondered what her answer would be.

Gabriella's eyes traveled to the family portrait above the fireplace and then to the open diary in her lap. Her gnarled fingers touched the yellowed pages as she looked up at the man standing beside her.

"I think I've always known. I just wondered why no one else saw the resemblance. Whenever you two were in the same room I saw it—the same intense look, the same half-smile when you were amused. And your temperament! Yours is very similar to his."

"It is not," Agostino shot back. "He's arrogant, opinionated, stubborn . . ."

I stifled a laugh.

"And loyal to his loved ones whatever the cost," Gabriella said.

Agostino did not look convinced. "Sometimes we see what we want to see. Before I gave you the diary, I read it over more than once, and still it isn't clear. You've had time to read it. How can you be sure? After all, you had no proof."

"You're right. It was just a feeling I had. And for many reasons, most of them selfish, I was happy to let you believe you belonged to *our* side of the

228

family. I always loved it when you called me *Nonna*. Then, when you discovered the letters and found out you were adopted, I just waited to see how the pieces would fit together." She looked at the both of us. "What was in the box you found in Cecilia's tomb? You never told me."

"Keepsakes and a letter," Agostino said then stopped.

Gabriella was alert. "What letter?"

I spoke up quickly, "From Elena. Mother-daughter correspondence. Nothing earthshaking, I'm afraid."

Agostino shot me a grateful look.

Gabriella looked disappointed. "When I sent you over to the cemetery that day, I was hoping you would find some proof of who your father was." She looked down at the book in her lap. "I guess we have it now."

"Do we?" he asked her. "In my opinion, the diary suggests that Angelina may have had more than one sexual encounter around the time of her pregnancy. Take the passage in the cemetery, for example. Did you notice any actual names?"

Gabriella flipped through the book, pressed open a page, and scanned it. "You're right. It doesn't mention her companion's name." She shook her head. "Rereading it now, it sounds more like a dream than reality. *'We walked among the graves, the early morning mist filling up the space like a presence...'*" Gabriella looked up. "Excuse me for being blunt, Agostino, but your mother was a romantic. You can tell from her writing. It may be a mistake to take everything in this book literally."

Agostino groaned. "Then how do we know if *anything* in here is real?"

"We don't. That's why I called this meeting. I am hoping we will get to the truth today."

The sound of the front door opening interrupted their conversation.

"They are here," Gabriella said, turning her wheelchair toward the center of the room. "Get ready for the fireworks."

Massimo Ladro stood in the doorway carrying a large briefcase and wearing a professional smile. "*Cara,* Gabriella. I still can't get over your amazing recovery. You look better every time I see you."

"I always knew you were a good liar, Max. Your concern for my welfare is touching even if it lacks sincerity."

Massimo attempted a laugh. "Now, now, Gabriella, you don't mean that. Everyone in the Urbino family cares deeply for you, and I am no exception."

Gabriella didn't answer.

Massimo took a few steps into the room. "I am here early to go over some papers and get your signature . . ." He stopped when he saw Agostino and me. "*Scusa.* I see you are occupied."

"Put everything over there." Gabriella pointed to the opposite side of the room where there was a writing desk and a chair. "We can look at them together."

Massimo cleared his throat delicately. "These documents are confidential."

"Agostino is an heir," Gabriella told Massimo. "Anything you have to say to me can be said in front of him."

"Technically . . ." Massimo started to say, but Gabriella's look silenced him. He changed the subject. "What about her?" He pointed at me.

Gabriella smiled. "As Agostino's fiancée, Anna has every right to be here."

Fiancée??? My knees felt like they were going to buckle.

Everyone moved to the desk, and Massimo spread the papers out so everyone could see them. He extracted a pen from his suit pocket and laid it next to the documents.

"As you can see, I have modified the wording to meet your specifications. The last time we met, you requested . . ."

The front doorbell rang. Massimo looked up, annoyed. Maria, the housekeeper, led a tall, clean-shaven man into the room. *"Quest' uomo . . .* he say he is invited." Maria looked at Gabriella for confirmation.

"Buon giorno, Signora, tutti." Sergei bowed his head slightly.

"Ma che . . . ?" Massimo exclaimed. "This meeting is for immediate family only."

Agostino cut in. "I asked him to come. He is here as a witness to today's events and to give clarification if needed."

Massimo's brows drew together, and he started shuffling his papers.

The doorbell rang again. After a few minutes, Brunetta wheeled an impeccably dressed and freshly coiffed Pepina into the room. Vito brought up the rear, looking uncomfortable in a suit that no longer buttoned in the front.

Gabriella stared at the new arrivals like she was searching through layers of brain matter. Then she broke into a grin. "Pepina! I haven't seen you since your papa's funeral. *Come stai?*" The two ladies were brought together in the center of the room. Pepina beamed and reached across her wheelchair to clasp Gabriella's hands.

"We must be the oldest *donnas* in Scheggino," Gabriella said. "How old are you now anyway?"

"Ninety-one last July," Pepina said.

Gabriella grinned. "I've got you beat by almost a decade."

Massimo's voice rose above the din. "This is most disturbing." He looked at Agostino. "How many witnesses do you need?"

Muffled voices were heard in the entrance hall, and a moment later Beniamino walked in, followed by Donatella. She glared at the group for a minute then turned to her husband and hissed, "Who are all these people?"

"If you spent more time talking to the villagers, you might know some of them," he hissed back. He stepped forward and shook Sergei's hand. "I enjoyed your performance the other night at our event. You added some other performers this year. Very effective."

I pretended not to hear.

Beniamino turned to Pepina. "This is indeed an honor. Dr. Sabatini's daughter and her family will always be welcome here. There are still villagers who remember his dedication to the town of Scheggino."

Pepina beamed and gave him her hand. Donatella dipped her head and kept her arms by her side.

We heard more voices, and Giovanni and Pamela appeared. Giovanni's jaw dropped when he saw the crowded room. Pamela went into full public-servant mode, working the room, shaking hands and murmuring pleasantries.

"Can I get everyone's attention?" An anxious-sounding Massimo called out. "Find a chair and get comfortable. Gabriella has a few things she would like to share with you."

Beniamino and Donatella took the two armchairs near the fireplace, and Giovanni and Pamela spread out on the settee. There were no more places to sit. "Maria!" Gabriella's voice rang out. "Bring more chairs!"

A few minutes later, Maria and another woman dressed in hospital scrubs returned with two chairs. Agostino pointed to an area near the fireplace where Brunetta and Vito were standing. He wheeled Pepina over to them and then walked to an unobtrusive corner behind the desk. He gave me a quick nod, and I joined him.

As everyone settled in, Massimo cleared his throat, straightening the edges of his documents like a trial lawyer preparing his opening remarks.

"Thank you all for coming," he began. "Gabriella called this meeting because there have been a few developments." His eyes flicked over the group. "She felt everyone should be informed."

The room was suddenly quiet. Sergei had removed himself from the action and was leaning discreetly against the wall near the doorway. Beniamino's face was a mask, his fingers moving restlessly in his lap while his wife swung her leg back and forth and stifled a yawn. Pamela stopped whispering to Giovanni and gave his knee a sharp pat like a parent's final reminder to a disobedient child to behave. Vito mopped his brow, watching Brunetta's fingers push the edges of a familiar-looking manila envelope farther down into her purse. Only the two old ladies seemed relaxed, knowing that they had lived long enough not to be surprised by anything.

Gabriella pulled herself up in her wheelchair, looking like a schoolteacher addressing a group of unruly children. "As you know, I've been threatening to die for years now..." Protests erupted throughout the room before she raised her hand for silence. "Someday it might actually happen. That is why I am taking care of some unfinished business now. When I married into this family eighty-plus years ago, Gregorio told me to be prepared for a hell of a ride. He wasn't kidding. My husband knew his brother was a man of incredible energy and foresight, and you, Ben, have been a great custodian of Claudio's legacy. Her eyes shifted to Giovanni. "The young blood has been good for the Foundation; your ideas reflect current interests and ways of marketing we never had in the old days." She paused and inclined her head over her shoulder. "And my grandson has done equally well without help from any of you."

She stifled a cough and stopped to catch her breath. Agostino went to the desk, poured her a glass of water from a pitcher and brought it to her. "Drink," he ordered.

Gabriella took a few sips and continued. "Because of an unfortunate situation Ben inherited upon his marriage"—Gabriella looked pointedly at Donatella—"the Foundation considered it prudent to transfer the business and all its assets into my name. It was meant to revert to Ben's family when I died, but … well … that has taken a little longer than expected. In recent months, certain facts have come to light that make another decision necessary. You all know by now that there are two children buried with Cecilia and that I was the one who helped bury them. What you don't know is the identity of Agostino's real parents."

I snuck a glance at Beniamino. Except for the tightened muscle in his jaw, his face remained impassive.

Gabriella took a sip, handed the glass back to Agostino, and surveyed the room again. "A birth certificate has been found with Agostino's name and that of his mother on it." She paused to let the information sink in.

"Who was she?" Pamela asked.

"Her name was Angelina De Glielci Lallo. She is the descendent of Cardinal Poli's noble family, the De Glielcis."

"The former owners of our house you mean," Donatella said.

"That's right."

The room fell silent. I could almost hear all the Urbinos thinking.

"Where did you find this birth certificate?" Giovanni's voice sounded skeptical.

Pepina signaled Brunetta to wheel her into the center of the room next to Gabriella. "I had it," she said. "My father acquired it from the hospital in Spoleto where Angelina died. My father was her physician, and he took care of her during her pregnancy and until the end of her life. She was like a daughter to him. We all loved her very much." Pepina's voice faltered, but she got herself under control. "Angelina also left behind a diary, one that chronicles the events leading up to her pregnancy and illness."

"What was wrong with her?" Donatella asked.

"She had metastatic breast cancer," Pepina replied.

Donatella's voice was tinged with sarcasm. "And she still gave birth to a healthy baby? Sounds like a miracle to me."

Pepina stared at her. "It was."

Giovanni snorted. "What about the father of her baby? Is *he* mentioned in this diary?"

Before Pepina could answer, Sergei spoke up. "A diary is hardly concrete proof."

Giovanni sat up. "I think I speak for all of us when I say we would like the opportunity to see the birth certificate *and* read the diary... just to confirm Agostino's true parentage, of course. There are, after all, certain important assets that would be affected."

Like Beniamino's house, I thought to myself.

Pamela and Donatella nodded their approval.

Pepina looked at the diary resting in Gabriella's lap and then up at Agostino. "The diary belongs to you. You may do with it as you like."

I watched Agostino's face. I was sure giving the diary to Giovanni was the last thing he wanted to do, but what choice did he have? If he refused, it would look like he had something to hide.

Agostino gently took the book from Gabriella, walked over to Giovanni, and handed it to him. "Just remember, when you look into the past, you cannot change what you find ... or go back to not knowing."

Giovanni's eyes narrowed. "*Who* is your father, Agostino?"

"I am," two voices answered at the same time. Everyone in the room turned their heads. Beniamino and Sergei were walking toward the center of the room.

"Oh my God," Agostino said.

The room erupted into eight voices talking at once. "This is outrageous nonsense!" Massimo's rose above all the others. "Ben, don't you say another word!"

Pamela held Giovanni back as he lunged toward his father. "You bastard," he cried. The diary tumbled to the floor. Donatella got out of her chair, walked toward the settee, and picked up the book. She sat down and started reading.

Sergei and Beniamino stood face to face now, inches apart.

"When?" Beniamino asked.

"Summer 1962. I was eighteen. I did the Via di San Francesco on a regular basis in those days. You?"

"Early August, the same year," Beniamino replied, looking shell-shocked.

"The squawking of the chickens grew louder," Donatella read aloud, *"I silenced them with one tap to the head and a tickle on their tummy. I reached for his belt and unbuckled it."*

"Stop!" Pamela put a hand over the page.

Donatella looked up at Beniamino. Her face was a deep red, and there was venom in her eyes. "You fucked her when you were engaged to me? *Mascalzone*! You will pay for this." She started out of her seat, and Pamela grabbed the diary before it fell again. Massimo rushed over and took it from her, retreating behind the desk.

Sergei stepped in and held Donatella back as her hands reached for Beniamino's face. "Let go of my mother!" Giovanni yelled, shoving Sergei and bringing the hysterical woman back to the settee. "Get ahold of yourself," he whispered in her ear. "Remember where you are."

As if a switch had been turned on, Donatella took a breath and composed her face into something that resembled normal. She smoothed her skirt with trembling hands and sat down between her son and daughter-in-law.

The silence that followed felt like the aftermath of a deadly accident, that moment of shock before the ambulance arrives.

"Is Sergei for real?" I whispered into Agostino's back. "Or is he trying to protect Wojo?"

"You mean distract them from looking at what's written on the birth certificate?" Agostino whispered back.

"Yes."

"Hell if I know." His voice sounded shaky. "I need to sit down."

I motioned for Massimo to vacate his chair. As soon as it was empty, I slid it under Agostino, and he slumped into it, his eyes glazing over.

Massimo came from behind the desk and stood between both ladies and their wheelchairs. "Everyone, stay calm. We need to assess the situation. It seems we have two men claiming to be Agostino's father. Both admit they had relations with Angelina Lallo, but we have no concrete proof that they fathered her child. I think we need to see this birth certificate." He turned to Pepina. "Does the certificate list the father's name?"

Sergei cut in quickly. "What does it matter whose name is on it? If we are both . . . uh . . . candidates, it doesn't make a difference. In those days, the early sixties, it was difficult to prove the father's identity—especially if the woman had multiple partners."

"He's right, Massimo," Ben said.

"Make them take a paternity test!" Giovanni cried out.

Massimo's face clouded over. "I'm not sure the Foundation wants that kind of publicity. There would be a public record of it. Sergei might not want that either." Massimo looked at him hopefully.

Glancing at Sergei, I could only imagine how thrilled he would be trying to explain it to his fellow seminarians.

Beniamino spoke up first. "For my part, I do not wish to take the test."

Sergei looked relieved. "Neither do I."

"You can be forced to take it," Giovanni told them.

"Young man!" Gabriella's voice rang out sharply. "Why are you so eager to pursue this? It wouldn't have anything to do with your inheritance, would it?"

Giovanni turned red and kept silent.

"Because, if it is, I might remind you of something. I haven't signed any of Massimo's papers, and as of this moment, I own *all* of The Urbino Truffle Foundation *and* the majority of shares. And don't forget, in the *comune,* there is a ledger stating that Agostino is my legitimate grandson. Unless it has been stolen, I am going to assume it's still there."

Pamela paled.

Giovanni spoke up quickly. "You can't expect us to believe that worthless piece of . . . ow!" Pamela was pinching his arm.

Gabriella continued. "That means, if things stay as they are, Agostino gets everything when I die."

Silence. The Urbino brains were doing overtime.

Massimo sighed. "Gabriella, what do you propose?"

"I propose you draw up documents that name Giovanni and Agostino Urbino as my designated heirs and distribute the company assets and my shares equally between the two of them."

"But that means dividing the Foundation!" Giovanni exclaimed. "This business has always been on *our* side of the family."

"There's a fifty-fifty chance that Agostino *is* your family," Gabriella shot back. "Why not keep the name of the business intact and divide the shares? You two can work together."

Agostino spoke up for the first time. "I'm in the hotel business, *Nonna.* I don't know the first thing . . ."

"Then you will *learn!*" Gabriella said. "Like Claudio learned from his papa. You boys can blend two worlds and expand. A chain of hotels offering truffle hunting expeditions; gourmet restaurants within the hotel, serving and selling the products. The possibilities are endless."

Beniamino looked at the two men glaring at each other from across the room. "It'll never work," he murmured under his breath.

"It'll work if they want it to. Financial success can be a big motivator."

Massimo gathered the papers together and put them in his briefcase. "Okay. It looks like we have a plan. If no one has any objections, I will make the necessary adjustments and be back in an hour." Before anyone could utter a word, he was out the door and gone. There was no sign of the diary on the desk.

I nudged Agostino. "You'd better go retrieve that diary. If he starts looking at it, you are going to have a lot of explaining to do."

Agostino dashed out after Massimo. A moment later he returned with the diary in his hands. "Thank you," he whispered to me.

Taking their cue from Massimo, Donatella and Giovanni rose and started for the door.

"Where are you going?" Beniamino asked.

"Mama and I will be at Avelino's Bar," Giovanni answered. "Commiserating."

"Remember you need to be back here in an hour," Pamela called out.

Giovanni didn't turn around.

"I'll keep an eye on him," Pamela said as she hurried after them.

Beniamino watched her leave and turned to Gabriella. "I'm not holding my breath on this idea of yours, *Zia*. Good thing I intend to be around to make sure my family behaves themselves."

Pepina chose that moment to clasp her old friend's hand. "I try never to wear out my welcome. If you won't be needing us further . . ."

They double kissed—two old ladies reaching across their wheelchairs to say goodbye. "Let's not wait so long next time," Pepina said. "We don't have all the time in the world, you know."

"Speak for yourself," Gabriella answered, her eye on Beniamino. "*I'm* not going anywhere. Someone's got to keep an eye on things."

As the Sabatinis got ready to leave, I made my way over to them. "Thank you for being here. I put my arm around Brunetta and ushered them out of the room. When we got to the front door, I pointed to the manila folder in her hands. "My advice is to keep that in a safe place and don't show it to anyone."

Vito reached for the folder and stuffed it into the inside pocket of his open sports jacket. I watched him lift his mother-in-law out of the wheelchair and help her down the steps to their car. It occurred to me that first impressions can be deceiving and perhaps Brunetta had chosen wisely after all.

The living room was quiet now; Beniamino and Sergei conversed by the fire, and Gabriella took the opportunity for a quick snooze. Agostino moved toward the two men. When he got there, he reached out to clasp each of their hands. His voice was emotional. "I would be proud to have either one of you as a father. And if it's all right, I don't mind having both of you."

The clasped hands became a three-way hug. As Gabriella's eyes opened, I slipped behind her wheelchair and guided her into the middle of the circle.

Agostino looked over his shoulder. "Anna, get in here."

As the group huddled together, I felt the warmth of a newfound family emerging. Ben's face, while still a bit shell-shocked, looked hopeful. Sergei's was full of joy.

"I'm so glad I decided not to die," Gabriella murmured, wiping her eyes. "I can't wait to see what happens now."

Agostino's arm tightened around my waist.

"And you never know . . ." Gabriella said, her gaze avoiding the two of us. "There might even be a traditional Umbrian wedding in the near future. The kind they used to throw a hundred years ago."

Chapter 33

Heart to Heart

BENIAMINO pulled up two chairs by the fire and gestured for Agostino and me to sit. He handed each of us a glass of Grappa Al Re. Shafts of sunlight from the arched windows slanted across the cavernous room.

Beniamino took a long pull of his drink. "It feels good to have you here, Agostino."

"It feels good to be here," Agostino responded. "I haven't been since I was a child. Claudio's funeral, I believe."

Beniamino flushed with embarrassment. "I'm sorry it has been that long. It looks like we have a lot of lost time to make up for."

Agostino looked at the man standing by the enormous mantel and smiled. "We do—and it feels like we've already started. He glanced around the room. "This house is so beautiful. The history, the décor . . . I am glad Anna has a chance to finally see it."

Beniamino and I remained silent.

Beniamino cleared his throat. "I think I'd better get this out in the open before *someone*—he glanced at me—lets it slip."

Agostino jerked his head in my direction. "If this is another secret . . ."

I hung my head. "There is something I haven't told you. I have been here before."

Agostino's eyes widened. "When?"

"The day we opened Cecilia's crypt. When you wanted time alone."

"You came here?" Agostino's voice rose. "You said you went walking."

"I *did* go walking . . . and ended up at Beniamino's villa. I saw the gate open and . . ."

"Let's just say she ended up being present for a certain shareholders meeting," Beniamino said, coming to my rescue.

"Anna was invited to a meeting with your family?" Agostino said, looking at the two of us incredulously.

"I wasn't exactly *invited* . . ." I started to explain and then gave up. "Oh, hell. I snuck in."

Agostino's eyes narrowed. "You snuck in?"

"I saw Giovanni, Pamela, and Massimo drive in after I had hidden myself in the garage, and I knew something was up. I went through a back door and up the servants' stairway . . ."

Beniamino intervened again. "Granted, her methods weren't exactly orthodox."

"More like criminal." Agostino's tone sounded anything but understanding.

Beniamino took his hand off the mantel and laid it on Agostino's shoulder. "Anna's actions were well intentioned. She felt that, by listening in, she could find out what my family was up to. She was trying to help you."

Agostino sat back and regarded me. "What did you learn?"

I swallowed hard. "I heard them discussing the future of the Foundation. That was when I found out that it was in Gabriella's name. Did you know about that?"

"No."

"Gabriella suspected something about your parentage. By including you as an heir, she felt she would be righting a wrong," I said.

Agostino sighed. "Look, the truth is, it never mattered. Don't take this the wrong way, Ben, but I never wanted to be in the truffle business. Money means nothing to me if I can't do what I love."

"That's why I have so much respect for you." Beniamino said. "When my grandfather started this company a hundred years ago, he did it because he loved it. You are so much like him."

Agostino seemed surprised. "Thank you, Ben. It means a lot to hear you say that."

The three of us settled back, sipped our drinks, and gazed into the fire. Beniamino put on another log.

"How did you get out?"

I looked up. Agostino was studying me. "The front door," I answered honestly.

"The front door," Agostino repeated, sarcastically. "You want to tell me how *that* happened?"

Beniamino took over. "After everyone left, Anna and I had a heart-to-heart talk." He saw Agostino's face and continued. "We talked about a woman named Angelina."

Agostino stared at me. "So you knew. Why didn't you tell me?"

Beniamino cut in. "I asked her not to. I wanted to be the one."

I waited for Agostino to berate me for sticking my nose into other people's business—again. I deserved it.

"Sounds like something Anna would do," Agostino said, his mouth twitching. After a moment, he turned to Beniamino. "You knew my mother. What can you tell me about her that I don't already know?"

Beniamino spoke softly, reverently. "She was a woman who needed to be loved, and she was deserving of it. Her misfortune was to be born into a family that did not know how to give her what she needed. I am also to blame. If I had been a stronger man, her life... and mine... might have turned out different."

"And mine?" Agostino asked.

Beniamino seemed unsettled. "There is something I must tell you. Angelina told me I was not her first. But there was blood. I thought she just didn't want to admit she was a virgin."

"Perhaps the blood was a symptom of her illness, and not ..."

Beniamino sighed. "We may never know without a paternity test. Do you want me to take one?"

Agostino rose and reached for Beniamino's hands. "I don't need a paternity test to know I want you in my life."

Beniamino embraced him. "Neither do I." He pulled back. "There is something else. I want you to have this house when I die. After all, your association with the De Glielcis is official now. It rightfully belongs to you."

Agostino shook his head. "Thank you, but I want Giovanni to have it." He turned and glanced at me. "I have other plans."

Chapter 34

Full Circle

A RAY of light shot through the half-open French doors and flashed on a gold cameo locket around my neck.

Terry's breath caught as she walked into my bedroom. "You're wearing Agatha's locket. The one she gave *Nonno* Spirito to remember her by."

I looked at her admiringly. "You remembered! It was our link to our great uncle SJ." My fingers flew to my throat, and I unfastened the tiny clasp. As the locket opened, it revealed the portrait of a young man.

Terry reached out and touched it. "It's SJ, isn't it?"

I nodded. "When we met for the first time in the cemetery, I was wearing it. That's how he knew we were related."

Terry closed it gently. "It is perfect you are wearing it now. To honor him." She stepped back and eyeballed my gown. And that dress is stunning. Where did you find it?"

Glancing in the full-length mirror, I did a little twirl. The long-sleeved satin gown billowed around me like a sheet of liquid silver. "It was Gabriella's wedding dress."

I remembered the morning she suggested I try it on. We were in her kitchen going over last-minute details of the wedding.

"I was married in 1935," she told me. "The flapper years. Dresses were form fitting—no flounces. We all wore wreaths of flowers with simple lace veils that hung down our backs." Her old eyes swept over me. "I was a skinny little thing back then. It just might fit you."

She had insisted right then and there on going to her closet and getting it out. As I wheeled her down the hallway, I was already formulating a way out in case the dress turned out to be hideous. When I unzipped the protective covering and held it up, I gave a little cry of delight. The ankle-length satin gown was cut on the bias with long tapered sleeves and an open back ending in a point at the waist.

"It's absolutely perfect," I told her.

Terry lifted the crown and veil to the light, looking at her handywork. She had been sewing fresh flowers and leaves into the dried ones all morning. "This is Mom's headpiece, remember? The orange blossoms she used are a bit faded, so I am giving it a refresh. I brought it with me in hopes . . ."

"It is beautiful." I cut in. "She is here with us, today. I just know it."

I flashed back to the day, five years ago, when Mom and I crossed the bridge into Scheggino and headed up the old Roman road to the Villa Urbino. A man had welcomed us with dust-covered clothes and open arms—a man called Agostino. How could either of us have known that he would someday be my husband? And what of my decision to make Scheggino my home . . . would she have approved of this new life I was poised to begin?

"She is here. There is no doubt." Terry held out the wreath. "You are taking a part of her with you down the aisle."

The leaves on the crown gave off a pungent odor when I touched them. "You chose well," I said. "These plants are called *elci*. They grow abundantly here. As a matter of fact, Angelina's grandparents' last name was originally Delci, 'of the elci' in English. Through the years it morphed into De Glielci." I laughed, shrugging my shoulders. "A little private lore that no one back home cares about."

"I care. I think it's wonderful. It connects both our families. The one you came from and the one you will now become a part of."

Suddenly my eyes filled with tears, and I reached out to touch her shoulder. "I am so glad you decided to come."

"What, are you crazy? *Not come to my sister's Italian wedding?* I'd quit my job if they wouldn't let me go."

"And if you don't get a move on, you're going to miss it!" Tino's voice called up from downstairs.

My wedding. The words didn't send me into paroxysms of terror anymore. I thought back to the morning Agostino and I hiked up the Via di San Francesco and stopped in front of the wrought-iron gates of the Eremo delle Grazie.

Right outside the gate, he got down on one knee and proposed. The ring he held in his hand was the one in the keepsake box, the sapphire ring given to Angelina by her mother. "Before I say yes, you'd better explain *that*." I pointed to the "sold" sign on the gate.

"It's your wedding present. As half owner of the Urbino Truffle Foundation, I was able to buy it from the Lallo family. I gave them fair market value even though I didn't have to. You should have seen the realtor's face when I made the offer."

"What are you going to do with it?"

"I was thinking of taking you up on your idea of turning it into a retreat, a place for people to get away from the stress of the modern world. We could turn the cells into bedrooms, meditation cells . . . my head is brimming with ideas."

"What about yoga and stretch classes?"

"I say yes!" Agostino grinned.

"Then I say yes, too!"

He took me in his arms and kissed me tenderly. "If it will keep you here with me, I will offer you the world."

"I don't want the world," I told him. "I only want you . . . and Scheggino." It was at that moment I knew. My home was here now.

Agostino's eyes were twinkling. "I have another surprise. Beniamino and I have been discussing plans to turn the original truffle headquarters into a community space. There will be rehearsal rooms for events . . . or ballet classes. We will begin work right after the wedding. Speaking of the wedding—it will be the biggest San Nicola has ever seen!"

"San Nicola? The Catholic church in the village . . ." My voice trailed off.

"But of course. It is perfect, right?"

"Remember when I told you I had some issues with . . . uh . . . that particular institution?"

Agostino's face turned serious. "You said you were . . . what was it?"

"A recovering Catholic," I replied.

Agostino thought for a moment. "Well, if you are recovering then you are getting better."

I gave a half laugh. "Maybe I am *getting better*, as you put it, but there are many things I don't agree with."

"For example?"

"The Bible is the base of Catholicism. Do you believe everything in it?"

Agostino answered right away. "I look at it as a kind of guidebook. The messages in it point me in the right direction."

"What is the right direction?"

"To be the best person I can be—honest, compassionate, faithful . . ."

"Don't you find it hard sometimes?" I asked.

"Of course. I am far from perfect. My jealousy has always been a problem. When I lose my way, I think about the messages again."

I had another question. "Do you live by God's will or your own?"

"When I get it right, they are one and the same."

I sighed. "How can you be so sure?"

"Because I *feel* it," he said simply. Seeing my puzzled face, he continued. "Some of our greatest philosophers have struggled with questions like yours. We are imperfect people; the answers are never easy. But as long as you keep an open mind . . . no . . . as long as *we* keep an open mind"—he tightened his arms around me— "the answers will come. One day at a time."

I flashed on a similar conversation I'd had with a certain theology student, walking the streets of Rome not that long ago.

"One day at a time—with an open mind *and* an open heart," I added, pulling him closer.

Terry was eyeing me skeptically. "Does this mean I'm going to lose a sister? There will be three thousand miles separating us. I may never see you again."

The sound of panting reached our ears, and a second later, my five-year-old chocolate Labrador trotted into the room. I reached out and rubbed her ears. Truffles had come with me this time, eager to start a new life with her best friend. When I opened her kennel after fourteen hours in the belly of the plane, I promised her it would be a one-way trip.

I patted Truffles's head and turned to Terry. "I will always be back. And next time, I will bring my husband with me."

"What about this apartment?" Terry's eyes were hopeful.

"I'm not selling it. We decided to keep it for friends and family . . . those who don't want to stay at the Villa Urbino, that is."

Terry nodded her head approvingly. "Tino will like that."

"And you?" I asked her. "Maybe we could get Mark and your kids to visit . . . ?"

"Maybe." Terry was smiling now. "Miracles do happen."

Looking out at the patch of blue beyond the window, I could see Cardinal Graziano's miniature garden catching the first rays of the morning sun. "In this part of the world, it seems, they happen all the time. Miracles, I mean. I certainly never saw this one coming."

"And what about the Urbinos?" Terry's eyes twinkled. "From what you told me, they are quite a handful. Are you ready to deal with them? It may be years, if ever, before they accept you as one of their own."

"I know it won't be easy, but if Agostino is prepared to bridge the gap and make a fresh start, then I must support him in making that happen. And don't forget, I have Gabriella as an ally."

"You'd better learn how to make minestrone and feed it to her every day yourself. You are going to need that alliance for a while." She crossed her arms behind her head and lay back against the pillows. "You know, I could get used to this place. A summer home in Italy doesn't sound half bad."

I looked at my watch. "It's thirty minutes to show time. Aren't you singing today?"

"Shit!" She sat up and swung her legs off the bed. "I was supposed to go over the duet Sergei and I had planned." She slipped on her dress and high heels and clattered down the stairs.

"Tino, you have been upgraded to man of honor as well as brother of the bride," Terry said before she disappeared out the door.

The walk from my apartment to the church was a harrowing one. Even though the distance between the two was minimal—La Chiesa di San Nicola was located within the castle walls—teetering along the cobble stones negotiating my train and a bouquet of spring flowers required finesse. Tino guided me; one hand on my elbow and the other firmly around my waist. Truffles trotted along behind, the second attendant in my wedding party.

We turned a corner and I had to blink twice. Half the population of Scheggino seemed to be standing right outside the church. The minute they saw me, they let out a cheer: *"Evviva gli sposi!* Long live the newlyweds! The sound was deafening. I looked quickly through the crowd. I saw familiar faces—residents I had nodded to on my way to and from the piazza; Sabrina from the *alimentari* with a smug "I knew it all along" expression on her face; the group of old ladies I had never been able to befriend—they were all smiling at me!

"Did you invite these people?" Tino whispered to me as we got closer.

"I don't think so. I have a feeling the invited guests are already inside. These are the *uninvited* ones."

"The whole town has turned out for this." Tino looked at me with admiration.

"Don't kid yourself," I said. "I'm sure this is standard procedure for village weddings."

"I love it!" Tino exclaimed. "In fact, I wouldn't mind having a nice Umbrian wedding myself!" As we walked up the steps to the church, he eyed the crowd. "Do you see the bags?"

I looked. Every person, including the children, was holding a white paper bag in their hands.

"If I'm not mistaken, there are almonds inside, sugar-coated ones. After the service, as soon as you and Agostino come out, you are going to get pelted with them."

I looked anxiously at my gown. "I thought they used rice now. Too many complaints from the brides."

"Agostino said you wanted it to be like a hundred years ago . . ."

I shook my head. "No, that's what *Gabriella* wanted."

Tino patted my arm. "Relax, experiencing the old traditions is what we came for . . . even if that means getting pelted with rock-hard almonds."

I lifted my chin. "Maybe this one time I will allow myself to hide behind my husband and let *him* get pelted."

High heels clattering up the stairs from the piazza made Tino and I turn our heads. "Anna, Tino, *auguri!*" Francesca Corti called out. Even from the top of the stairs I could see the red lips.

I shot a glance at Tino and raised an eyebrow.

Tino grinned awkwardly. "I invited her. She and I have been having some great conversations about our families . . ."

I started to object and then stopped. *Tino was a big boy.*

Francesca brushed the lint off Tino's sport coat and grabbed Truffles's leash. "I'll take care of her," she said, winking at me and heading toward the church entrance.

I turned back to Tino. "You might want to do a little research before things get too far along. In case you two are related."

Tino blanched.

"Anna! *Aspetti!*" I looked down the passageway. Flavia and Mari were hurrying up the cobblestone steps. Flavia reached the top stair holding her side. "*Scusa.* We are so late. We have the car waiting down in the piazza. As soon as the service is over, we must get back to the Villa Urbino. The guest list is up to one hundred and fifty now."

I waved my hand, shooing them into the church. "Take a back pew and leave early," I told them. "Right after the 'I dos.'"

"I think you will be saying '*sì*' instead of 'I do,'" Tino whispered into my veil. "And knowing the Italians, I wouldn't be surprised if you will be asked to 'love, honor, and obey.'"

I frowned. "Maybe I can arrange for Agostino to say those words instead."

As we entered the church, the organ in the choir loft filled up the space with its gorgeous sound. Terry, her voice clear and strong, was singing "Ave Maria." Up ahead, at the altar, Agostino waited with Sergei and Beniamino on either side of him. My heart skipped a beat. *Two fathers are better than none*, I said to myself.

"Ave Maria" ended abruptly, and the strong opening chords of Mendelssohn's "Wedding March" took over. I looked at Tino as a sudden sense of loss washed over me. "There are a few people missing here today."

Tino nodded. "I feel it too. Mom and Dad would be here chatting up the Urbinos and getting themselves invited to brunch. And SJ! I'm hoping he has a front row seat in heaven and Giulia is right there with him."

I gripped Tino's arm more tightly and took my first step down the aisle.

The bright faces turned toward me were not those of strangers who lived in a town halfway around the world. They were friends—friends in the hometown of my ancestors. Gabriella's wheelchair hugged the front row pew, and as I approached, she reached out her hand and touched my dress. *"Bellissima,"* she whispered.

Next to her were Donatella, Giovanni, and Pamela, their expressions resigned but hopeful. It wouldn't be the first time the family had to deal with an unforeseen turn of events. The legions of Urbino cousins, uncles, and nephews crowding the pews behind them would no doubt have to follow suit. It would be a challenge winning them over but, as I reminded myself, I liked challenges.

On the bride's side, I could see Pepina, Brunetta, and Vito standing straight and proud in the front pew, and a little farther down were GP and his family. My neighbor, Leonia, was there too, her mop of red hair standing out from the crowd. She had been the first friend my mom and I made in the village. Next to her, Renata was dabbing her eyes with a handkerchief while Georgio searched the groom's side for suspicious characters. I knew he would always be looking out for me even if he didn't have to.

Reaching the altar, Tino released his grip on my arm. "Piece of cake," he said, then quickly walked to a waiting seat in the first row. I took a deep breath and turned to Agostino. His eyes looked straight into mine. *You can do this, I have faith in you,* they seemed to be saying.

That warm comforting feeling came over me . . . again. I realized the journey I had taken with my mom to find my roots had really been a journey to find myself. In getting to know my ancestors I had learned that they were people just like me: strong and courageous but vulnerable and uncertain when faced with the emotional challenges of life. Their legacy of perseverance had shaped not only the person I was but also the person I would become. My grandfather Spirito and his two brothers had crossed the Atlantic and braved the unknown in America at the turn of the twentieth century; Spirito's bride Marianna had been willing to leave a promising career in education to follow the dreams of her husband. But the legacy did not end there. It also included those who had stayed behind like my great aunt's daughter Teresina and Dr. Sabatini, the village doctor who contributed to the welfare of his community, one patient at a time. It included Spirito's first love, Agatha Altarocca, the woman who turned an act of violence into an opportunity for a better life. And SJ, her son, the man who taught me how to live every moment as if it were my last. We were all connected to a rich and rewarding past, to family members separated by time and distance and circumstance. We shared the same hopes and dreams, the same mistakes and triumphs. Among the villagers, the stories of my ancestors had gone beyond just words strung together—they had become a part of my life. With patience and understanding, the people of Scheggino had guided me through fear of the emotional unknown, taught me lessons in humility, and helped me open my heart to love.

The irony of it all did not escape me. I had come here in search of my past, and in doing so, I had found my future, a future I would not have been able to experience if it weren't for the courage of a woman named Angelina. Her fight to outpace death so that her son might live had brought Agostino to me.

I was where I belonged, and everything that had come before prepared me for this moment. My past and my future—and Agostino's family and mine were now connected forever.

I looked up. The church was quiet, and the priest was looking at me expectantly. I hadn't heard a word he'd said for the last ten minutes.

Agostino mouthed the word *"sì."*

"Sì," I said loud and clear.

The priest looked relieved. He put a hand on each of our shoulders and said, *"Vi dichiaro marito e moglie.* I now pronounce you husband and wife."

Agostino bent down to kiss me, and the entire church erupted in a deafening roar of pure joy.

Epilogue

Vatican City, Rome, June 2017

A GROUP of men in black robes and white collars were entering a side door of Saint Peter's Basilica. At a glance, they all looked identical.

"Do you see Sergei?" I asked Agostino as we attempted to follow them.

A guard stepped in front of us. "The line is that way." He nodded to the block-long queue of people waiting to go through security.

"But we are here to see one of the deacons being ordained," Agostino explained, pointing to the last figure disappearing through the doors.

"Only immediate family can join them inside," the guard said.

"We *are* immediate family," Agostino replied.

The guard looked us over. I was desperately hoping he didn't ask us how we were related. *I am his son* would not have gone over well, I suspected. It might have been the sincerity in Agostino's face or maybe the fact that if we had to wait in line, we would surely have missed the ordination. Whatever the reason, the guard made a split-second decision to step aside. "Third Chapel on the right," he called out to us as we hurried up the steps and entered the church.

The grandiose scale of the basilica's interior never failed to take my breath away. To our right, set well back from the railing, the pristine sculpture of Michelangelo's "Pietà" lay half obscured in the vaulted shadows of a grand chapel. Farther on, niches containing gigantic sculptures of popes, cardinals, and saints adorned every inch of space. As we walked toward the center, I saw the canopied "Baldacchino" rising from its gilded pillars, and below it, groups of tourists hovered around the railing, hoping to catch a glimpse of the grotto where Saint Peter's remains are buried.

A realization, like a bolt of lightning, hit me. I turned to Agostino. "I'm thinking of something Angelina said to Pepina before she died. She was talking about where she saw God. I understand it now. When I look around this great cathedral, one of the greatest ever created, I realize this is not where I feel closest to Him. He is not sitting on a cloud looking down on us from a frescoed ceiling or enshrined in a gold encrusted chapel, He is in an *eremo's* hut and in the middle of a forest at the top of a mountain. He lives in a child's laugh—and in a mother's dying wish." I reached for Agostino's hand. "It was Angelina who showed me, in the way she approached her life and the things she believed in, that God is not only in the world around us—He is *inside* us."

Agostino's eyes shone. "If she could teach you that, it is proof that my mother's life had meaning. It is part of the miracle, isn't it?"

Still clasping hands, we turned away from the altar. Everywhere there were priests and nuns clustered in groups or striding across the marble floor. God's messengers intent on a job they had to do.

Agostino sighed. "We'll never find him in here."

"The guard said third chapel on the right," I reminded him.

We walked over to where a crowd of lay people stood behind a roped-off area. Elbowing our way to the front, I caught sight of the same group of white-collared men that had entered the basilica earlier.

"Just look for the gray hair," Agostino whispered to me.

It took me a while, but I found him. One gray head among a sea of blonde, black, and brown ones.

"Shall I yell, 'Hey dad?'" Agostino shot me a grin.

I punched him in the arm. "Not unless you want to get excommunicated on the spot."

I looked beyond the crowd to the interior of the chapel where the ordination was to take place. On the apse wall was a large mosaic depicting an early Christian martyr, and underneath the marble altar rested a simple white sarcophagus with "Sanctus Johannes Paulus PP. II" inscribed on it.

I sucked in my breath and looked at Agostino "This is the tomb of . . ."

Agostino cut in. "I know."

"Unbelievable," I said.

An important-looking man in a purple robe and tall, rounded hat climbed the steps to the altar. He turned and made the sign of the cross to indicate the service was beginning. The white-collared deacons moved toward him, filing past the relatives and well-wishers straining against the cords. As if sensing our presence, the gray head lifted, eyes searching the crowd, and then a smile of recognition formed when he caught sight of us. His eyes rested for a long moment on Agostino before they moved to me. He winked, and like a ray of sunshine, a flash of the old Sergei emerged before he lowered his head in prayer.

I nudged Agostino excitedly. "Did you see that? He winked at us!"

Agostino's eyes filled. "He's going to make one *helluva* priest."

"The Lord be with You," the bishop intoned, his arms lifted in a benediction.

The deacons were moving away from us now, toward the altar. The crowd pushed against the rope, straining for one last look.

A sudden sadness came over me as I watched the families saying goodbye with their eyes. An invisible barrier now separated them from their loved ones—a barrier that hadn't been there before. They were witnessing the end of a relationship and the beginning of another. I realized I was feeling it too. What link would we find to bridge the gap between our two worlds?

As the deacons began to recite The Apostles' Creed, the path opened up before me, and the way became clear.

"I believe in God . . ." the voices began.

The crowd took it up like a chant, "The Father Almighty, Creator of Heaven and Earth . . ."

Instinctively, Agostino and I joined in, the words echoing through the Cathedral. It filled the vast space with a sound that resonated with conviction and hope for the young priests ready to face the world with only the armor of faith to guide them.

I looked at the man next to me—his eyes were focused on one upturned face in the group of white collared men.

"You haven't lost him," I said as if reading his thoughts. "Your relationship with Sergei and Beniamino is just beginning."

Agostino squeezed my hand. "I know."

I watched my husband's gaze move to the white sarcophagi under the altar and upward to the vaulted ceiling—and beyond.

Acknowledgments

A SPECIAL thanks to my brother Tony Wilcoxson and my sister Tess Wilcoxson Nelson for their continued indulgence in allowing me to unearth the secrets of our family's past one skeleton at a time—and with more than a little creative license.

To my dear friend, Sergio Proietti, who is never too busy to lend a supporting word, translate a phrase, or inspire me with yet another tall tale of his beloved Italia.

To my editor, Molly Lewis, whose insight and attention to detail continue to astound me and whose rare compliments mean more to me than she will ever know.

To the team at Acorn Publishing for giving me the opportunity to grow as an author.

To Tess Wilcoxson Nelson for helping me maintain my social media presence despite my protests that I would rather just sit home and write.

About the Author

ANNA WILCOXSON grew up in San Diego, California, in the 1960s and began her career in 1975 dancing with the original San Diego Ballet, The Santa Barbara Ballet Theatre, and the International Ballet Company of USIU. In 1991, she received her BFA in dance at the USIU's School of Performing Arts. In addition to owning her own ballet school, Miss Wilcoxson has served on the faculties of Mira Costa Community College and Chula Vista Middle and High Schools.

In 2009, when she assumed the role of caregiver for her 95-year-old mother, Anna's creative passion shifted, and she began writing short stories based on her life and experiences in the performing arts. A trip to Italy with her mother in 2010 sparked the idea for her Secrets and Promises series, which includes *Secrets and Promises: The Story of an Italian American Family* and its sequel, *The Deathbed Game.* The novels center on the stories she heard as a child about her immigrant ancestors. *Sinners and Saints* is the third book in the series.

Anna divides her time between San Diego and Scheggino, Italy.